Taming of a Wolf

Viking Wolves Book 2
CJ Ravenna

CONTENT WARNINGS

Parental death (off-page) and main characters experiencing grief due to that loss

Brief violent attack on main character

Flashback of a car accident with fatalities

Brief references to torture that occurred before the start of the book

A child experiencing hospitalization after breaking an arm

CHAPTER 1

JAMIE

You know your love life is lacking when the characters in your latest romance novel are getting more action than you.

I mean, damn! It's just been chapter after chapter of nonstop smut, plot simmering on the back burner while the leads resolve their sexual tension. Meanwhile, I, Jamie Sullivan, can't even stick around until the end of one of the rare dates I go on. But hopefully, that will all change tonight. My good friend and coworker Jess set me up with a vet tech who is a friend of a friend. She had nothing but good things to say about this guy, and I hope he lives up to his reputation.

I want the kind of love I read about in books, but at this rate, I'm becoming more and more convinced that it's just not going to happen. For a while, I settled for one-night stands, but I want the real deal. I'm twenty-two. It's time I stopped *thinking* about meeting Mr. Right and got around to actually finding the guy. For my little brother's sake, I need to take my future seriously. Jace deserves stability, a family. I can't give him any of that on my own.

Setting down my e-reader on my lap, I check the time. This guy, Matt, should be here at any minute, and then we can head to the restaurant. It's a cute place on a boat moored along the harbor with fairy lights strung up and twinkling.

Matt. I wonder what he's like. He has to be a nice person if he's a vet technician. Anybody who cares about animals must have a heart of gold. From the pics Jess has shown me, he's super handsome. I exhale some of the nerves from my belly. I'm hoping we'll hit it off. Although being fifteen minutes late isn't the best first impression...

While I wait, I check my phone. No texts from Kate or Jace. Must be a good sign, right? My little brother is having a sleepover with Kate's daughter since I said I'd be out late. Hopefully, all is well—unless something has happened. My nerves return full force.

I shoot my little brother a quick text.

Hey. Everything good?

He doesn't reply right away. Biting my lip, I try and get back into my book, but now my mind keeps tugging me toward my phone. When it buzzes in my pocket, I snatch it up.

> **Jace: No! The house is on fire and everyone's dead!! lol yeah every-thing's fine jeez**

When did my little bro become such a sassafras? I'm impressed.

"Jamie! Hi, I'm so sorry I'm late!" A gorgeous man, tall and dark-haired with neat stubble, rushes up to me.

"Matt, hey!" My heart skips as I jump up to greet him, giving his hand a shake. "Nice to meet you. Jess has told me so much about you."

"Same, same!" He's panting, like he ran all the way over here. It's sweet that he was in such a rush. "Want to go grab a table?" He points at the boat.

My growling stomach says yes, please, so we make our way there. The heaters keep the cold away as the host seats us at our table. "Have you been here before?" I ask as I pick up a menu.

Matt thanks the server when she delivers our water. "No. It's really cute, though. Love the vibes."

When the server returns, we give her our order, and I buy a bottle of wine for the table. As we drink, we get to talking. Matt asks me all sorts of questions when I tell him I own my late grandma's bookstore, and he tells me about some of the cute, furry patients he's met at the vet's office.

My stomach flips when our eyes meet, and already, I'm imagining a future between us. He's sweet and handsome, easy to talk to, and a great listener. From his scent, I can tell he's genuinely enjoying himself. A few years back, I somehow gained the ability to... sense people's emotions through their scent. It's super strange, and no amount of googling has produced any answers. Emotions have a scent to them. Anger is spicy. Shame is sour. Happiness is sweet, while sadness is heavy and dark. Weird, I know, but it can be helpful in figuring out people's genuine feelings.

I have a good feeling about Matt. Maybe, just maybe, he and I will really connect. I can see it now: we'll go on a few more dates, I'll introduce him to Jace and they'll hit it off, maybe in a few months, I'll ask him to be my boyfriend, and then—

My phone rings in my pocket just as our food arrives. When Kate's name flashes on my screen, my heart lurches. "I'm so sorry. I need to take this."

Matt shrugs. "Sure." He tucks into his spaghetti and meatballs.

Rising, I pace across the deck. "Kate? Is everything okay?"

When my brother's distressed sobs reach my ears, I have my answer. "Hi, Jamie, I am so sorry, but Jace had a really bad nightmare, and I can't calm him down. He really needs you."

Glancing at Matt, I fight back a sigh. I'm only conflicted for a second before I know who I'll choose. Jace. Always my little brother. "Can I talk to him?"

"Of course! Jace, sweetie, it's Jamie. Do you want to say hello?"

For a moment, there's silence. "J-Jamie?" My brother's breathless, shaking voice breaks my heart.

"Hey, bud. Kate says you're having a rough night. What happened?"

But he blurts out, "Can you come home? Please? Right now. Please." His hysterical sobs make my chest tighten with guilt. If I'd known he'd get so upset, I'd never have come on this date.

I'm being selfish, putting myself and my wants before his. "Yeah, buddy. I'll be right there. Promise. Do you want me to stay on the phone with you?"

He sniffles. "Y-yeah."

"Okay. I can do that. Just a second, okay?" Lowering my phone, I march to the host stand, explain that I'd like to pay and leave, and he prints my receipt. After swiping my card and signing, I jog back to our table. Shit. He's going to be upset. Hopefully, he'll understand.

"Hey, so, I am so sorry, but something's come up."

Matt's smile falls off his face. "Oh no. What happened?"

Dragging a hand through my hair, I say, "My little brother's having a tough time. I'm sorry, but I need to go make sure he's okay. I've paid for dinner, and I'd love to go out with you again another time."

When a scowl creases Matt's face, I lose hope in an understanding response. "Are you serious?" Before I can respond, he chucks his napkin on the table. "I came all the way from Jersey to meet you, and you can't stick around for dinner?"

Heat flames my cheeks. "I'm sorry, but—"

"Your brother's what, ten, right? Tell him to man up."

Anger burns in my veins. "You don't get it!" I snap. Fuck being polite. Nobody gets to talk about my little brother like that. "I'm all he has left of our family. He needs me."

Screw this guy. I can understand being disappointed, but insulting a traumatized ten-year-old is a low blow. If this is how Matt reacts before he's even met Jace, that's already a red flag.

"Forget it," I snap. "Don't call me again."

Turning away, I march from the boat and back toward Kate's house near Hudson River Park.

I need someone who will prioritize my brother like I do. If I can't find that person, then I'd rather be alone the rest of my life.

Jace is in the middle of a panic attack when I arrive at Kate's. "Oh, Jace." I throw myself onto the bed and hold him tight as he sobs, his little body shaking against mine.

Kate gives me a sad smile, holding her own concerned daughter close.

"Did you have the dream again?"

Gasping, he nods frantically against my chest. He grips at my shirt, nails biting into my skin. God, poor kiddo. I hate this for him.

"D-don't leave me all alone," he whimpers. "Please, Jamie."

Like our parents did.

Even though it's been four years, tears sting my eyes, and a lump aches in my throat. "It's okay, bud. I promise." I rub his heaving back as he sobs into my shirt, soaking it with his tears. "I'm here. I'm alive. I'm not going anywhere. Ever."

God, I am so stupid. While I was out on some stupid date, my brother was suffering.

Can't I do anything right? If our parents were still here, they'd know what to do.

Mouthing a silent thank-you to Kate and her kiddo for being there for him, I lift my brother and carry him downstairs. When Jace starts squirming, I set him down. He wipes his face dry.

"Feeling better?" I ask.

Jace shrugs and doesn't look at me, cheeks red from crying or embarrassment or both.

"Want to take a walk over to the river before we go home? The water always calms me down."

I don't get a reply, but Jace doesn't resist as we walk away from the car and toward the river. The water sloshes peacefully, and gulls cry in the night. Turning my face to the sky, I count the few stars I can see and try to calm myself down. I need to be strong for Jace.

"I still miss Mom and Dad," Jace says.

I take in a deep breath that hitches around a sudden sob. "Me too."

I miss our parents. I wish they were here to tell me what to do. To help me raise my brother and protect him. I can't do this alone. "But it's going to be okay." Kneeling down, I squeeze his shoulders. "I'm here. We've got each other."

Jace nods, sniffling.

I pull him in for a tight hug, and he tenses in my arms. "What's that?"

I look back into the murky depths of the river. There's something shimmering within the water. It almost looks like... some kind of light? The longer I stare, the brighter the light becomes until it's almost painful to look at. What the hell's going on?

Bubbles form on the river's surface. My lizard brain screams to run, but I'm frozen in place. Something's happening. Something big. There's a tugging in my chest, like a hook's fastened in my skin, urging me closer, forcing me to watch and wait.

An explosion of water showers up into the air and sprays me right in the face. Shrieking, I wipe water out of my eyes just in time to see a shape soar in front of the full moon. It looks like a... a rowboat. And it's flying straight at me!

"Holy shit!" I hurl myself and Jace out of the way just as the boat crashes down on the pavement where I was standing. Chunks of wood fly everywhere, bouncing off my body. Shaking, I lower my hands away from my face.

"Are you okay?" I ask Jace.

He looks shaken but unharmed. "What *was* that?"

The scattered remains of the boat are everywhere.

And lying atop the remains is a man.

He's huge, even lying down, or maybe the bizarre armor he wears makes him look bigger. His long black hair is plastered to his face, and water glistens in his thick bushy beard. Little beads are woven into his hair and beard, parts of which have been braided.

"H-hello?" I squeak, then clear my throat.

"Is he dead?" Jace asks, peering closer.

"No! I'm sure he's fine." To myself, I mutter, "Please be fine..." I inch close enough to tap him with my foot. He groans, and I exhale in relief. Okay, he's not dead. What the hell do I do? I should probably call an ambulance, right? Oh god...

I drop my phone with a panicked curse as the massive man slowly sits up. He tosses back his head, his hair flying out of his face. The greenest eyes I've ever seen pin me in place and steal the breath from my lungs.

I position Jace behind me just in case.

Parting his lips, he speaks in a low rumble like thunder. "Where am I?"

I open my mouth, but no words come out.

His nostrils flare, his eyes shining in the dark as he takes me in.

"Who are you? What is that…" He draws in a deep breath through his nose, and his eyes fucking glow like an animal's under a flashlight. "That scent. What *is* that?"

My legs quiver as he rises and comes toward me, his armor rattling with every slow step.

The winds change, and there's a smell unlike anything I've ever smelled before. It's like… I don't know how to describe it. Like all of my favorite smells rolled into one. Coffee and cinnamon. The whiff of parchment when you open a well-loved book, the spine cracked and the pages slightly yellowed from age.

"It's…" He comes toward me, sniffing frantically.

"You," I say, breathless as he stops mere inches from me.

Bushy brows furrow as those green eyes hold my gaze.

The hook in my chest tugs and burns, urging me toward him.

And somehow, I know nothing will ever be the same again.

CHAPTER 2
ANDERS

ISLE OF ULFHEIM, YEAR 831

"Don't you dare say it," I growl, glaring at my twin.

Lyall sighs. "I told you so."

Snarling, I slump back onto my bedroll. Beyond the window of my cabin, the distant chatter of the village reaches my ears. The fisherman calls out about today's catch. Children laugh as they run through the streets. Wolves howl in the forest as they prepare to hunt. The little girl who sells her flowers will just be getting ready to go home. I wonder if anyone bought her flowers. Normally I do, but I've been confined to my home.

Who will buy them after I am gone?

"Damn it!" Jaw tight in a rare display of frustration, Lyall paces the bedroom. "I cannot fathom how in Odin's name you thought challenging Wulfric for his position would end any other way!"

Shame burns the back of my neck. My actions, justified as they may have felt at the time, have brought my twin pain. That is not something I ever wanted. "What was

I supposed to do, pray tell? Let Wulfric and that filthy human mate of his change our way of life? Humans are the enemy, in case you have forgotten, brother!"

Whether they're trying to slaughter us and christen our corpses, conquer us and force us to give up our god Fenrir, or invade my pack's village, humans have been nothing but trouble.

"Not Kieran!" Lyall snaps.

I normally respect my twin, and we've had a good relationship most of our lives. Today, though, my temper rises at his words. Somehow, he is just as blind as my worthless little brother Wulfric.

"Do not presume to know his intentions! Or any human's. They slaughtered our father. Tortured me. How can you forgive them so easily?"

With a bitter laugh, Lyall sweeps his golden hair back from his face. "You've let your hatred blind you. This isn't about Wulfric's mate, just admit it! This is about your childish feud with Wulfric!"

My mouth falls open. "Childish? We both know if I had been Alpha instead of that runt, I could have protected our pack!" Instead, my father was murdered, most of my pack was slaughtered, and Wulfric packed us up and moved us to an island we came to call Ulfheim.

And yet, after all the pain humans have caused us, there came a day when Wulfric brought a human into our pack when he should have simply killed the foul creature.

Kieran Grove. A human from the future, who'd somehow wound up in our timeline. Worse yet, the human was Wulfric's *mate*. He'd claimed the gods had chosen a damned *human* as his mate, after all the harm they'd caused our kind.

My brother had lost his mind ever since the human came to our shores. Not only had he accepted the human as his mate, but he'd dared to give him the furs of a wolf and make him one of us! How could my brother so easily forgive their crimes against our kind?

Wringing his hands together with a frustrated sigh, Lyall says, "The past is the past! Tyr's beard, brother, you have got to let this go! Isn't it enough you've divided our family?"

My mouth falls open. How dare he! "*I've* divided our family? It's Wulfric who—"

"Enough!" Lyall's voice fills the cabin. The birds outside stop twittering, and in my shock, I have been silenced as well. Lips trembling, Lyall takes in a breath, then another. As his eyes dampen, my anger cools. "Father and Mother would be ashamed. Their sons, fighting like children. They would have wanted us to stick together as a pack. Instead, you... you're leaving." Voice thickening, he ducks his head and conceals his face behind a curtain of hair.

Oh gods. I truly wasn't thinking. I wanted to hurt Wulfric, it's true, but I never wanted to hurt Lyall. I let my anger and my own personal lust for vengeance cloud my vision. "Lyall—"

"Don't!" he snaps, finally looking at me, eyes bright with anger and swimming with tears. Sniffling, he dashes them away. He always was the softest of us, but seeing him so upset makes my throat tighten.

"I didn't know this would upset you."

"You had Kieran beaten bloody! Of course it fucking upset me!" Even the human's language is rubbing off on us. It makes my skin prickle. "If you had a problem, you should have taken it up with Wulfric! You're a gods damned coward! What would Father—"

"Stop." I snarl the word but fail to hide my plea.

I know exactly what Father would say. By beating Kieran to hurt Wulfric, I disgraced my family name. No matter how justified they may have been, my actions were not honorable. They were the actions of a craven, not the son of an Alpha. If he could see me now...

There's a quiet knock on the door. One of the thralls pokes her head in, face streaked with dirt. "Pardon. The Alpha is ready for you." Her words hang heavy in the air as she departs.

My time in this world has come to an end. I have been exiled, and it's time to face my punishment. Wordlessly, I rise and hold my head high as I shoulder past Lyall. "Wait." A firm hand to my chest makes me freeze. Lyall's voice wavers when he says, "Your sword. I must take it from you."

Wolf's Tooth. The blade I've had since I was a lad. It hangs heavy at my side. There's an unexpected ache in my chest at the realization that I will never feel its cool grip in my palm again. "Go ahead."

Lyall removes the sword from my belt and sets it on the table. What will become of it? "Give it to someone worthy." I hate the softness in my voice, but Lyall doesn't mock me for it.

"I shall, brother."

This may be the last time I see my twin, hear his voice. I should apologize for hurting him, for not being the brother he deserves... but the words just won't come because that would mean acknowledging how inadequate I really am.

Tearing my gaze away from him, I step out into the chill of the evening. The thrall hands me a sack of apples and salted meat and a flask of water for my journey. On the horizon, Sol, goddess of the sun, guides her chariot beyond the ocean. Her fading light deepens the shadows and colors the skies in vibrant hues. Somehow, the coming darkness fills me with despair. It feels like I will never see her light again.

Forcing my head up high, I walk in the direction of the beach. Though I can sense Lyall following me, I keep my eyes fixed on the horizon. I shouldn't have expected him to understand. There is no animosity between him and precious Alpha Wulfric.

As we leave the village behind, my brother Gunnar comes into view. I return his glare. "I'm so pleased you've dragged yourself from the woods long enough to say goodbye."

Gunnar grabs my arm hard and tugs. "Shut up."

There's a wild gleam to his eyes, likely his berserker tugging at him. If I ever see him again, he'll be on all fours as a savage beast. It's what he gets for being foolish enough to open his heart to love, only to lose it.

Love always ends in tragedy, after all.

"How long are you going to wait to find and claim the mate the gods have chosen for you?"

"Not your concern," he bites out, sounding more wolf than man. It... scares me, I admit. He's going to lose himself unless he finds his mate, yet he won't even bother looking.

"Would you listen to me? You've got to move on. Leif wasn't even your fated—"

"Enough!" Gunnar snarls, eyes flashing as he draws back a fist.

"Stop this, both of you!" Lyall shoves me back, simultaneously seizing Gunnar's fist. "Gods, can we have one day without throwing punches?"

"Not my fault our brother is a fool," I huff.

They await us on the shore. My skin prickles, and anger burns me up from the inside as I meet Wulfric's steely gray gaze. Expression unreadable, he turns away and walks toward the rowboat moored on the shore. He stole so much from me: first, my father's love and adoration, and now, he steals me from my home and my pack. He will pay dearly for this. I don't even bother looking at Kieran.

As the waves crash upon the shore, I approach the boat and try to ignore my aunt Helga's tear-streaked face. To avoid seeing the pain I've caused those I love written all over their faces. Why can't they see things as I do? I only wanted to keep them all safe. I have already lost my father to humans. I won't let my brother's foolishness threaten our pack. No matter what, I must find a way to return and end the threat Kieran poses.

Lyall's hand trembles at my back as he pushes me down into the boat. Through our bonds, he whispers, *"Goodbye, brother."*

Wulfric keeps his eyes on the horizon as he says, "Farewell, brother. May the Father Wolf guide your path." Then he pushes the boat out into the water, and the waves pull it the rest of the way into the sea.

Aunt Helga starts to chant, and her voice carries over the ocean. The icy wind freezes the tears I hadn't realized were on my cheeks. Ahead of me, a portal bursts into being, and I look back over my shoulder at my twin.

"Lyall. I'm afraid. Please, I—"

My boat flies through the portal in a burst of water, propelling me high into the air. My cry of alarm echoes into the night sky. The bag of provisions goes flying out of the boat and disappears as some strange-looking bird flies up to me and squawks in fright. For a moment, I'm transfixed by the view laid out before me.

Wherever I am, this world looks nothing like my own.

The buildings are as tall as the highest mountains, if not taller. Though it is nightfall here, everything is so bright. Everywhere I look, lights sparkle in the darkness like stars. I could spend an age taking in the sights of this strange new world... but then the boat hurtles back toward the ground.

I curl into a ball and brace myself, but I'm not prepared for when the boat shatters all around me. The collision with the hard ground stuns me. For a few seconds, all I can do is fight the urge to pass out. I can't. I must stay awake. Who knows what threats await me in this strange place?

A voice calls out to me, and a scent unlike anything I've ever smelled before pulls me from the dark depths, trying to drag me down into unconsciousness. This smell... I must find out where it is coming from. Who it belongs to.

The ulfhednar within me stirs to life, filling me with the strength I need to find my feet and rise.

A man stands before me. He's shorter, the top of his head reaching my chest, with a lithe, lean build. He must not be a warrior, then. It looks like he lives a soft, comfortable life. How pathetic, and yet I must admit he is stunning. I usually prefer the company of women over men, but I'd be blind to deny his beauty. I've never seen hair such a color in one so young; it's as light and bright as polished silver, though his brows and beard are as black as my own. And his eyes... so light and blue they look like shards of ice.

"Who are you? What is that..." I ask, and then the winds blow that delicious scent to me again. "That scent. What *is* that?"

As the man's nose twitches, mirroring my own fascination, I come closer.

"It's..." I whisper.

As his scent floods my senses, the wolf inside howls for him with a yearning so deep it takes my breath away.

"You," he breathes, his voice full of the very same awe coursing through me.

He smells like the woods where I roamed with my father, like leaves and soil warmed by sunshine. Even more intriguing is the scent of his wolf, however faint. He is ulfhednar, like me. But where are his furs? I must know more about him.

He smells like...

Mine.

He *is* mine.

"What is your name?" The words escape me in a growl. I'm surprised by how foreign my words sound. I'm not speaking the language of my people but an unfamiliar tongue similar to my mate's. The portal's magic must have given me the ability to speak and understand his tongue. A useful skill.

"J-Jamie Sullivan. Uh. Maybe we should get you to a hospital, or—" He yelps as I grab the front of his coat and haul him in close. With my nose to his neck, I breathe in deep and practically groan as that sweet, luscious scent fills my lungs. "Dude. What the hell? Let go!"

"I understand why I arrived here of all places," I say against his skin. "It was so I could meet you, Jamie, son of Sullivan."

It's then that I notice the wooden necklace protruding from the gap in his coat. Is that ash wood? It is! I would recognize it anywhere. Yggdrasil itself is an ash tree, and my people use branches or parts of ash trees to travel between the realms. This necklace could help me return to my time, overthrow my worthless brother, and lead my pack into the future they deserve.

Just as I close my fist around it, Jamie shoves me hard in the chest and sends me stumbling back.

"Whoa there, buddy." Jamie holds up both hands. "Usually, strange men buy me dinner before they tell me how good I smell."

There's a laugh, and I notice a young boy has been hiding behind Jamie. "Were you having a cosplay party on a boat or something?"

I have no idea what the lad's talking about. "A... party?"

"Are you dressed up as a Viking? Your clothes are so cool!" The boy's eyes light up.

"Jace, chill," Jamie hisses.

I think the lad is complimenting my clothes, even if I'm not sure what this "cool" means. "My clothes are quite warm, I assure you." I can't tear my eyes from the necklace. Even the symbol carved into the wood is one all ulfhednar would recognize: a wolf slumbering at the roots of Yggdrasil. The symbol of *my* clan. How did he get such a priceless gift?

"Where did you get that necklace?" I ask.

He closes a fist around it, clutching it to him protectively. I can tell it means a lot to him. "It was a gift from my grandmother."

"And her name was?" I wonder if I'll recognize it.

"Astrid."

A fairly common name. My clan has quite a few Astrids, but only one was a traveler. "Did she travel?"

Jamie squints at me. "Sure? I guess. She was always adventurous."

"I knew her when I was a lad."

Shaking his head, Jamie takes an even bigger step back from me. "No. I don't think you did."

Why does he insist on arguing with me? Leveling a scowl at him, I say, "She had a saying she'd tell us boys before going off on one of her journeys. 'Not all those who wander...'"

"'...are lost.'" Jamie's eyes widen to twice their size. "Her favorite quote from *Lord of the Rings*."

"Lord of the what?"

Jace huffs. "You've gotta be kidding. Everyone knows *Lord of the Rings*!"

Jamie leans back and catches himself on the railing. "Oh my god. How did you know my grandma?"

"She was a time traveler. As I am," I bitterly add. I'd much rather not be here, contrary to how pleased my wolf is at finding our mate in this bizarre place.

Jace gasps. "A time traveler? That's so awesome! I knew people like you were real!"

Jamie's mouth opens and closes like a fish. Finally, he laughs. "Okay. I'd better be going. Have a good night." He grabs the boy's shoulders, ignoring his protests as he tries to push Jace ahead of him.

He's leaving? He's mad if he thinks I'll let him walk away after I've only just found him—his necklace, that is. My place isn't here, it's back in my time, and that necklace is my key to getting home. This man is a complication I can't afford.

Just as Jamie spins on his heel, I grab his wrist and haul him back to me. "Hand it over. Now."

Jamie's face whitens even further, the scent of his fear making my stomach churn. I've scared him. Damn it, why is guilt gnawing at me? I need that necklace. Nothing else matters. I've stepped over others all my life to get what I want. Using others is how I've survived.

"What the hell is your problem?" Jamie squawks.

"I need it!"

"You're freaking crazy!"

A growl rumbles in my throat, and I yank him in closer. "Hand it over, or I'll… I'll…" But at his panicked gasp and the widening of his terrified blue eyes, the words lodge themselves in my throat. The growl cuts out as quickly as it began. My fingers loosen around his wrist of their own accord. My body, my very mind, can't even comprehend hurting him, no matter how important that necklace is.

How am I supposed to take it from him if not by force? Damn it!

Oh no. Do I have to ask nicely? Must I beg?

I'd rather hurl myself back into the river.

"Would you…" I grind my teeth, trying to hold back the revoltingly weak words. "May I—" I clamp my jaw shut and squeeze, grinding my teeth. I have never asked anyone for anything before. All I could possibly want has always been given, and gladly, or I've taken it by force with my fangs, claws, or sword.

"May I please have your necklace?" I can't even look at him and snarl the words at the ground, ears and face burning. "I need it to return to my timeline."

There's a long, breathless pause as Jamie and Jace look at each other, then back at me like I've grown five heads.

I swear to Odin, if I have to repeat myself, I may die from humiliation.

"Sure," Jamie says, tone light and breezy.

I jerk my head up—and yelp as his fist crashes into my nose.

"Stay the hell away from us, you creep!" Grabbing Jace's hand, Jamie tears off into the night as if Odin's Wild Hunt itself is after him.

My nose heals in seconds, though I wish I could say the same for my pride, and I wipe away the blood with a scowl.

My mate just punched me and ran away.

Since when does anyone run from me?

Gods. Can I do nothing right in this place?

Well, I can't let him get away. Not before I've gotten my hands on that necklace. It's not because I'm drawn to him in any way. That would be foolish.

Get the necklace. Get home. Nothing else matters. If I have to, I'll take a chosen mate the instant I'm back in my time. Nothing is coming between me and my goals, not even fate itself.

Drawing in a deep lungful of Jamie's scent, I pursue him away from the river. His trail leads to a strange metal contraption I've never seen before. Jamie climbs inside, and the contraption roars to life, making me jump. What in Hel's name is that *thing*? Is it a horse? Is that how people get around in this world? I don't see any horses to ride, so that must be it. Gods. Horses are terrifying in this timeline. The metal horse speeds Jamie away from me, moving faster than any horse from my time.

Damn it! I can't lose him.

Ahead of me, a woman opens up the inside of her own metal horse thing. I cover the distance in moments. "You there! Step aside! I have need of your horse!"

"Get away from me!" She whips something small from her pocket, and the next thing I know, my eyes are on fire. Yowling, I cover them, wiping frantically to try and clear my vision. Tears stream down my face, blurring my sight as the woman climbs into her metal horse and hurtles away.

My eyes may be compromised, but my sense of smell has only heightened to make up for it. Jamie's scent lingers on the breeze. I must follow it. Nose to the air, I pursue Jamie's scent, wiping my streaming eyes as I go. My vision slowly clears as my healing repairs whatever damage that woman did to my eyes. What was that substance she sprayed me with? It burned like silver. Could she have been a hunter? How else would she have known silver is our weakness?

Unease twists in my belly. I round the corner onto a street bustling with activity. People flood the streets, some carrying small children, others walking dogs of all sizes. They rush past, chatting to each other or into strange handheld objects I've never seen before. Humans, all of them. I'm surrounded by humans, my clan's greatest enemies. Not a single one of them smells like I do or even looks like me. They're all different, and where I'm from, anything different is a threat.

My wolf snarls below the surface, and my heart races faster than a rabbit. Sweat dampens my palms. Jamie's scent is lost to me among a sea of other smells. I try and swallow, but my throat is dry as a bone.

What is this feeling?

Those strange metal horses emit loud, blaring noises that make my ears ache. A man wearing rags shakes coins around in a cup. Someone slams into my shoulder. "Watch it!" the man snarls as he bares his yellow teeth, but I barely hear him over the strange music blasting from some sort of wheeled instrument he's dragging along behind him.

My gods, but this place is noisy!

It's too much.

Kill them all. The wolf inside grows into a berserker beast as my fear turns to red-hot rage.

I can't. There are too many of them. I am outnumbered. I am a lone wolf without a pack, and lone wolves never last long.

I grip at my chest as my lungs constrict.

I must follow him, get the necklace, and go home.

A huge metal horse lets out a booming blast that echoes through the street and drags me from my thoughts. Some guy yells at the metal horse to "Shut the fuck up!" How odd. As if a horse can understand them. A familiar splash of color grabs my attention. It's Jamie's blue horse, and I can just make him out through the window. As Jamie races off, I pursue him like the moon chases the sun.

He makes several twists and turns, and the crowd ebbs and flows until the streets are at last quiet and relatively deserted. Jamie hitches his horse along the curb and steps out, but he's unaware of my presence. I slow my steps, knowing I must plan my next move carefully. I don't want to frighten him again. I can't use force. Not against my mate. I must try another tactic. But what? I know nothing of gentleness. Where I'm from, kindness and consideration will get you killed.

There's never been a time in my life I've needed to rely upon anyone. Relying on others means trusting them, and in my world, trusting the wrong person can end with a blade in your back. But Jamie is my only anchor in the sea of uncertainty I've found myself in. My only chance of returning home. I must not lose him. I must swallow my pride, be calm, and do whatever it takes for him to give me that necklace.

Jamie walks around the side of the horse and opens one of the doors. "Come on out, bud. We're home."

Yawning, Jace drags himself from the horse's insides.

"Feel okay?" Jamie puts his hand on the boy's shoulder and guides him toward a tall house I assume is his home.

"A little. Tired." He rubs his face as they stop before the front door. Their backs are turned, so neither sees when a man in a mask steps out of the shadows, blade in hand, and lurches toward Jamie.

The man presses the blade against Jamie's back and says in a low, commanding voice, "I want everything you're carrying. Phone. Wallet. I don't fucking care. Hand it over or else."

"Jamie!" The boy clutches Jamie's arm with a frightened whimper.

Jamie's entire body stiffens, and the scent of his fear bowls over me. "I-it's okay, Jace. Listen, man, I'll give you whatever you want. Just leave my brother alone."

A red haze descends over my eyes, and my blood begins to boil. My fingernails lengthen into claws, and my fangs gnash in my mouth. The wolf within bays for blood.

I can't fight the fury a second longer. I throw my fur hood up over my head, and the shift takes hold. I drop down onto four huge paws as my body transforms. The wind roars in my ears as I charge. Jumping upon the craven thief's back, I sink my fangs into his coat and hurl him off the stoop. The boy screams, and Jamie puts himself between the boy and me to shield him, his eyes huge and full of fright.

The boy has nothing to fear from me. I direct my fury at the thief, who is scrambling backward, smelling of fear and urine as he says, "Oh shit!" All I want is to rend flesh from bone and lay the threat broken and bloody at my mate's feet so he knows without a doubt that he is safe. That he will always be safe.

Pulling back my shift, I grab the dropped knife in my hand and hold it to the thief's throat. "Lay a single finger on them, and I will kill you. Understand me, fool?"

"Oh my god," the thief babbles. "I'm sorry! I'm so sorry. Please, let me go."

"Silence!" I snarl, digging the blade in until beads of blood form on his skin.

"W-wait!" Jamie says. "Don't kill him. Let him go."

I turn a glare on Jamie. "Why should I?"

"He's just some idiot kid. Let him go. I don't want his death on my conscience."

"He tried to hurt you." I can't fathom my mate's intentions. How can he be so forgiving?

"But he didn't. You were here. You stopped him. Just let him go. I'll file a report with the cops. He can be their problem."

I don't know who these "cops" are, but I suppose Jamie knows the ways of this world better than I do. If he thinks killing him will bring more trouble down on his head, then I don't want that.

"Fine." I pocket the blade. "Get out of here, thief. If I ever see you again—"

"You won't!" the thief babbles, springing up. "Thanks, man, thank you so much!" He dashes off into the night. The wolf in me longs to chase him down and kill him away from Jamie's prying eyes, but I'm distracted when Jamie says, "Stay back. I appreciate what you did, but—"

"But he helped us!" the boy interjects, poking his head out from around Jamie.

"It's all right. I won't harm either of you." I sweep my gaze over Jamie, relaxing when he doesn't appear harmed, just frightened. The rage inside cools to a simmer as I let my gaze linger on his full, soft lips and pert button nose.

"Are you hurt?" I ask.

Jamie shakes his head. "N-no. Thanks to you." His throat bobs when he swallows. "Just so we're clear... I really saw you change from a wolf into a man, right? I'm not crazy?"

"You saw correctly."

"Oh..." Jamie sounds faint as he leans his head back against the door. "Wait. No. Stop. This is weird."

The boy looks from Jamie to me, wide-eyed. "That wasn't weird! That was awesome!" A big grin lights up his face. "You totally went all Jacob on his ass!"

"Language!" Jamie huffs.

I normally don't like children, but the lad's enthusiasm makes the corner of my mouth tip up. "Who is this Jacob? He sounds like a fearsome fighter."

"A werewolf from this book series my friend likes called—"

But Jamie says, "Is that what you are? A werewolf? Or a wolf shifter?"

"We call ourselves ulfhednar. Why? Is there a difference?"

Jamie nods, moving his hands animatedly as he speaks. "So, yeah. In fiction, werewolves are usually men or women who are forced to change into a wolf when there's a full moon. Like a curse. Wolf shifters can assume their form at will and are generally more sympathetic than werewolves, especially in romantic fiction."

Fiction? What in Odin's beard is he talking about?

Jamie laughs. "You don't understand most of what I just said, huh?"

I scowl. "I understood fine." I didn't, but like hell I'll admit to feeling so utterly lost.

"That's okay. You said ulfhednar, right?" He butchers the pronunciation, but I nod. "Okay, so that's what I'll call you. Wow. This is wild!"

"What time are you from?" the boy asks, venturing closer to get a better look at me. "You look like a Viking!"

"Aye, I am." The boy's big, bright smile confuses me. Their reactions are not what I was expecting. Aye, Jamie is ulfhednar himself, and so is the boy, but they've grown up among humans. I'm surprised he hasn't been told awful things about us or taught to hate himself. "You aren't afraid of me?"

The boy shakes his head emphatically. "No way! This is awesome. You're a Viking werewolf! How cool is that?"

Jamie considers my question. "Not really. You saved my life. Or my belongings, at the very least. Besides, I've always thought werewolves—uh, ulfhednar—were really cool. Especially in romance novels." His cheeks flush pink.

He thinks we're... cool? "How exactly do ulfhednar and the weather relate to each other?"

"What?" He barks a laugh. "No! I mean... I like ulfhednar. I definitely don't hate you."

For someone who grew up among humans, he's more open-minded than I expected. But how doesn't he know he's like me?

"Thanks for saving me. I'm sorry I punched you in the face. You were kinda creepy, but you made up for it." He shakes his head. "I feel like an asshole now."

I just shrug. "I've had much worse. You've got a good arm! You'd make a worthy warrior where I'm from, pet."

Jamie's cheeks color at the nickname. Gods above, but he is lovely. He returns my smile. "All right. How about we start over, then?" He clears his throat, then sticks out his hand. "I'm Jamie Sullivan. I like reading, baking, and cozy sweaters."

I stare at his hand. "What are you doing?"

Jamie laughs softly. It's a sweet and musical sound. His smile is more radiant than any sunrise I've ever seen. "You're supposed to shake it. Oh, wait. Wolf shifters usually smell each other, right?"

The boy tilts his head. "Like, sniff each other's butts? Gross."

It's true we like to scent each other, though not our asses, but if I'm going to be here long, I should get used to these human customs. "Shake it? Oh." I grasp his hand and shake. Hard. Jostling his arm up and down, I say, "I am Anders, son of Erik and Matilda."

"Whoa, you've got a good grip!" Jamie says, voice breaking as I vigorously pump his arm. He frees his hand and shakes it out, laughing as he pulls a ring of keys from his pocket. "A man who can shift into a wolf and time travel. What a strange night."

"Why is that so strange?" I ask him. "You're ulfhednar yourself."

Jamie drops his keys. "Wait. I'm what?"

I thought it was strange that he'd go out and about without his furs, but his utter confusion is even more unsettling. How can he not know what he is?

"Jamie," I say slowly, "you're ulfhednar too. I can tell by your scent."

Jamie snorts, scooping up his keys. "No, I'm not."

"Did your grandmother give you any furs, by chance?"

"No, why would my—" Jamie's mouth goes slack, his eyes bulging. "How... how would you possibly know about—"

He's quiet for so long I start to think he's frozen from the cold.

Finally, Jamie blinks a few times, then plasters a smile on his face. "I could really use a hot drink. Do you want to come upstairs?" His voice is decidedly casual. It worries me.

"Aye, sounds good. Have you got any mead?"

"What? Uh. Yeah. Sure."

I don't think he has any mead.

Chapter 3

Jamie

Holy shit.

Wolf shifters, I mean, *ulfhednar*, are real! Time travel is real! I decide to gloss over what Anders said earlier, something about me being ulfhednar too. Because that's just not possible—I'd know for sure if I was able to turn into a wolf.

Except if he's wrong, then how did he know my grandma? How could he possibly know she gave me her treasured furs?

I really don't want to go there. A time-traveling Viking just flew out of the Hudson River, hit on me, and tried to rob me, only to end up saving my life. Tonight has been crazy enough. Anders prowls around my living room, nose to the air, sniffing frantically. It would be funny if it weren't so strange.

Even with his odd antics, he is the most gorgeous man I've ever seen. Sure, he's grumpy and hotheaded, but he's not so bad. There I was, lamenting over my lackluster love life, and he burst out of the river and landed right at my feet.

When Anders plops down on the sofa, my little brother bombards him with questions, his voice high and squeaky with excitement. "Jamie's a wolf shifter, right? Does that mean I'm one too? When will I shift?"

He's taking this way better than I am.

For such a gruff-looking guy, Anders is quite patient with my brother, smiling good-naturedly as he says, "Aye, lad, you will. But not until your twelfth winter when you don your furs for the first time."

"I'm almost eleven!" Grinning, Jace leans over the back of the couch and shouts, "You hear that, Jamie? I'm gonna be a wolf shifter!"

My head is freaking spinning as I lean on the kitchen counter. What shifter romance did I wake up in? "I heard you, bud. Would you like hot chocolate?"

"Yup, with lots of marshmallows," Jace chirps.

Anders jerks his head toward me. "Chocolate? What is that?"

Oh, right. He doesn't know what half the stuff from my world is. He's probably so confused. Oh man. How do I describe chocolate to him? "It's sweet. Mine comes in a powder, and I mix it into hot milk." I make the powder myself at my café, so I know it's good.

"A sweet powder?" He wrinkles his nose. "Fine. I'll try it."

"Do you want marshmallows or whipped cream?"

Anders looks bewildered. "What in Odin's beard is a marshmallow?"

I don't have the brain cells for this... "You know what, I'll just give you some."

Jace lightly punches Anders's shoulder. "You'll love it, trust me!"

Once I've mixed the drinks, I pop in some marshmallows and add a dollop of homemade whipped cream on top. Carefully, I carry the mugs into the living room. I join Anders on the sofa, Jace sprawled out on my left. "Careful, it's hot."

He gives me a narrowed look. "I know that." After sniffing the rim of the mug, he takes a cautious sip. Whipped cream gets stuck in his thick mustache. He takes a huge gulp. "What witchcraft is this? It's delicious!"

"It's called sugar, dude," Jace says, popping a marshmallow into his mouth.

Those bushy brows furrow. "My name is Anders. Not dude."

"You've got cream in your beard."

"Where?" He feels around, completely missing the spot.

Without thinking, I reach out and swipe my thumb over his upper lip. His sharp inhale makes my heart trip. Those dark green eyes glance at my thumb, and then, curiously, he leans in and licks the cream from my finger with a swift dart of his tongue.

"Eww," Jace says, making a face.

Holy shit. I must be more pent-up than I thought because my dick jerks just from feeling another man's tongue on even the smallest part of my skin.

I'm having hot chocolate with a Viking werewolf, and now he's looking at me like he wants to devour me, piece by piece.

This is... normal. Completely normal.

"I quite like the cream, actually." A heated smile lifts the corners of Anders's mouth. "It's delectable, especially on your skin."

Oh hell. How did I go from getting no action to suddenly being the object of a Viking werewolf's affection? I'll take it. I'm not gonna complain. Even if the guy is obviously playing me to get my necklace.

"Uh, bud? How about you go brush your teeth, wash your face, and get ready for bed?"

Giving us a weird look that makes my ears burn, Jace goes into the kitchen and puts his mug in the sink. Before he goes into the bathroom, he looks back at Anders. "Will you be here tomorrow?"

I turn to Anders. "You're welcome to stay the night. It's the least I can do."

Anders offers a smile. "Thank you."

Jace closes the bathroom door.

"You don't have sweet things where you're from?" I ask, voice cracking from nerves as those emerald eyes gaze into mine.

That indulgent smile widens. "Nothing quite so sweet as you, pet." Those low words, uttered in that sexy Scandinavian accent...

No, Jamie! Have some self-respect.

A flattering snort escapes me. "Oh, come on, man. Be less obvious, at least."

Anders tilts his head. "About what?"

"We both know you really want my necklace." I motion at the wooden necklace resting against my beige cable-knit sweater, the green collar of my plaid shirt flaring out above the neckline.

Anders frowns at me. "You think I am trying to deceive you?"

"I don't think. I know."

When Anders leans in closer, my heart jumps into my throat, but it sure isn't from discomfort. As much as I wish I could have some self-respect, the fact of the matter is Anders is smoking hot, and I've been unintentionally celibate for weeks now.

"I don't lie, pet. Nor do I waste my time on those beneath me. And most everyone is beneath me," he growls. "I do want your necklace. However, I want to earn it. Normally, I would simply take it, consequences be damned. No one has ever come between me and something I want and lived." A shiver runs down my spine. He's being completely honest; I can see it in the coldness in his eyes. "But I can't do that. Not with you." He doesn't sound happy about this at all and glowers at the floor. "When I say I like the way you taste, it is not a lie. Nor is it a lie when I say you're the most breathtaking creature I have ever laid eyes upon. It is simply the truth."

My mouth goes unexpectedly dry. It's overwhelming, being someone's sole focus like this. But I really like it.

"Oh," I say, too flustered to speak. "Well, uh... You're pretty breathtaking yourself."

"So I've been told." He smirks.

This fucking guy...

"It appears I must... earn your necklace." He looks physically ill at the thought. "And then I shall leave for my home. So, tell me what I must do to earn it. I can work well, and I'm skilled with a blade."

I gawk at him. "What do you think I'm going to ask you to *do*?"

He shrugs those big shoulders. "Whatever it is that needs doing. I'm a skilled hunter, so I can provide you with any game you need. I can also work. Household chores are usually attended to by my thralls, but my fool brother and that pup of his freed them. Mayhap it is good that I left." Disgust curls his lip. "I am not above doing simple chores if that is what you'd prefer." He looks like he'd rather throw himself back in the river than subject himself to menial household chores.

I suck in my lips so I don't laugh. Is this guy for real? He wants to cook for me? Clean for me? Hell yeah. "Let me think!" I flop back on the sofa, pondering all the things I could ask him to do. "So many tasks! How can I possibly choose?"

He scowls. "Don't look too pleased about it. If you were anything other than my mate, I wouldn't even consider stooping so low as to indenture myself to you."

"You could do my laundry, color-code my bookshelf, vacuum... Oh! Maybe you could—wait, *whaaat*?" What did he just say? If I weren't such an avid romance reader, I wouldn't have even picked up on what he'd just said. He's a wolf shifter, ulfhednar, whatever you want to call it. And in every paranormal romance I've read, wolf shifters have—

"Mate?" I croak, edging farther away from him on the couch. "As in... fated mate?" That explains why he's so fixated on me, so attentive, why he stuck out his neck for me. Wait. Why am I acting like any of this bullshit makes any sense! It doesn't! At all!

Anders sighs like he's on his way to the gallows. "Aye, lad. It would seem I arrived in your timeline for a reason. The Norns themselves preordained our meeting. The ladies of fate and destiny wished for us to meet."

Oh my god. If I hadn't seen this guy shift into a huge wolf, I would be calling 911 right now. Maybe I should do it anyway. "Wait. Hold on a sec!" I lurch from the couch and nearly knock my drink off the coffee table.

Anders pursues me, his nostrils flaring, eyes dark and fixated. It should be fucking creepy, and yet some animal instinct deep inside is preening at the knowledge that this strong, gorgeous Viking wolf has picked me of all people.

"I'm human," I finally say, as if that makes any sense.

Anders growls, "No, pet. You're not. I've told you, you're ulfhednar. As am I. The Norns would not be so daft as to pair me with my kind's greatest enemy."

Anders corners me against the TV stand and lowers his head, breathing in deep. Oh god. Do I have some special scent to him, like in the books? And wait. *He* also had some weird scent when I first saw him. That moment replays in my mind, and I remember how everything in my world narrowed down to him the moment I caught his scent.

"Do you doubt our bond, pet?" Anders rumbles in my ear. "Must I prove here and now that you're meant for me as I am for you?" Big, warm hands glide down my sides and grasp my hips, urging me closer. "The effect you have on me... it's unlike anything I've ever known."

And he isn't lying. The proof is pressing hard against my hip. To my dismay, my own body is reacting right back. His scent is spicy with desire and longing, so potent and overwhelming that it makes my brain go all fuzzy. An odd, low whimper escapes me, and to my horror, I tip my head back and show him my neck. Like I'm... submitting to him.

Oh no. Is he right? Ever since my eighteenth birthday, I've had an odd sense of smell and been in tune with others' emotions because of the change in their scents. Did something about that day change me? I think back. "Wait... my gran gave me wolf furs for my birthday. Furs that look a lot like yours."

I wore them to make her happy that day, but I'd internally squirmed at the thought of wearing fur. So I'd put them in my closet and never wore them again.

"Oh shit..." I whisper, knees shaking. "I... oh my god. I think you're right." His scent and the heat of his body are like a magnet, urging me closer, but I jerk back and stumble to the couch. Collapsing, I fold over and hide my face in my hands, trying to think rationally.

"I've had dreams," I say at last, "where I'm running as a wolf. Not all the time. Always on a full moon. I hear another wolf howling to me. I run to them, because I have to. Because I know that the moment I see them, smell them—the loss, the guilt, the damn grief will all go away, and everything in this fucked-up world will finally make sense. I'll finally be whole." My eyes sting, the longing in my dreams so visceral, even in my waking moments.

"It's not a dream, pet." Anders's fingers card gently through my hair, and his touch calms the storm in my head. "It's your wolf, crying out to be set free."

"Can I free him?" I lift my head, gazing up at Anders with a desperation I've never felt before. "How?"

"I will show you. Is there a forest around here? Somewhere we will be undisturbed?"

I snort. "In New York City? Not likely... Although we have a few large parks. I'll take you in the morning after Jace has gone to school."

Anders grins. "I can hardly wait. Your wolf will be as beautiful as you are."

Nerves ripple through my stomach. I woke up this morning thinking I was just a normal guy. Turns out, I'm ulfhednar. I have so many questions. Will it hurt? Are there any complications? Is it dramatic like in the movies?

I guess we'll find out.

CHAPTER 4
ANDERS

I DON'T SLEEP WELL on Jamie's sofa. It's far too small, and my feet dangle over the edge. How can Jamie sleep with people all around him? The village back home was spread out, but here, I can hear every cough, sneeze, and bark of a dog from the floors above and below. Worse yet is the couple down the hall on their second—third?—round of sex for the night. The gods must hate me.

Normally, I can tune these sounds out, but I'm too restless. My wolf stirs, making my claws prick the cushions and my fangs sharp. He wants to be in the next room with Jamie. Our mate. I still can't believe it. The ladies of fate must have it out for me to not only lead me to my mate but to make him the key to being able to return home. Mayhap Loki is controlling my fate and laughing at my expense.

When I open my eyes, the room has brightened. I managed to sleep, but not much. It's a struggle to leave the sofa as my body cries out for more sleep.

"Jace, I'm ready!" Jamie barrels out of his room, arms flailing at the shirt caught over his head. "Hurry, we've gotta go to school!"

A snort answers him. The little lad sits at the counter, munching on something sweet-smelling in a bowl. "Been ready for, like, ten minutes." He smirks proudly and puts his bowl in the sink.

"Who put sass in your cereal?" Jamie says with an amused smile. He jogs to the door. "Eat up, we've gotta go."

He's barely finished speaking by the time Jace is by the door. "Beat you to the car!"

Jamie sighs like he's already exhausted.

I grin at him. "The lad's keeping you on your toes, eh?"

"Tell me about it." Jamie chuckles. "You can either wait here or come with us. We'll go to the park after I drop Jace off."

I rise, muscles cracking as I rotate my neck. "Grab your furs, pet. It's time to show you who you're meant to be."

Jamie drives us in the metal horse—no, the *car*, that's what Jamie called it. Not a horse at all but a machine, whatever that is. It's faster than a horse, louder too, and we sit inside instead of riding on top. I tried to climb on the roof, but Jamie yanked me down and made me get inside.

In any case, Jamie drops the lad off for his lessons, then drives us to some place called Inwood Hill Park. My wolf bristles beneath my skin as my mate's sweet scent tugs at me, so potent in the enclosed space of the car. All wolves feel the urge to mate on the full moon, and although the full moon above is outshone by the sun, the urge is still so potent.

I've never liked the idea of soulmates. Oh, I know they exist, but the idea of needing someone, some so-called better half, has always terrified me. I understand why they're important, but when I was a boy, I learned that having someone only means having someone to lose.

Father was never himself again after Mother died giving birth to Wulfric, the precious Alpha. Father changed, closed himself off even from us children. The softness Mother brought out in him died when she did. I'd do anything to avoid knowing that pain myself, even if it means leaving behind the man my wolf demands I mate with. Mate or not, Jamie is a tool. Nothing more or less.

No. I'll earn his necklace and return home to challenge my foolish little brother.

There is no room in my plans for anything... any*one*... else.

"Anders? Earth to Anders." Jamie waves at me. "We're here."

I jolt out of my thoughts. "I heard you the first time," I snap, shoving open the door. "Get your furs." Once Jamie has retrieved the furs from the trunk and thrown his bag across his shoulder, I follow him farther into the park. We walk for a bit until we're surrounded by trees and there's no one else around.

The wolf pelt he carries is a darker shade of silver than his hair, mottled with brown, black, and white fur.

"You had better not be playing a prank on me," Jamie says, his scent souring with unease.

"A prank?"

"You know, a joke. You're not gonna make me wear these furs, close my eyes, then run off on me?"

"I once killed a traveling jester who tried to rob me. The only good jokester is a dead one."

Jamie laughs nervously. "You're... serious, aren't you?"

"No. I'm Anders." All these words he uses confuse me. I haven't heard of most of them.

"So, where're we going?" Jamie inquires, throwing me a playful smile.

That smile does something to me. Makes my heart skip and my stomach lurch, like I'm under attack. But by what? *Feelings*? Not bloody likely. "Does your chattering ever cease? Keep walking. I'll tell you when to stop."

"Sir, yes, sir!"

The gods must be punishing me for failing to overthrow my brother.

Once the distant noise from the streets has faded, I'm confident we're far enough. The only human scents in the air are stale. A lake reflects the sun, and the park is unnaturally quiet. There should be more birdsong, but I suppose not many birds live in the city. I keep expecting to hear the howling of wolves. The absence of their song only reminds me how far away I truly am.

"Here should work." I turn to Jamie and find him clutching the furs close, biting his full lower lip. He could make himself bleed. Scowling, I march up to him and reach out, brushing my thumb over his lip to remove it from between his teeth. A lovely flush springs to his cheeks. "Don your furs and get ready."

"That's all?" He frowns as he shrugs the furs on over his shoulders.

"Usually, there is an initiation ceremony. You would consume the heart of a wolf you hunted yourself."

Jamie's eyes widen. "Oh shit."

"What?"

"My gran made me try a wolf's heart once. You're telling me that was part of this ceremony?"

"Aye."

Jamie shakes his head wildly. "Why didn't she just tell me? Why be so cagey about it?"

"She truly told you nothing?"

Jamie screws his eyes shut. "No. She *did*. I just never believed her. She'd tell me stories about how our Scandinavian ancestors had wolf's blood in their veins and the ability to shapeshift. I thought she was just spiritual or something, so I played along. I accepted her furs, even though I only wore them a few times when I went to see her. I ate a wolf's heart once. It was gross. But what was I going to do? Insult her beliefs? It made her happy. But still, if I technically did the ceremony without realizing it, why did I never shift?"

"Your wolf lies dormant. All it needs is something to wake it up. As your mate, my presence should be enough."

Jamie shakes his head. "I don't even know what that means."

"You said you've heard stories about my kind, haven't you? Did your grandmother never tell you of mates?"

"Like I said, I never really believed her stories." The guilt is evident in his scent.

"The stories my people tell always have a lick of truth in them."

Jamie groans and smacks his forehead. "I feel like such an ass. My grandma was trying to tell me so much about myself, and I just blew her off."

"Do not hurt yourself." I cup his cheek in one hand, brushing a thumb over his short, dark beard. "Once you have assumed your true form, you will understand."

Jamie blinks rapidly. "This is crazy..."

"Just close your eyes and focus on the parts of yourself that have always been there, lurking within you."

Looking more uncertain than ever, Jamie closes his eyes.

"Tell me what you're thinking."

"I'm thinking... I really wish I'd had more coffee."

"Focus!" I snap.

"Okay!" he gripes back, brows scrunching. "I... I've had a really great sense of smell since I was eighteen, when my grandma gave me her furs. In my dreams, I'd run as a wolf. I was looking for something. Looking for... for you. I think I was looking for you."

Something glows warm in my chest. The thread of a pack bond, blossoming into life. I'd felt it there before, but it was subtle. Now, it's burning brighter as Jamie's features change before my eyes. His ears are pointed, and white fur streaks his cheeks.

"You were, pet. You've found me. I'm here. Find our bond. I know you can feel it." I throw up the hood of my fur cloak and let the change flow through me.

"A bond? I don't know what you're... *Oh.*" Understanding floods his voice with sudden emotion. "Wow. Oh wow. That's... What *is* that? It's warm. It feels amazing."

The bond between us grows taut, drawing us toward each other. On four paws, I go to Jamie as he drops to all fours with a pained groan. I touch my nose to his forehead and growl, deep and low in my chest.

"Find us, mate. Find our bond."

Gray fur covers Jamie's face, which forms into a snout. The shift happens in only seconds, and then a beautiful wolf stands before me with eyes as bright and blue as the sky. Our bond blazes like the sun in my chest.

"A-Anders?" Jamie's voice blooms in my mind, sweet and confused.

"I can hear you."

Jamie turns his snout toward his paws, and his eyes grow wide. He lifts one paw, then the other. *"Holy shit. I'm a freaking wolf!"*

"No. Truly? I thought you were a puffin."

Jamie bumps his head into my shoulder. *"Shut up, you jerk. Whoa. This is so cool! I have a tail!"* He proceeds to chase said tail, spinning around like a puppy until he grabs it, bites it, and yelps in pain.

"Aye. And what a fearsome wolf you are." He's so energetic, like a pup instead of the fierce servant of the wolf god Fenrir that he is.

"Dude. I'm gonna be the coolest wolf! I—Whoa. Wait. What's that smell?" Dropping his snout to the earth, he sniffs frantically. Leaves get stuck on his nose, making him sneeze.

My tail thumps, betraying my amusement.

Jamie sniffs around until he runs right into me. Nose twitching, he inhales a deep lungful of my scent. *"It's... it's you. Why do you smell so freaking incredible? You smelled amazing before... but now..."* A shiver racks Jamie's wolf body. My mate circles me, sniffing eagerly as he rubs his body along mine. Shoving his head beneath my chin, he scents at my throat and rumbles low.

"You smell like... mine. *"*

The notes in his scent make me growl eagerly. He wants me just as much as I crave him.

Suddenly, Jamie drops to all fours, tail in the air. He yips playfully, then dashes off into the woods.

A primal hunger rises in me. He wants me to chase him. Catch him. Claim him.

And oh, I will delight in it.

Chapter 5

Jamie

Being a wolf is awesome so far.

I'm fast, faster than I've ever been.

The colors of the world are different in this form, but my eyesight is sharper, like I'm looking at everything through HD lenses.

Then there's all the scents... The world has never smelled sweeter, a kaleidoscope of aromas that bring color and life to the world around me.

And then there's him. Anders. And he smells the best of all. Cinnamon and coffee and that used-book smell that always brings a smile to my face. Except now his scent is driving me wild. I want him to chase me, catch me, and do whatever the hell he wants with me.

The moment I caught his scent, it was like everything clicked into place. I understood why no guy has ever worked out for me, and it's because they weren't him. My mate. Mine.

Of course, I still barely know the guy, and he's got a crap personality. But honestly? The big grump isn't that bad.

He had no reason whatsoever to save my neck when he could have just taken what he wanted. He sure didn't have to teach me about this amazing side of myself I never knew existed. He's, dare I say, kind of a sweetheart. Even if he pretends not to be.

I lose momentum as I run, worry suddenly weighing on my shoulders.

This... isn't good. I've always been the kind of guy who wears his heart on his sleeve and dives in headfirst, regardless of the consequences. I fall hard and fast, often giving my all and receiving nothing back. It's gotten me badly hurt in the past. I shouldn't like Anders, and yet, damn it, I do. I think beneath all that scowling and grumbling, there's a big, frigid heart waiting to be warmed up.

Shaking my head, I take off running again, needing to leave these pesky thoughts behind. Don't go there. No matter what these weird wolfy instincts are telling me, Anders and I can have our fun, but that's all it will be. Fun. He's made it clear he has every intention of returning to his timeline and leaving me behind, regardless of our bond.

The wind whips through my fur as I run, spraying leaves and dirt behind tame. Pursuing paws thunder the ground. He's gaining on me, and my heart races in exhilaration at being caught, at being claimed.

The wind goes out of me as Anders leaps onto my back, pinning me beneath him. His breath scorches my neck, his low growls vibrating against my skin and forcing a shiver from me. All my instincts scream to submit, to give him everything he needs until I'm all used up, but only in the best way.

The shift recedes as I surrender, prey grateful to be caught. A cold nose brushes the back of my neck, and his hot breath scorches my skin. Anders's growl vibrates over me. The predatory sound makes my heart gallop and my breath hitch. Somehow, though, I know he won't hurt me, even though I realize I might want him to.

I roll over and submit, baring my throat to my mate. "Please," I whimper, and I hope he understands what I'm asking for—everything he can give me.

The wolf above me shifts to Anders the man. His emerald eyes are black with lust, fangs sharp as he bares them at me. "Please what, pet?" He purrs the words as he sweeps his fingers down my jaw.

"Please, just... I need—"

I need him, all of him, with such intense, primal yearning I can't hope to put it all into words. My body burns hot, my cock so hard it aches.

"What is this?" I rasp, hips gyrating against him before I can control myself. The answering response of his cock, grinding on my own, has me arching up for more.

"Your wolf recognizes his mate. He's gone into heat. Wants me to claim him."

Embarrassment flames my cheeks. *That's* what's happening to me? It feels like I'll burn to ashes unless he shoves his cock in me. "I... There's no pressure. You can ignore it."

Anders snarls above me. "Ignore it? How am I supposed to walk away when I can smell your cock leaking for me, pet?"

"I just mean if you don't want to—"

"I have never wanted anyone more. I wouldn't leave your side if Ragnarok itself were upon us."

"A-and Ragnarok is?"

Anders nips the shell of my ear. "The end of the world and the beginning of another."

That's what being with Anders feels like, the end of my normal, empty life... and the beginning of something brand-new and exhilarating.

"Want you," I say with a groan, rocking my hips against his. "Now. Hurry."

I know I've pleased him when he yanks down my jeans and boxers in one go. His hand is around my cock, squeezing and stroking. A cry escapes me as I buck into his fist, chasing the pleasure, but it isn't enough. I don't want to take things slow.

"Fuck me, Anders. Please. Need it." I fumble in my bag, which is strapped around my shoulders. It somehow didn't fall off when I shifted, nor did any of my clothes rip. It was like the fur cloak grew over everything I was wearing.

That's convenient, though right now, I'd really prefer to be naked.

"What is this?" Anders asks, inspecting the lube I hand him.

"It's lube. It'll make things slick and painless. Oh, I've got condoms in there too." I'd stuffed those in my bag last night, hoping my date might end on a pleasurable note. Looks like I'll get to use them after all.

"And those are?"

"To protect against STDs. That's diseases you can get during sex."

Anders tilts his head. "Ulfhednar do not get sick or diseased."

He's immune? Huh. That's really convenient. "Then forget the condom. Want to feel every inch of that heat you're packing, big guy."

I fumble with Anders's trousers, practically salivating at the outline of his impressive cock straining the fabric taut. Tugging them down to his knees, I'm gifted with the sight of the holy mother of all cocks. It's so long and thick, the shiny, leaking head protruding from his foreskin. I have got to taste him, make him come in my mouth, but not tonight.

I help him out of his shirt, and I hiss at him to be gentle when he almost rips my shirt to shreds in his haste. With a curious expression I shouldn't find endearing, Anders gets the lube open and drizzles some in his palm. He sniffs the slick, then rubs it over his cock. He gasps, eyes fluttering shut. "Gods. This is… it feels so good." He strokes himself, marveling at the easy glide of his hand up and down that thick length.

"That's the wonders of modern sex life for you. You have got to try sex toys sometime." He's in for a treat.

Slicking his fingers with more, he presses them between my legs. I lift my knees up, biting my lip to stifle my groan as he slides them easily inside me.

"Gods above, pet. You feel like Valhalla itself. So perfect," Anders breathes, eyes falling shut as he swirls his fingers. The full sensation makes me whimper, rolling my hips to take him in deeper.

"Want you inside me. Now," I pant.

Anders's mouth quirks against mine. "Then roll over, pet. Offer yourself to me."

I'm embarrassed by how quickly I'm on my hands and knees for him. I arch back, presenting myself. Little pants escape me as his bare thighs knock against my lower body. The blunt head of his cock pushes against me, then in, and I whimper as he stretches me, fills me.

A thunderous growl escapes Anders, and his claws dimple my hips. "Feel how well you take my cock, pet?" With a groan, he rocks his hips, sinking deeper into me. My body burns with the intrusion, even as pleasure sings through every nerve and has me clawing up the grass beneath my palms. "So gods damned perfect for me."

The fire in me only burns hotter at his words. Having him inside me is the only thing that will extinguish this roaring flame. I grind my teeth, fighting back the urge to demand more of him as he rocks into me agonizingly slowly. I'm not a demanding guy. I give and give, never liking to take or ask for more. But with him, I can't help myself. "Anders," I croak, unable to hold back.

His thick fingers curl in my hair. "Tell me what you need."

I arch back against him, smacking my ass against his pelvis. "Fuck me. Please. I can take it. Don't hold back. I need... I just—" But words fail me as Anders tugs my hair, shoving my face into the dirt.

With a snap of his hips, he slams into me, his balls slapping my ass. My hoarse cry echoes into the woods, a mix of pain and pleasure that feels so right, it brings tears to my eyes.

"This what you want, pet?" Anders snarls in my ear as he pounds back in. "To be taken, bred by my cock?"

"Anders," I gasp, "yes, yes, *yes*—oh fuck!" I cry out again as he drives into me, and this time, he doesn't let me catch my breath. Anders sets a brutal pace, gripping my hips hard enough to leave bruises as he pounds me with speed and force no human guy could ever hope to match.

I can't speak. All I can do is moan again and again until I know my voice will be hoarse. Anders takes me apart, leaving me drooling in the dirt, completely mindless with pleasure. I submit everything I have, all my thoughts, all my worries and cares, and let him take care of me in a way I hadn't known I needed.

All my life, I've taken care of other people. Finally, just for this moment, I can trust someone else to give me what I crave. It feels selfish to have something all my own, something just for me. But damn it, I don't fucking care.

All I care about is Anders's heaving chest against my back, his animalistic grunts and snarls in my ear that would be terrifying under any other circumstances, his thick, hot cock stretching me full to bursting.

"Close," I pant. "So, so close. Please. Don't stop."

To my horror, Anders pulls out, leaving me gaping and empty. Suddenly, I'm flipped onto my back. Anders looms over me, cock flushed red and leaking, slick with lube. "Want to see that beautiful face when you come for me, pet," he says, then shoves my knees to my chest.

He practically folds me in half, but it's worth it when I can watch the blissed-out look on his face as he slides back in, chasing away that horrible emptiness. It sucks that this one time is all I'm allowing us to have. I'd love to have his big dick rearranging my insides every day and night.

My eyes roll to the back of my head, and I fist my cock and stroke. Every muscle in my body coils tight, ass clenching hard around Anders's cock. I'm so close, but only Anders can push me over the edge.

"Have I pleased you, pet?" Anders's eyes glow preternaturally, his fangs sharp in his mouth.

"Yes, Anders, yes!"

He curls his hand around my cock and squeezes. "Then be a good pet and come for me!"

His name escapes me in a hoarse scream as I come, splashing his chest and stomach with my release.

Anders's pace never falters as he relentlessly pursues his own orgasm. "Gods, Jamie. Want to knot your tight, perfect ass."

Yes. That. It all sounds perfect. "What?" I slur.

"My knot will tie us together. It will give you the relief you need. I promise."

Wow. My life really is a smutty shifter book.

"Give it to me, all of it. Please."

With a low, desperate groan, Anders slams all the way in, and something at the base of his cock expands. The pressure inside me, the way I stretch around him, is all too much. The fire beneath my skin erupts as I come again and again, clutching onto Anders.

A bestial roar escapes him as with one final slam of his hips, he comes inside me, flooding me with his thick, hot seed. His knot swells inside me. A gasp escapes me, and when I squirm, I'm alarmed to find our bodies are stuck together. Anders kisses my hair and whispers, "Be still. It will not hurt. Breathe."

He's right. It doesn't hurt. It feels amazing, actually, to be so full, to be tied to him in such an intimate way. It makes my wolf howl in delight, so I decide to trust my animal instincts. Finally, the beast within me knows nothing but sated relief.

We catch our breath on the forest floor, bathed in warm sunlight. Anders drapes his furs over both of us. Big, warm hands cradle my head with tenderness no hookup has ever shown me. Chest tightening, I fight to remind myself he's only being nice because he wants my necklace, and I'm surprised by how much that hurts.

"Did I please you?" Anders asks, voice hoarse and satisfied.

I smile, curling my fingers in his wild mane of dark hair. "Yeah, puppy dog. You did."

His indulgent smile makes my heart sing, and I know I made the right choice to end things after this. I always fall too easily, hope too quickly, dream too big.

Anders can never be mine, no matter how sweetly my wolf sings for him.

Chapter 6
Anders

Jamie's face is the first thing I see when I open my eyes a little while later. The warmth of my furs keeps out the chill of the day, but nothing is warmer than Jamie's body pressed so close to mine. His silver hair is tousled, his plush and slightly swollen lips parted while he sleeps. Gods above, but he is beautiful. The Norns chose wisely when they led me to him.

Then I see the necklace, and my pride curdles and dies in my chest.

So what if I fucked him? It's not as if we mated, though my wolf came terribly close to biting him. If I'd done that, it would have been an unnecessary complication. Leaving would have been impossible. Now is my chance. I could take the necklace and run, right now. It would be so easy. Jamie wouldn't even notice it was gone until he wakes. In only hours, I could be back in my timeline. I won't have to worry about going berserk if I leave now, defeat my brother, and take a chosen mate once I am Alpha. All I have to do is take the damn necklace.

My fingers twitch, itching to reach out.

Mate, my wolf whines, and a surge of longing hits me.

No! I must not give in. I care nothing for this man. He was a pleasant distraction, I'll admit. The gods brought us together so I could find his necklace, not because I have any feelings for him.

I trace the black rope around Jamie's neck, then let my fingers close around the ash wood. I squeeze it so tight the symbol carved into the wood is surely embedded in my palm.

Why? Why can't I steal it from him? What foul spell has this man cast upon me? I've always used others, always done whatever I could to come out on top. In this world, you kill or are killed. You use others, or you get used.

I must return home, and yet my wolf is pulling me in another direction. He wants us to stay here in this wretched place, here with Jamie. I can't. My home is not here; it will never be here. Home is Ulfheim, and unless I return, I won't have a home when my brother's idiotic human mate betrays them all.

Jamie stirs beneath me, and I jerk my hand back like his necklace burned me. His ice-blue eyes should look cold, but they radiate warmth as he cracks a sleepy, pleased smile that obliterates every wall I've built around myself. Somehow, this man has enthralled me, body and soul. How will I find the strength to fight our bond if just one look in his eyes breaks down all my resolve?

"Hey, puppy dog." Jamie's gravelly voice makes my prick jerk in my trousers, threatening to fill.

"I'm not a puppy," I growl at him, but it comes out petulant rather than pissed. I can't even sound irritated by him. What is wrong with me?

A happy little hum escapes Jamie as he twines his fingers through my beard. "I didn't realize I'd fallen asleep. You really wore me out, big guy." He winces and rubs his behind.

"Did I hurt you?" Why do I care? I've never cared for the satisfaction or well-being of any of the men or women I've taken to my bed before.

"Oh, you did, and I loved it." Jamie sprawls out on his furs and stretches. Gods, the way he looks beneath me… tousled hair, dried seed on his belly and chest, slender cock soft and vulnerable between his plump thighs. I've never seen a more tempting sight. "But surprisingly, I feel okay." He digs beneath him and chucks a rock into the trees. "Much better. Amazing, actually. Nothing hurts."

"It shouldn't. You're a wolf now. You'll heal most any injuries as long as they aren't fatal."

"I think I like being a wolf." He scratches the back of his head. "So, uh… I'm not great at morning-after stuff."

"Neither am I."

"Really?"

"No. Usually, I just leave. But… it's awfully hard to walk away when you still smell like my seed."

Flushing, Jamie turns his face away. "I should really get going…"

No. I won't let him run from me—not until I've gotten that necklace. That's the *only* reason. "You telling me you don't want to take advantage of your newfound stamina?" I run my hand down the dried seed on his belly, then stroke a finger over his stiffening prick.

Jamie whimpers and rocks against me. We're both hard, and as we grind together, longing for him possesses me.

His jaw tightens, lust and indecision plain on his face. "Fuck it. Here." He shoves the bottle of lube at me. "Make me beg for it."

"You will, pet. I won't stop until you do."

I drench my hand in the slick stuff. Once I coat my cock with lube, I blanket him with my body. I take both of us in hand and stroke, making Jamie moan. His hot, hard cock against mine has a growl rising to my lips. I grip us both tight and thrust, groaning at the sensation of our flesh becoming one. Jamie arches beneath me with a cry, hips rolling to match my own thrusts.

The tight, hot grip of my fist coupled with the sensation of his cock grinding against mine with every thrust has my head spinning. A few more thrusts and I could spill just like this. But I won't. Not until Jamie has begged me to give him the release he needs. I separate our bodies, and Jamie whines beneath me. "No. What—"

I grab his wrists and pin them above his head. "Told me to make you beg, pet. I am a man of my word. You will not spill a drop of seed until you have begged me for release. Am I clear?"

Jamie shudders and nods. "Yes."

Squeezing his wrists, I let my tongue trail down his chest. I circle and suck on his nipples, both of which are pierced. I flick one of the rings with my tongue, then give it the gentlest of tugs, but Jamie writhes like he's been struck by lightning.

"I like these rings, pet. Very much." I tug the ring again, and Jamie spits out a curse.

"Anders. Pl—" He bites his lip hard, silencing what would have been a sweet plea.

"Going to make me work for it? Challenge accepted." I lick my way down his body, tasting the dried cum on his skin, licking until I've cleaned his chest and belly. Jamie pants beneath me and rocks his hips, trying to get me to pay attention to his cock, which is weeping drops of seed onto his abdomen.

"Patience. I must make sure you're clean." I lick and lick, moaning at the taste of him. Jamie writhes and whimpers, biting his lip so hard to keep from begging I fear it will bleed. I must work harder, it seems.

Finally, I reach his cock, hard as iron and flushed a furious red. Parting my lips, I flatten my tongue against the base and lick all the way to the weeping head. Jamie bucks beneath me with a strangled shout of "Yes! Right there. Just like that. Fuck, puppy dog, that's so good."

Opening my jaw wider, I swallow him down, then wrap my lips around the head and suck hard. When Jamie curses and cries out, I know I've pleased him. I've never sucked another man's prick before, but I must be doing a good job to have him so close already.

"Yes," Jamie breathes. "Yes, like that. Don't stop. So close. Oh god. Anders, I'm gonna—"

So he likes it but not enough to beg for more. I haven't done enough, not yet. I pull off his cock and leave him thrusting into empty air. Jamie chokes out a dismayed cry.

"Haven't made you beg, pet. Not yet," I rasp, throat sore from sucking him so deep. I let go of his wrists and hold down his thighs, preventing him from taking control of his pleasure.

"You're a bastard," Jamie croaks.

I grin. "You wanted to beg, pet. If you want to come, you will beg."

Jamie grins. "Make me."

Once I can tell he's no longer about to blow, I take him in my mouth again. Jamie sighs and tangles his fingers in my hair, squeezing and stroking as I bob my head. I take him deeper and deeper, letting him work my throat open. I gag once or twice, but I don't stop pleasuring him. Jamie's whimpers become moans and pants as I let go of one thigh and caress beneath his balls. I press inside his tight hole, groaning as his heat wraps around my finger.

As I suck, I swirl my finger, stroking and curling. Jamie cries out above me, and I smile around him. When I go to pull off, Jamie groans and pulls my hair. "No. Don't. Let me come. Anders, please let me come. Please, please, *please*!"

A growl rumbles through me. I curl my finger inside him and bow my head, taking him in deep. I suck as hard as I can, bobbing my head faster, and that's it. Jamie cries out above me and spills down my throat. He shudders and shakes until he's emptied every drop. Jamie collapses back against his furs, gasping and shaking. I lick him clean and swallow my reward, though I still have yet to finish.

The need to spill my seed eclipses everything else. Grabbing his hips, I flip him onto his stomach. I position myself between the cheeks of his perfect round ass and thrust. I dig my fingers into the meat of his ass and squeeze his cheeks together, creating a tight sheath. My eyes roll back, and my thighs tremble as I let loose, straining for my release.

"Gods, pet, you feel so good," I snarl. "So good for me. So perfect."

Jamie rocks back, aiding my efforts. "That's it. Use me. Make me smell like I'm yours."

His words light me on fire. With a roar, I spill all over his back, pearly ribbons of seed spattering his beautiful, fair skin. Jamie groans beneath me, gasping with me through my release. Even after I've spilled every drop, I continue to rock against his ass, chasing every sensation until I'm sensitive and overstimulated.

Panting, I run my hand through the mess on his back and smear it into his skin. He'll smell like me, like mine, like mate. Turning in my arms, Jamie plants a sweet kiss to my lips. "Man. I'm gonna need a coffee if I wanna stay awake after that. You've worn me out, big guy."

I ask, "What is this coffee?"

Jamie gapes at me. "What the hell did you just say?"

I tilt my head, confused at his shock. "I believe I asked you a question. Answer it. What is coffee?"

"No. I can't believe you've never had coffee. We need to fix this. Now!" He's on his feet. "I can hear a lake in that direction. Let's clean up. Then I'm getting you the best cup of joe you've ever tasted."

Together, we go to the lake. We wade in and wash ourselves clean with cool water. Once we're clean, though still faintly smelling of our lovemaking, we return to our clothes and dress.

"Where are we going?" I ask.

Jamie zips up his coat. "Well, I'd love to take you to my café over in Brooklyn, but that's quite a trip. There's a diner nearby. They should be open even this early. I make the best coffee in the city, but this place is pretty good too.

Besides, I need pancakes. Like, now." He takes my hand and pulls me along after him.

"What are pancakes?"

"Oh man. You don't know what you're missing!"

This "diner" is a boxy building. Inside, there are only a few tables. It's an open space with little room to conceal attackers. "It appears safe for now." I vow to stay on my guard. The air is thick with delectable smells. "Is that... bacon?" I begin to drool, to my disgust. Gods, how I love bacon.

"You can get so much bacon. Hey, Wanda! Can I get a table for two?"

An older woman behind the counter smiles. "Sure thing, kiddo. Have a seat." She gives me a dubious look as I trudge past, armor rattling. I make sure to sit facing the door, then throw a cautious look behind me.

Jamie arches a brow. "What are you looking for?"

"Wolf hunters," I snap. "They could be anywhere, even in this time. By turning you, you could have a target on your back."

Jamie's eyes widen. "Oh shit. I didn't know. I really do think we're safe, though. Wanda is a good person, and her staff treats me like family. We're safe, puppy dog. I promise." He rubs my clenched fist.

A man garbed in black approaches our table. "Good morning!" In his hand, he grips a bundle of weapons. A snarl tears from me, and I leap to my feet.

"Get back!" I snap, shielding Jamie with my body.

The man screams and drops the weapons to the ground.

"Anders, chill!" Jamie leaps up and puts both hands on my chest. "He's our waiter. He's just come to take our order."

"Jamie, get away from him! He's armed!"

Rolling his eyes, Jamie grabs the fallen weapons and shoves them at me. "It's just forks and knives, you dummy!"

And... it is. I only saw the tip of the knife protruding, which isn't even sharp.

"Oh." My shoulders slump.

"Sorry about that." Jamie helps the man up.

He shakily drops some stiff papers onto the table and darts off.

"Gonna have to leave a big tip," Jamie mutters, picking up one of the stiff things.

"What is that?"

"It's a menu. It's a list with all the food items on it."

I pick it up and sniff it. It smells strange. I flip the menu upside down, hoping that will make sense of it. I can't read anything that's written here. I don't recognize the writing. It's all strange symbols, nothing like the runes my pack writes with.

"Uh. Anders? You good?" Jamie's looking at me like I'm the strange one.

"How do you read this?" I ask. It seems while the portal has made it so I can speak the language of this time, it hasn't given me the ability to read these odd runes.

Jamie gawks at me. "You gotta be kidding."

"There are no children here, Jamie. Now, tell me how to make sense of this."

Jamie rubs his eyes. "I'm too tired for this..."

"H-hello." The timid man from a few minutes ago jumps when I glare at him. "Can I get you started with anything?"

"I'll have some coffee, milk on the side, and banana pancakes with a side of sausage and scrambled eggs, please," Jamie says. "Also, some chocolate chip pancakes to go, please."

"And you, sir?" The man inches away from my glare. "What would you like to eat?"

Since I still have no idea what the menu says, I say, "Boar stew and a mug of mead. Some bacon as well."

"I... I'm sorry?"

Jamie hides his face in his hands for some reason.

"What are you sorry for?" I snap. "I told you what I want. Now, get it." If he were my thrall, I'd have him flogged for making me repeat myself.

"Anders," Jamie hisses.

"W-we have pancakes, oatmeal, granola..."

I don't know what any of those things are.

"He'll have what I'm having! But with bacon instead of sausage," Jamie chimes in, grinning a wide, fake smile.

"I will not—" But he kicks me beneath the table, and I'm shocked into silence.

The man leaves us alone. Jamie slumps, sighing.

"Did you just kick me?" I growl at him.

"Someone had to."

"I should take you over my knee."

He bobs his eyebrows. "Don't threaten me with a good time, puppy dog. Anders, you need to understand that nothing here is like what you're used to. Otherwise, you'll stick out, and this world is nasty to people who stick out."

"If you'd just give me your damn necklace, I wouldn't have to worry about fitting in," I grumble at him.

Hurt sours Jamie's scent. "Just because we had a good time doesn't mean you've earned my grandma's necklace yet."

Suddenly, I wish I could swallow my words. I didn't mean to hurt him. I never want to hurt him, in fact. "I... I feel comfortable with you," I say, focusing on tearing the paper napkin into strips to give myself something to do. "But everything else is..."

"Different, right?" Beneath the table, Jamie runs his foot up and down my ankle. His touch soothes me, at least a little.

I nod, grinding my teeth. Shame burns my neck from admitting such a weakness.

"Okay. I get that."

I jump when our waiter arrives with steaming mugs in hand. The scent is bitter and makes me recoil. Whatever drink this is, it's served with a side of milk and some packets. I tear open the packets and pour something white and granular into my palm. It smells good, so I lick it, humming in delight at the sweetness. "This is delicious. What is it?"

"Sugar. You had it last night in the drink I made you." Jamie smiles, watching me. "You're like an angry toddler."

"What is all this? How do I drink it?"

"You can take it as is, or you can add milk, sugar, whatever you like," Jamie says.

I cautiously lift the hot mug to my lips and sip. The bitter taste is so strong, I spit it all out. Jamie covers his mouth, his shoulders shaking with laughter. "Here. Try it with milk."

Lifting the little pitcher, I pour in milk, and the black solution in my cup lightens to a brown shade. It looks like muddy water. When I taste it again, the bitter flavor has been diluted, but only somewhat.

"Better?"

I smack my lips and nod. "This tastes amazing!"

"Here. Try this." He pours some of the sugar into my mug and stirs it with a spoon.

This time when I taste the drink, the bitterness is hardly noticeable. I hum my approval, then add another pack of sugar. Then another. It's almost as sweet as honey now. Perfect.

Jamie's eyes grow wide. "That's an awful lot of sugar."

I sip the coffee and moan at the sweet taste. "Much better."

Jamie chuckles, like he finds me amusing. "Loving your enthusiasm, tough guy. It's pretty cute." He pours milk into his coffee and drinks it. Somehow, the bitter taste doesn't bother him.

"Cute!" I've never been so bewildered! "There is nothing cute about me." I should tell him to stop calling me a puppy, but the fact is it doesn't bother me. Neither does being called cute. If anyone else did it, I'd lop their head from their neck. But when Jamie says it, it doesn't get me on the offensive.

Swallowing his coffee, he says, "I beg to differ. You're adorable. Especially in your furry form. Those big ears, that boopable snoot! So precious."

I growl at him lightheartedly, and he just laughs. The things I'd do to hear that sound…

Plates of food arrive. The "pancake" things look like stacks of flat, fluffy bread. I'm familiar with such things. What I don't expect is for them to be so sweet! They are so soft they melt in my mouth.

"Are you gonna eat them plain?" Jamie grins at my enthusiasm as I tuck in. I haven't eaten in hours.

"Why not? They're delicious!"

"Here. They're even better with butter and syrup. Real syrup, not this fake diner stuff. I'll have to make some for you at home sometime with the real deal."

I spread the butter and drizzle thick amber syrup over the pancakes. When I take a bite, it's like a taste of Valhalla in my mouth. "I imagine Odin himself must eat such fine things."

Jamie's grin widens. "Never heard somebody love pancakes so much."

I clean my plate in seconds, saving the crispy bacon for last. Oh, how I love bacon... This world may be different, but the food is incredible. My stomach feels like it will burst by the time I'm done, and still I eye Jamie's remaining pancakes with zeal.

"Want some? I'm stuffed." Jamie spears a piece of pancake.

I eat it right off his fork, moaning my satisfaction.

Jamie's smile is soft when I open my eyes, and it makes me scowl. I don't like how easy it is to let my guard down around him. I feel like a different person when I'm with him, someone weak, soft, vulnerable.

"What kind of food do you eat where you're from?" Jamie asks me.

"Nothing so complicated as all of this." Even the bacon tastes different. "Everything has more flavor."

"How did you even end up here anyway?"

A growl escapes me as bitter feelings sour the sweet aftertaste of pancakes. "My brothers exiled me."

Jamie's eyes get wide. "Why?"

"They betrayed me in every sense."

Frowning, Jamie reaches across the table and takes my hand. All the anger drains out of me, leaving nothing but soothing calm. I don't like it. Nobody has ever been able to affect me so easily. It feels like trickery. If Jamie wanted to, he could use the effect he has on me to his advantage and harm me.

And yet... I don't think he's capable of such cruelty. My wolf knows this, and his judgment has never been wrong. Although he and I are not always in alignment.

"Want to talk about it?"

I am a man of action, not words, but it's only fair he understands why I need his necklace.

"I have three other brothers. Lyall, my twin. He and I are the eldest. Gunnar, the second born. Wulfric, our youngest brother. Our Alpha." The words are like acid in my throat.

"Alpha?" Jamie wrinkles his nose. "Oh, like in shifter books. Wow. The books are pretty accurate to real life."

"I cannot say what is in these books of yours, but where I am from, Alpha is a title given to one who rules over not just his immediate family but the entire pack. It can be earned through strength alone or bestowed at birth. He or she will make the decisions that impact the community and help keep our kind safe."

"And that's what your brother Wulfric is?"

I grimace. "He is undeserving of the title."

"You think you should have been Alpha."

"I don't think. I know." To my horror, I realize I want to tell Jamie everything about my family history. I want to tear open old wounds and bare the most painful parts of my past to him. He wouldn't judge me. He'd understand, I'm sure of it. For so long, I've carried these scars, and all of a sudden, they're too heavy to bear alone. Grinding my jaw to keep my painful secrets locked inside, I decide to keep things short and simple. "Wulfric has weakened our pack. Because of him, our father was murdered by human hunters."

"Oh my god," Jamie whispers. "Anders, I'm so sorry."

"Don't," I say through gritted teeth. "I don't need or want pity. What's done is done."

Jamie winces, and instantly, I want to kill whoever made him look hurt... except it was me. So I'd have to kill myself. Damn it. "It wasn't pity. Just sorry you had to experience that. I also lost my dad. My mom too. I know how much it hurts."

I didn't know he'd also lost family members. We have more in common than I realized, despite our many differences.

I want to tell him everything. How the memories some-times rear their ugly heads late at night when I try to sleep. How I've reimagined that day every single day, tormenting myself over everything I could have done differently. How the guilt sometimes consumes me piece by piece. It was because of me that he was killed. Because I wasn't there. I wasn't strong enough. If I'd just been there, I—

I force those poisonous thoughts away with a harsh clearing of my throat. "We dealt with the hunters. Wulfric took over after Father's murder. He's a poor imitation. Nothing like either of our parents."

"I'm sure it must have been hard for him too, Anders. He's probably doing the best he can."

I shake my head, refusing to let go of my anger. I need that anger to fuel me so I can return home and challenge him. "You don't know a thing about Wulfric, pet." I try not to be angry at him. He knows little of our world. "Trust me when I say he's been a poor leader, and his actions have weakened our pack. He brought a *human* into our pack. After everything they'd done."

"Where'd this human come from?"

"Your time. He'd traveled to ours, no doubt with the intention of hunting us all down and killing us. Humans can't be trusted. They hate my kind. Always have."

"But I don't," Jamie reminds me. "You're super cool."

I'm caught off guard. I'm not used to having my be-liefs questioned like this. If it were anyone else, I'd bleed them for questioning me, but I'd never hurt Jamie. "That's true," I admit. "But you're an exception, pet. You're ulfhednar at heart. Humans hate and fear us. Our gift of the change makes us untrustworthy in the eyes of many. Savages."

Jamie's shoulders slump. "Sorry to hear that. I'll be honest, a lot of humans even now hate wolves."

I snort. "Unsurprising."

"But a lot of them also really love wolves. For so many, wolves are considered a vital part of our ecosystem, and some people have dedicated themselves to preserving the species."

I narrow my eyes. "Preserving? Why would wolves need preservation?"

"Humans hunted wolves almost to extinction."

"So, things truly have not changed. If that's how they treat wild wolves, can you imagine how they would treat ulfhednar? They are the true monsters."

"I won't argue with you there. Humanity disappoints me more than it surprises me." One side of Jamie's full lips curve up. "But I think for every lousy person, there's a few trying to make the world better for the next generation."

How interesting. I'd never thought of it that way, that good could rival or even outweigh the bad. My mate has a unique way of looking at things.

"Anyway, your brother's mate was human?"

"How did you know he was my brother's mate?"

He shrugs. "It's not hard to guess."

I take a sip of my coffee. There's a buzzing growing under my skin, and I'm itching to move. I tap my feet beneath the table to relieve the restless energy. "That's what Wulfric believes." I sneer the words. "As if a human could ever be one of us."

"But I was human."

"No. The Norns would never choose a human for my mate. They did it for Wulfric as a sign to tell us all he was unworthy. I am not. You were *raised* human. That's different. Your grandmother was born to ulfhednar parents. All you needed was another wolf to bring out your innate shifter abilities. You would have manifested shifter abilities from a young age, even if you or your parents lacked the ability to change forms. Heightened senses, for instance."

"Yeah. That makes sense. My senses have always been really strong. Still, you shouldn't paint humans with such a broad brush, Anders. All of my friends are humans, and they're really great. I bet if they knew—"

"No." I slam a fist down on the table. "You can never tell them what you are, Jamie. Never. They would hate and fear you, desire nothing more than to see you dead."

"That's not true." He shakes his head, anger spicing his scent. I've upset him. Best to change the subject.

"Kieran tried to change everything about our way of life. Modernize us. First by getting rid of our thralls. Eventually, he'll convince Wulfric to give up Fenrir's gift. Wulfric will obey, I know it, and then he'll force us all to do the same! He will doom our pack."

Chewing his pancakes thoughtfully, Jamie swallows. "I don't know, Anders. It sounds like you're making assumptions. I don't blame you at all after everything humans did to your pack, but how can you know Kieran will do all of that?"

I sigh and don't argue. Jamie is newly changed. He can't understand. While my wolf may have insisted we trust our Alpha, I knew better than to obey my animal instincts. "Even if there was only the slightest chance Wulfric would weaken us and expose us all to hunters, I had to do everything in my power to prevent it. So I challenged him."

"And you lost," Jamie says, guessing correctly.

I growl out a yes. I can't tell Jamie all the conflicting thoughts that warred in my head as I faced my brother. How angry I'd been and then how sorrowful. Old wounds had torn wide open, and I'd been forced to acknowledge my own guilt, my own helplessness and failings. I'd let my emotions cripple me.

"Wulfric should have killed me. Instead, weakling that he is, he chose exile as my punishment. He let me live, and it was a mistake." My knuckles whiten as my fingers tighten around my utensils. "I will return, and this time, I'll win. Once he's dead and I claim the title of Alpha, my pack will never be threatened again, not by rival packs or hunters."

Jamie bites his lower lip. "Anders—never mind. I'll just say that sometimes, how we feel isn't always a reflection of reality."

I don't know what he means.

"Will Wulfric kill you if you return?" Worry taints his scent.

I flash my teeth in a feral smile. "He can try, but he won't be successful."

"Why? What are you going to do that is different this time around? You should have a plan."

"I will not fail. I promise you. But I will do what must be done to save my pack, and for that to happen, you must give me your necklace. I am willing to earn it. Just tell me what I must do."

Jamie's eyes brighten. "I do have an idea, actually." He pulls out one of those handheld objects humans seem so fond of. "Come on, let's get the rest of this to go. I've got somewhere to be, and you're coming with me."

Curiosity compels me to my feet. "Lead on, then."

CHAPTER 7

JAMIE

"Where to next?" Anders asks.

I drive out of the parking spot. "Brooklyn."

"What's there?"

"When my grandma died, she left me her bookshop."

Anders hums. I'm not sure if he knows what books are. After we drive across the Brooklyn Bridge, it's only ten minutes to the shop. Once we park, Anders follows me into the little blue shop with big glass windows. The sign over the shop welcomes us to Moon Beans and Books Café.

Every time I unlock the doors, memories of Gran rush back to me. When I was a kid, if my parents were busy, they'd drop me off here. I'd study at one of the tables while Gran baked fresh pastries, or I'd while away the hours reading fantasy books or blushing over a steamy romance novel. She always had the latest bestsellers. When I was a college student studying to earn a degree in entrepreneurship, Gran gave me a job and helped put me through school.

After Grandma died a year ago, I worried the café would lose much of its heart and soul, but I've done my best to keep her spirit alive. I've created my own coffee blend that flies off the shelves and expanded our stock to include books by indie authors rather than just the latest bestseller from the big publishing houses.

My bookshelves full of diverse stories by queer and BIPOC authors are the highlight of the store. I always wanted to read more books with queer characters like me when I was growing up, and I know so many people crave that representation too, so it's important to me that my shop helps provide a platform for those much-needed voices.

This shop is my baby, so it really pisses me off when people try and take advantage of me and mess with my store. Like my former employee. I tried to be understanding, gave her chance after chance, but she kept missing work and coming in late if she came in at all. Just a few days ago, she quit without any notice and left me searching for her replacement.

Then, a Viking werewolf burst out of the Hudson River and landed at my feet. Anders wants to earn my grandma's necklace? I have an idea for where he can start.

"How would you like to work here?"

Anders almost drops a book he's lifted from a shelf. "You want me to work? Here?" His eyes go wide as he looks up and down the shop.

"It's a simple job," I assure him, hoping I don't give the guy a coronary. "Nothing complicated like making coffee. I just need someone to stock shelves and keep the store clean. Do you think you could do that?"

Anders huffs and crosses his arms. "Do I *look* like I'm incapable of manual labor to you?"

I throw him a wink. "Puppy dog, you look capable of throwing me over your shoulder and carrying me off to your den to have your wicked way with me. So that's a yes?"

He shrugs said shoulders. "Just tell me what needs doing."

"Like I said, just cleaning and simple stuff like that. If you want, we could work up toward you being a barista."

"For how long would I be indentured to you?"

Oh, right. Our time together has an end date. Anders will want to go back to his time. My wolf whines in my chest. I cough to try and hide the pitiful noise that escapes me. I barely know Anders. Why do I care if he leaves? "Until after the New Year, if that's all right, so about three months. The holidays are the busiest time of year for us."

Anders runs a hand through his thick beard, considering my offer. "Very well. I accept your offer on the condition that you give me food and lodgings until I can return to my time."

"Of course. I'd be happy for you to stay with me." More than happy, actually. If I were shifted right now, my tail would be spinning in circles.

"When can I start?"

"We're closed today. There was some flooding in the basement, but that's all cleared up. But how about to-morrow?"

Throat bobbing, Anders says, "T-tomorrow?"

Fighting back a chuckle at his nerves, I flick some of his long hair out of his rugged but handsome face. "Re-lax, puppy dog. You've got this. You'll shadow someone and they'll show you the ropes."

Anders's shoulders loosen. "Oh. Aye, I can work with ropes."

A laugh escapes me before I can stop myself. "No, not those kinds of—never mind."

Ah, he's too much fun.

If I'm not careful, I could really see myself liking this guy.

Crap.

Jace is bursting with excitement when I pick him up from school. "Mr. Gladston wants us to pick our own subjects for a presentation."

His excitement makes my chest warm with affection. Mr. Gladston is his history teacher, and Jace adores him. "That's cool! What do you want to give a presentation on?"

"Duh, Vikings! Hey, Anders!" Jace sprints toward the car. Before I can warn Jace not to pester Anders, the big Viking squats down to Jace's eye level and offers my brother a smile that makes me almost trip over my own feet. How is such an intimidating guy capable of looking so... sweet?

"Aye, lad? Have a good day at your school?" His deep voice is soft and warm, making my chest hitch.

"It was great! Hey, Anders, can you come do a presentation with me at my school? I want to tell my class all about Vikings!"

It's not a *terrible* idea. Nobody will actually believe he's a real Viking from another time, but a Viking werewolf in a classroom full of rowdy children doesn't sound like the best combination. Anders will probably be overwhelmed by the environment.

Anders says, "I'd be happy to. What is a presentation?"

The last thing I want is for Anders to put himself in an uncomfortable situation. He's already stressed as is. "Jace, hey, bud. How about you get buckled in? We can discuss this at home."

Once Jace is in the car and buckled up, I drive us home. Jace challenges Anders to a race up the stairs, and I'm surprised when Anders obliges, grinning like a big kid as they race each other to the fifth floor. Huffing a laugh, I jog after them.

Anders hasn't known Jace for even a full day, but he's already better with him than most guys I've dated for weeks. Chest tightening with longing, I halt on the stairs. Anders isn't staying. He isn't. Staying. I can't afford to get attached to some guy who clearly has his own motives and priorities.

"Yes!" Jace slaps his palm against the front door. "Beat you!"

"Jace," I scold lightly, then glance at Anders. He's panting exaggeratedly. There's no way my kid brother could have beaten a Viking werewolf. Did Anders let him win?

Damn it. That's so sweet. And I'm supposed to *not* daydream about a future with him?

"That you did, lad," Anders says, ruffling Jace's hair when he comes to stand beside him.

Unlocking the door, I let everyone inside. "Are you hungry?" I ask Jace. I made sure to pack him his usual lunch, so he shouldn't be.

"Nope. Can I play video games?" He flashes a charming smile.

"For an hour, but then you need to do your homework, okay?"

Jace boots up the PlayStation, then throws himself on the sofa. "Got it!"

Chuckling, Anders says, "He's a good lad."

"The best brother a guy could ask for," I say, smiling as Jace starts playing *Rachet & Clank*.

Anders sniffs his underarm. "Where is the nearest hot spring?"

"We don't have those here, but you can use my shower."

"A... shower?"

"Yeah. You know. A bath."

Anders cocks his head. "Is it Laugardagr?"

I have to google on my phone what the hell that word means. Turns out it's an old Norse word for Saturday. "No. Why?"

"It's wash day."

"Nowadays, most people bathe at least every day."

His eyes widen. "Every day? But that's such a waste of water!"

"No, no! It's okay. We have plenty of water here." I show Anders where the bathroom is. "How about you give me your clothes. I'll wash them."

Anders arches a brow. "You do this all yourself? Don't you have any thralls to do your chores for you?"

"You mean like a maid or something? Yeah, I wish I could afford to pay a cleaner. This place seriously needs it."

He sighs. "Fine. I suppose I can wash my own linens. Is there a river around here?"

A snort of laughter escapes me. "I have a washer and dryer in my unit. Just strip. I'll take care of it."

Anders undresses, grumbling about how I shouldn't be washing his clothes. His eyes widen when I turn the tap and water gushes into the tub. "You don't have to gather water? It fills itself?" He marvels at the water, running a hand curiously through it. "It's so warm!" He adjusts the knob and gasps when the temperature drops. "Hot and cold at the turn of a knob! Odin's beard, this is astonishing!"

I grin at his enthusiasm. For such a scary-looking guy, he really is adorable. "There are towels on the rack, and I have a spare comb there. I'll do your laundry." I leave Anders to his own devices and get the washer running.

With the washer cleaning his linens, I collapse on the sofa and watch Jace play games. He's good at gaming, but I was never really into it. Books were always my go-to escapism. "You're feeling better, huh?"

Jace's fingers slip on the controls, making his character fall to their death. "Darn it! Uh. Yeah. I'm fine." Thanks to my shifter senses, I pick up the way his heart skips and his scent darkens with something like... guilt?

"Hey. Pause the game a sec. Talk to me."

Sighing exasperatedly, Jace sets down the controller and stares into his lap. "I'm sorry." He rubs his nose. "For messing up your date."

Jace thinks it's his fault? I had no idea he was blaming himself. "That wasn't your fault."

"Yes, it was," Jace huffs, blinking fast. "I always mess things up for you."

Shaking my head, I touch his shoulder. "You do not. It's not your fault you get anxious sometimes, Jace."

"But you were really looking forward to it." Jace's lips tremble, tears brightening his eyes. "You were happy. You're never happy."

Is that what he thinks? Horrified, I stay silent as I churn over the past week or so, trying to remember what kind of a mood I was in. Sure, I try to be upbeat and positive, but lately, a lot of it feels like an act. Rent is tight, and I've basically got two full-time jobs—the bookshop and being a parent to my little brother. Maybe there was one time I cursed when I screwed up dinner, or maybe I sweat over little mistakes too much, but I try to stay positive for his sake.

So he doesn't realize how fucking deep I'm drowning some days.

The truth is, I don't know if I can keep the bookshop going *and* raise Jace, but I've got to. It's hard when, after an exhausting day burning the candle at both ends, I come home to a cold, empty bed. I can't remember when I last had time for myself or even finished a book. Most days, I don't think I'm a good caretaker to Jace. My parents were so much better at this than I am, and they're gone.

I have no one to rely on, no one I can trust with my brother but myself, and a lot of the time, I don't even know if anything I do is good enough.

Swallowing the lump in my throat, I make myself smile. "Jace."

He stubbornly avoids my gaze.

"Hey." Reaching out, I tip up his chin and look him in his watery eyes. "That guy I went out with? He was a jerk."

"You're just saying that," Jace mumbles, picking at a loose thread hanging from his jeans.

"I mean it. He was a big, nasty chicken butt." Jace snorts, and I grin. "Listen to me, kiddo. Nobody is coming between us. If I have to choose between you and some guy, I'm choosing you. End of story."

Jace makes a face like what I said was gross, but happiness blooms in his scent like sweet spring flowers. "What if they're Henry Cavill?"

I gawk at him. This kid... "Okay, if I have to choose between you and Henry Cavill, I'm picking Cavill, but anyone else gets the boot!" When Jace erupts into giggles, my own laughter bubbles out of me. "Get over here."

"No!"

"Come here!" I yank him against me and tickle him until he's gasping for breath. Breathless with laughter myself, I give him a squeeze. "Love you, little bro."

"You too," he says grudgingly, but he's smiling when we pull apart.

"Now, go do your homework."

Pouting at me, Jace does as he's told. The bedroom door closes behind him, and I fall back against the cushions. I meant every word. I will always put Jace first. Our little family is broken and unconventional, but we're all we've got.

Nobody's coming between us, even if I have to be alone for the rest of my life.

Chapter 8
Anders

Later that night, Jamie orders us something called pizza. It's flatbread sprinkled with cheese and something called tomato sauce and cooked until it is crispy. It is delicious. I ate half of it. The human world may be full of savage, hateful creatures, but they do know how to cook.

After we've eaten, Jamie calls Jace and me into the bathroom and shoves a little brush at me. "Here."

It's so tiny I can't fathom what uses it has. I take the brush and run it over my hair.

Jace erupts into laughter.

"What are you doing?" Jamie is gawking at me.

"It's a brush. I'm brushing my hair."

Jamie covers his mouth but can't suppress a snort. "No, it's a brush for your *teeth*! In my time, we brush our teeth after meals." He hands me a tube. "This is toothpaste. You scrub it over your teeth, then rinse and spit."

"Ah. Is that why your teeth are in such fine shape?"

He nods. "I'm surprised your teeth look so good," Jamie says as he takes the tube back and squeezes the paste over our brushes.

"Ulfhednar have strong and resilient teeth, and if we lose them, it's usually in fights. But plenty of humans from my time are missing theirs."

I begin to brush. The paste makes me gag at first and tastes like one of Jamie's mints. He instructs me on which direction to go in, and by the time I spit and rinse, my breath smells as sweet as his.

Jamie's patience, I might even describe it as an *eagerness*, to teach me the ways of his world is... Well, it's a kindness I wouldn't have expected to find in a place like this. He fed me, cleaned my clothes, put a roof over my head. My mate gives so much of himself so willingly. He should be careful. Doesn't he know how easy it would be for someone to take advantage of his kind heart?

Someone like me.

"Want us to read together again?" Jamie asks Jace as we approach the lad's room.

He shakes his head. "That's okay. I can do it myself."

"Okay, if you're sure..."

Jace grins. "Good night!" He waves to both of us and heads into his room.

Jamie sighs. "Man, I miss the days when he would pester me for a bedtime story. He's growing up so fast."

"You read together?" I ask, following Jamie to his room across the apartment.

"Not as much as we used to." Jamie jumps when I bump into his back right outside his door. "Oh. You want to sleep with me?"

"And why wouldn't I?"

Jamie huffs. "You know, I may be ulfhednar, but I was raised human. We tend to take things slow."

"I know nothing of slow."

"Clearly." He holds the door for me, and we go into his room together.

Jamie peels off his shirt, and I wet my lips, admiring his fair skin. My mate kicks off his pants, revealing his strong legs, perky ass, and the swell of his cock. It feels like ages since I had my hands or mouth on his skin, but it was only this morning.

"Does it unsettle you? I can show restraint if you'd like."

Jamie's throat bobs when he swallows. "It does," he admits, and something inside me shrivels. There's a flush to his cheeks, and arousal spices his scent. There's something he isn't telling me.

I discard my breeches and peel my shirt over my head. Wrapping my arms around his chest, I pull him to me and press my nose into his neck. "If I unsettle you so, then why do you smell like you'll die unless I touch you, pet?"

Jamie shivers and leans his body into mine. "I, uh... Can we just talk, actually?" He wiggles out of my grip.

I'm disappointed but shrug. "If that's what you wish."

Jamie lies in bed and pats the space beside him.

"Move over," I insist.

"Why?"

"I want to be between you and the door, pet."

Jamie scoffs, smiling like I'm amusing. "Why? To protect me from the dust bunnies in my living room?"

A furious snarl erupts from me. I don't know what these dust bunnies are, but if they seek to harm my mate, I will tear them apart! "Are these dust bunnies dangerous?"

Jamie hides his face in his hands, laughing for some reason. "Oh no. What have I done? Anders, I'm fine!"

"I cannot let you sleep near the door if these dust bunnies lie in wait! Move over. I will watch the door."

Still laughing for some unfathomable reason, Jamie scoots over and lets me lie on the side of the bed nearest the door. "Keep the light on. Beasts fear light of any kind. Dust bunnies must be no different."

Jamie's still giggling. I'm not sure why. Eventually, he quiets while I continue to glower at the door. If anything tries to enter this room, my wolf will rip them to pieces.

"You wished to talk?"

Jamie hums thoughtfully, hooking one leg over my waist. "Were you close with your parents? I know you and your brothers have a difficult relationship, but what about your mom and dad?"

An odd lump forms in my throat as I think of them. I haven't allowed myself to dwell on their memories, not in years. Yet I can't seem to deny Jamie anything. "Very close. I only knew my mother a few short years, but... she was a kind woman. Stronger than anyone I've known."

Warm hands rub my chest, almost soothingly. I close my eyes and bask in the warmth of Jamie's touch. It's good we aren't mated. Otherwise, he could sense these disgusting feelings tearing me apart. How weak they make me feel...

"She died birthing my brother Wulfric." Why am I still speaking? "I hate him for that. For taking her from me."

"Anders," Jamie begins, and I despise the sadness in his voice.

"I will kill him for killing her. For taking my father from me."

"Hey." Jamie grips at my chest, but I squirm out of his reach, curling my body away from his. All I want is to bare my heart and soul to him while he holds me tight until all my broken pieces cease to ache. I can't. I can't let him numb my anger. I need my fury to do what must be done and save my pack.

"Go to bed. I will keep you safe." Even if I could stay, I would never be a worthy mate for Jamie. He is too kind, too trusting. When I leave, it will be for the best. I don't deserve someone like him, not when I can't even keep my own family safe.

Jamie hums softly. "Okay. Good night, puppy dog." I ignore the hurt in his voice as best as I can, curling my fingers in the sheets so I don't reach out to him.

I focus on guarding the door and try my best to ignore the empty space between us.

The next day, after more delicious pancakes for breakfast, Jamie drops the lad off at his school, then drives us to his bookshop. It's warm inside and smells of parchment and Jamie himself. The wolf in me yawns and stretches out, longing to curl up and nap in this place that smells so much like our mate. His apartment smells even more divine.

I'm tense as the door closes behind us, and I reach back to lock it. Jamie insisted I wear the clothes of this time, which are soft and unsuitable for combat. He dragged me to this place called Goodwill on the way to the café and let me pick out my own clothes but insisted on picking my outfit for work. The jeans, dark shirt, and green apron fit comfortably, but if we're attacked, how will I defend myself?

"Everything okay?" Jamie looks back to watch me curiously.

A scowl twists my mouth. "I should have brought my furs." We left them at home, hidden in Jamie's closet. Gods willing, they'll be safe there.

"Anders, we went over this. You need to fit in, and walking around looking like you walked off the set of HBO's *Vikings* will intimidate customers."

Jamie's voice is placating, but I'm still irritated. "What do I care what some peasants think? Your safety is all that's important to me."

My mate throws me a teasing smile. "We both know you don't need your furs to protect me, puppy dog. You're strong enough, aren't you?"

"Of course I am!" As if I'd let anything happen to him.

Smiling, Jamie walks back to me and rubs my arm. "Then don't worry so much. You've got this."

His touch and sweet smile ease the tension from my body. "Did you build this all yourself?" I am impressed with my mate's craftsmanship.

"Oh no. The building was already here. But my grandma did all the work turning it into a bookshop. I'm not sure what it was before."

Still, it is remarkable that he has his own business. The Norns chose well. My mate is hardworking and kind. With a start, I force down the thought. I've got to stay focused, work hard, and get the necklace. Jamie is a fun distraction, nothing more or less. Although he is very nice to wake up next to. And suck off in the shower. And eat breakfast with. Jamie is lovely, like a sunrise at the end of a long, cold night.

"And you sell books?" I ask.

"Romance books specifically. I was never satisfied with the limited selection most big chain bookstores have. I have all kinds of subgenres of romance. Contemporary, dark, rom-coms, stories with LGBTQ+ and BIPOC characters, fantasy, paranormal. You name it."

"And you read for fun?"

"Yup. It can be a good distraction but also a great way of learning about other people's experiences."

I run my finger along the spine of a book. Pulling it from the shelf, I'm astonished by the artwork of a man and woman sharing a kiss while they ride on a horse into the sunset. It's beautiful, and the pages are soft as I flip through them. The runes inscribed within are not futhark. The language is unknown to me. "Fascinating."

Jamie's smile is soft and sad. "You've never read a book? At all?"

"We did not write our stories down. We told sagas and poems to our family and friends to teach valuable lessons the gods have passed down to us. Tales of honor, glory, and even warnings of how the world would end. I learned to wield a blade as soon as I was old enough to walk and talk. Survival was more important than simple pleasures." I close the book and push it back into place. "Now, what are my duties?"

"Basically," Jamie says as he leads me around the shelves, "you'll keep the store clean. Customers can be sloppy, so if they don't clean up after themselves, you'll have to wipe down tables. At the end of the day, you'll sweep and mop so everything is nice and clean for tomorrow."

"Easy enough." It is an honest job, if not the most exciting.

"You don't sound very happy."

"I'm not. Such menial tasks are the work of peasants. I am the son of a jarl."

Jamie claps me on the back, making me grimace. "Time to get down and dirty with the rest of us working-class folk, puppy dog."

As degrading as this work is, it sounds like child's play to me. I've always excelled at everything I've done. This shall not be any different, no matter what time I am in. Jamie shows me where the cleaning supplies are, though the store was cleaned the night before.

Someone knocks on the door, making me growl at the unseen threat.

"Chill, Anders. It's just Bailey." Jamie jogs to let whoever this Bailey person is inside. "Morning!"

I peer around my mate at the woman. She has rich umber skin, a face that strikes a balance between masculine and feminine, a strong jaw, full lips, and a button nose. A brimmed black hat sits atop a curly head of short black hair that is dyed pink at the tips. A black dress, heeled boots, and a black-and-white striped sweater complete the outfit.

"Morning, love!" Bailey says, sweeping my mate into an embrace.

I freeze in place as dread sinks into my stomach like a rock.

A growl rumbles up my throat as Bailey leans in and presses her mouth to Jamie's cheek.

Fury ignites within my soul.

Nobody is taking Jamie from me. I have never in my life had someone who was mine and mine alone. Wulfric had our father's adoration and then the love of his human mate, even though he deserved none of it. Gunnar had Leif, his chosen mate, and their child. Lyall had his mate for years, since boyhood. I had convinced myself I was happy sharing my bed with whichever tavern wench or village lad would have me.

It was a lie.

I have finally found someone made just for me, and I am not losing him.

Jamie is *mine.* Fury courses through me as the berserker within roars to life. My muscles grow thicker. My shoes threaten to split. Fur grows thick on my arms, creeping up slowly toward my face.

"Hands off!" I roar, making them both jump. I yank Jamie against my chest and bare my teeth at this Bailey.

How dare this person touch my mate so intimately? True, I haven't claimed him yet, but once I have, none would dare touch him!

Wait. What? I'm not here to claim Jamie. I'm here to charm him into giving me his necklace. Not to mate with him. *By the gods, stick to the plan, Anders!*

In a deepening voice, I snarl, "Touch him again, and I will cleave your arms from your body."

"Anders, what the hell?" Jamie glares at me, and then shock erases his anger. "Holy shit. What is happening to you?" he hisses.

Fury makes me pant. My clothes tighten as my muscles swell. If I transform into my berserker form, I will be hunted. Fear twists like a knife in my chest. "Can't... can't hold back the rage." Damn it! If I'd only claimed him that first night we were together, this wouldn't be happening.

"What's that, Anders? Oh, okay. Let me show you where we keep that!" Jamie whirls me around and shoves me toward his office. In seconds, he crams me in it and locks the door. "What is going on? Is this some weird ulfhednar thing?"

I pant through my fangs and make myself breathe in his scent. To my relief, the rage begins to fade. My claws become blunt, and so do my fangs. My muscles shrink back to their normal size. The fur growing across my body retracts below my skin.

"Anders," Jamie snaps.

I growl at him. "All wolves from an Alpha bloodline tend to be stronger than regular wolves, but this power comes with a cost."

"What is this cost? It had better not involve you ripping my employees' limbs off."

Collapsing into his desk chair, I glower at the floor. I don't like his harsh tone, a reminder that I have disappointed and upset him. "We risk becoming berserkers. We'd lose control of ourselves and become beasts capable of great and terrible destruction."

Jamie's face pales. "Is there a cure?"

"The only thing that can cure a berserker's rage for good is by claiming his fated, or chosen, mate. We would have to exchange bites."

Jamie's mouth falls open. "O-oh..." He rubs the back of his neck, his cheeks reddening. "So, if we, uh... bit each other, then you'd be okay?"

"Aye, but—"

"—but you're not staying." There's no accusation in his voice, but his words hit me like one. "Because this is temporary, like we've agreed, and mating would complicate things."

I hesitate for a moment, willing to say anything to save his feelings. "True."

Jamie worries at his bottom lip. Have I hurt his feelings? Before I can sniff him to parse how he feels, Jamie asks, "So what can we do instead?"

I shrug. "Being around you is helpful. You're my mate. Your scent is calming. For now, that could be enough."

Jamie eyes me hopefully. "Are you sure?"

"Yes. Unmated wolves are most at risk of going berserk when we're overwhelmed or angry. We wolves are very possessive, and we do not take kindly to anyone touching what is ours."

"So that's what triggered you." Jamie huffs a laugh. "Anders, Bailey is just a friend. They're dating Jess. They aren't interested in me. Honestly. So can you cool it and try to get along with my employees?"

"Aye."

Jamie smiles. "Good."

It seems I have convinced him I'm not a threat. But I know better. Until we're mated, which will never happen, my wolf will be close to the surface. It would be so simple if I could just claim him. My wolf craves to make him mine, to leave my mark upon his skin for all the world to see. Proof he wants me and no one else. I can't. My only choice is to hurry and earn his necklace as fast as possible. Before I lose myself for good.

I follow Jamie from the office, vowing to keep my wolf on a tight leash.

"Anders, this is Bailey. They're my barista. Bailey, this is Anders. He's going to be working here. Hey, would you let go?" He wriggles, but I only crush him tighter to my body, glaring at this Bailey person.

Bailey cracks a grin. "Ooh. Mixing business with pleasure, Jamie?"

I growl.

Bailey snorts. "Don't worry, I'm not going to steal your man. Nice to meet you, Anders. How'd you and Jamie meet?"

"We're mates," I declare.

Jamie coughs loudly and elbows my ribs, forcing me to let go. "He means roommates!"

"They were roommates!" Bailey gasps, then winks at Jamie and walks around him to the counter.

"Anders, what the hell?" Jamie glares at me. "You can't just stake your claim on me in public like that!"

His words strike me in the chest. "Are you... ashamed of me?"

Jamie's mouth falls open. "What? No, not at all."

"Then why can't I let others know? You're mine, and I'm yours."

Sighing, Jamie rubs the back of his neck again. "Bailey is a human. They won't understand. Besides, we're not..." Whatever he was going to say, he doesn't finish. Good. I don't wish to hear it.

"I do not like her." I glare at Bailey.

"Them. Bailey's a great person. Give them a chance."

"Them?" As far as I can tell, there is only one of Bailey.

"Bailey isn't a man or a woman. They're nonbinary."

I've never heard of such a term before. "So... in between?"

Jamie laughs softly. "No. Not in between. They exist outside the gender binary."

I still don't understand, not quite. "So instead of he or she, Bailey is they?"

"Yeah, exactly. So, you know you're a man. Right? If someone called you her or she, that would feel wrong, wouldn't it?"

I nod. "Aye."

"Bailey has never felt like a man or a woman. So they identify as neither."

I'm still not sure I understand. "That's strange."

"It's different, but different doesn't always mean bad." Jamie frowns. "That's not a problem, is it? Anders, I can't let you work here if you're going to harass Bailey."

"Why would I harass her—them? I don't mind if Bailey is a they. I was angry that they touched you. There's nothing going on between you two?"

Jamie snorts. "Not at all. Like I said, Bailey's got a girlfriend."

Good. For a moment, I thought I was going to lose him to someone else.

"Are you okay?" Jamie asks, frowning up at me. "You took Bailey's affection toward me pretty personally."

"Hardly." The feeling wasn't only rage. It was dread, like nothing I've felt before. Jamie is mine from now until the moment we part ways.

"We're open!" Jamie calls.

In a few moments, people enter the store. They order drinks at the counter, and Bailey prepares them swiftly and with confidence. They really are skilled. Jamie was right, customers are sloppy. Not only do they leave crumbs all over the tables, but they also leave books lying around the shop, forcing me to gather them up and stuff them back on the shelf. A plump woman with piercings in her nose and green highlights in her hair enters the shop. She removes her sweater, revealing tattoos on her arms. Jamie and his friends are a colorful bunch.

"Hey! So you're the new guy?" she asks, striding up to me.

"Aye," I answer. "Uh. Are you a they as well?"

The woman laughs. "Nope. Boring old she/her right here. Name's Jess." She thrusts out her hand.

"Anders." We shake.

"Nice to meet ya, Anders. Just a friendly critique, you're stocking those books wrong."

I grimace. "I am not."

"You're mixing the dark romance with the rom-coms."

"So?" She's the one who is wrong. I know exactly what I'm doing!

"Hey, no need to frown. We all were newbies once." One by one, she removes the books and points down the aisle. "Dark romance goes over there."

"I knew that..." My cheeks burn hot with frustration. It's a simple task. Can't I do anything right? "I can sort the books on my own." I snatch them from her arms and stalk toward the proper shelves, where I shove them into place.

Jess goes behind the bar to work with Bailey, and the pair chat, smiling and laughing. Jamie engages in their comradery as well. It's clear the three of them are close. Something twinges in my chest that feels a lot like longing.

I miss being somewhere familiar, around people who know me. I never got along with Wulfric, but my twin, Lyall, and I were thick as thieves as soon as we were old enough to get into mischief. I... I miss him. Gunnar too. I miss Helga, my aunt. Do they miss me? They must. I know Helga got more and more ornery toward me as I challenged Wulfric, and Lyall was exasperated with me more oft than not. But surely they still thought of me as pack, family?

How I wish I was home in Ulfheim.

"Excuse me!" a woman snaps, blonde and angry. She waves her paper cup at Bailey. "I asked for almond milk! This is regular milk. Pay attention!"

A small child at her side stamps her foot. "Mommy! Muffin!"

"Just a moment, sweetie. Honestly, I don't know why I come here when you always get my order wrong. You're lucky this is the only café down the street from my apartment!"

"So sorry, Karen." Bailey starts making another drink.

"It's Lauren!"

Bailey doesn't seem to care.

Jess catches my gaze and rolls her eyes. It seems like this Lauren is someone they deal with often. I endeavor to ignore the noise and focus on the simple task of stocking the books. At least, it should be simple. More fools have left books lying around. These have men riding horses on the cover. Are these dark romances too?

The child screams, "Mommy, I want!"

The scream pierces my ears, making me gnash my teeth.

"In a second, baby. Hey, hurry up with my drink!" Lauren snaps, her loud voice further irritating my sensitive ears. The coffee machines make all sorts of noise. The child shrieks in protest. A dog someone brought into the store barks, making me wince. Some old man sitting by the window sneezes shrilly. It's too loud. Too much. Too confusing.

I pile books in my arms to bring them to the proper section, only I can't remember where these damn books go. Was the dark romance section next to the potted plant or by the sofa in the back? Gods damn it! How did I go from being the best at everything I do to not even knowing where to put some bloody books?

A furious snarl builds in my chest as the noise swirls around me. Out. Need out. Need to run, now!

"Anders?" Jamie calls as he walks out from the kitchen, a tray of baked goods in his hands, a concerned look on his face. "Sorry, I know I said you could shadow me today. Things got busy, but I'll be there in a second. Do you need anything?"

"Where do these go?" I hold up the books.

Jamie squints at the spines. "That's a historical romance author, so they go in the way back to the left on the top shelf."

Repeating the information in my head, I turn around. "Whoa, Anders, look out!"

I slam right into Jess. She shrieks, and something hot splashes all over my chest. A yowl of pain escapes me as the liquid sears through my shirt and burns my skin. Somehow, I didn't drop the books, but there's coffee all over my shirt.

"Oh crap. I'm super sorry, man." She reaches out, and panic flares within me.

The burn of hot coffee on my skin reminds me of the silver *they* used to carve into my body. They invaded our village, set our homes on fire. Smoke had choked the air. With a crash, the door had blown wide open, and the hunters swarmed in. They'd bound me with silver. The pain had never ended. Every time I'd healed, they cut me open again and again.

I'd screamed for my father to come and save me.

I'd cried out for my brother Wulfric. My Alpha. The only time I'd ever thought of him that way.

No one had come.

"Get back, wench!" My roar fills the café before I can stop it.

Everyone stares at me. Their judgment, their mistrust, makes cold sweat break out over my body. I've backed up into the bookshelf. The breath saws from my body in ragged pants.

"Hey, I didn't mean—" Jess begins, her wide-eyed face etched with concern.

"Stay back," I snarl at her. "Do not make me tell you again!"

Fear widens her eyes, and, strangely, I want to take the moment back. My father's voice rings in my ears. I'd asked him once why Wulfric would be Alpha even though I was older and stronger. He'd told me, *An Alpha is chosen for more than the strength of their arms, Anders. He or she must be able to put the needs of others before themselves when necessary and never use their superior strength as a weapon against the weak.*

Is this... regret I'm feeling now? Wulfric would never have intimidated a peasant for such a simple mistake. A wave of inferiority crashes over me, dragging me down to the blackest depths. Is it really any wonder Wulfric was chosen instead of me?

I do the only thing I can and run from the shop.

CHAPTER 9

JAMIE

What in the hell just happened with Anders? At least he didn't wolf out again, but still, he seemed pretty freaked-out.

Jess gawks at the door he fled through.

My wolf, his urges faint without my furs, is pushing me to pursue our mate and make sure he's okay, but I've got to check on Jess. She's a wounded party in this too.

"Hey, you okay?" I squeeze her shoulder.

"What bit him in the ass?" She looks as bewildered as I feel. "It looked like he panicked."

"You know how it is. A new job is stressful."

"You're not the one he called a wench," she grumbles. "Who even talks like that anyway?"

A Viking time traveler who is in over his head and out of his element. It's a good thing he left his furs at home, or he might have shifted.

"I'll talk to him, Jess. It won't happen again."

Bailey hurries over with a mop in their hands. "I've got this, Jess. You go and take care of the customers."

It seems they're okay. Anders completely blew his first impression with my friends. I just hope he can fix it. I rush past the line of customers and out the door, only to find Anders sitting hunched over on a bench, face in his hands. A twinge spasms through my chest seeing him so downtrodden. I want to give him one of my famous Jamie hugs—my friends always say I give the best hugs—but I don't want to overwhelm him even more.

"Hey, puppy dog. You good?"

Anders growls, the sound very un-puppy dog of him.

"What happened back there? Jess didn't mean to bump into you. It was an accident."

"I know that," he says, voice muffled through his hands.

Tentatively, I lower myself onto the bench beside him. I want to touch him but ball my hands into fists in my lap instead. "Then what was it?"

A sigh deflates his shoulders, bitter as the chilly October wind. "I don't want humans touching me ever again."

My breath catches. Again? My poor puppy dog. "It's okay to set boundaries. We'll all understand and do our best." A sudden thought makes my stomach twist. "Is it okay if I touch you?"

Anders nods, and relief warms me.

"Can I touch you now?"

"If you like." Anders makes it sound like he's going to the gallows.

"It's not about what I like. Do you want me to touch you?"

He sighs. "Must I really spell it out? Aye. Of course. So just do it already."

Unable to fight back a smile, I scoot over so our sides are touching and slip my arm over his wide shoulders. The tension seeps from his body, and my heart melts when he leans into me.

Oh, I'm screwed. We slept together only yesterday, and yet my heart is all about this guy. I want him to keep opening up to me, to shed that tough-guy skin and show more of that soft heart I know is underneath. This isn't good. I'm going to get myself hurt if I keep giving pieces of myself away to him so fast. "Is that all that upset you?"

Anders angles his head so his chin is on my shoulder, his face out of view. "Just tell your human friends not to touch me."

"They wouldn't hurt you, Anders. I promise. They're good people. A lot like you, actually."

He jerks away with a scoff. "They're human. Nothing like me."

"I meant that they know what it's like to be outcasts. Jess's family disowned her after she told them she was bisexual. Bailey's family is great, but they've dealt with bullying for years because of their gender identity. Being ulfhednar isn't all that different from being queer, I guess. I promise Jess and Bailey would never hurt you. Neither of them have a mean bone in their body... Okay, maybe Jess can get a bit hotheaded, but that's just because she's protective of all of us."

Anders sets his jaw in a scowl. "I will never befriend humans. They are the enemy, and my fight is with them."

"Oh my god." I roll my eyes to the sky. "Do not try and fight Jess. You'll regret it, trust me. And Bailey teaches self-defense, so they could put you on your ass."

"Like to see them try."

How is this relationship going to work if he wants to beat the shit out of my friends? Wait. Is this a relationship?

"Anders. Just give them a chance."

His entire face turns red with fury, his jaw grinding so tight I worry he'll break his teeth.

"Please?" I add.

With an enormous sigh, Anders's rage leaves his body. "Fine." He spits the word like poison. "But only because I like it when you beg, pet," he says with a smirk that shouldn't be as sexy as it is.

I really want to get him alone, and soon, but only once I'm sure he'll be on his good behavior with my friends. "I know first days are always stressful."

"Wasn't stressed."

I ignore that because it's obvious he was. "I'm sorry I left you alone. I should have stuck close to you until you felt comfortable, but I had to get some baking done. For the rest of the day, I'll be right there if you need me."

Those beautiful emerald eyes finally meet mine as his shoulders loosen. "Truly?"

"Yeah. Promise." Standing, I hold out my hand.

Anders clasps it, and I tug him up with a strength I didn't have a few days ago. It must be the ulfhednar's influence. I expect him to pull away, but he keeps my hand firmly clasped in his as we head inside. The coffee has been cleaned up, Jess and Bailey are bantering behind the counter, and all seems well.

Returning to the box of books, I kneel and grab a few titles. "Okay. These are both rom-coms. Take a guess at where they go."

Anders scrunches his brow, then takes them from my hands and marches over to the correct shelf. "Here."

"Exactly."

Anders looks away, but not before I catch a glimmer of a pleased smile.

True to my word, I stay by his side for the rest of the day. We organize shelves, clean up after customers, and I run out to grab us some lunch from the deli around the corner. Since Anders is more in touch with his wolf than I am, I get him a sandwich loaded with meat and an egg salad on a roll for myself.

We sit on the sofa together and unwrap our sandwiches. Anders sniffs his. "Bacon!" He digs in with such eagerness I know I chose well.

"Hey, I made plans with everyone to go out tonight. How about you come out with us after work?"

Anders licks grease off his fingers. "Where to?"

"There's a bar we like in the West Village. We can all grab drinks, and you can have a fresh start with Jess and Bailey."

Anders glances over at Bailey and Jess with obvious reservations. "That would not be wise."

"Oh, come on, Anders. It'll be fun. Trust me, once they get past your scowling face and horrendous personality, they'll love you. At least stay for one drink."

"Very well." Anders leans in, and his lips tickle my ear. "I expect a reward for my good behavior later."

Noticing Bailey arching a teasing brow, I shove Anders away. "Later, when we're alone."

I can't wait for tonight.

At home that evening, I get ready for our night out. I squeeze into my sluttiest jeans, super tight and just barely covering my ass crack. A sheer top that displays my pierced nipples completes the look. Anders will definitely appreciate this. We went shopping for him on our way home. He seriously needed some more modern clothes.

It's cold tonight, but we'll mostly be in the car or inside the bar, so I finish the outfit off with some boots and a leather jacket. Jess usually helps me add some dark, dramatic eyeshadow, but we'll have to do that at the bar since I'm awful with makeup. I always make myself look like a goth clown without her expert touch.

Anders is lounging on the sofa in the living room. He's wearing the new clothes I bought him: a leather jacket like mine, tight ripped jeans that hang low on his hips, and a V-cut shirt that hugs his luscious pecs. I want to climb him like a damn tree.

"Hey. Ready to go?"

His eyes go wide at the sight of me, and he lurches off the couch. "By the gods. It's as if you're wearing nothing at all." He sounds absolutely scandalized, his hungry green eyes roaming every inch of my body. "I can practically see your... your..."

"Penis?" I add helpfully. "These pants *are* awfully tight." I give them a hike up so the fabric hugs my crotch even more.

He swallows, his Adam's apple bobbing. "I can't let you out of the house dressed like that. Every man in that place will be all over you."

Prowling over to him, I run my hand between his pecs and up to grip his chin, hauling him close so I can say against his lips, "I guess you'll have to protect me, then, puppy dog."

He growls low in his throat. "I'll tear the arms off any man who touches you and flog them to death with them."

"Easy there, fella."

Anders leans in, then pauses. A curious frown puckers his brow as he runs a hand along my hip. "What's this?"

All the desire heating my blood evaporates because I know exactly what he's asking about. His thumb brushes above my hip, tracing a scar I've tried so hard to forget about. Anders drops his gaze, and suddenly, I feel naked and vulnerable.

"How did you get this?" Anders asks, voice low and dangerous. "Who did this to you?"

I laugh because it's not a who, it's a *what*, and I can't go there. Not tonight, not ever. If I let myself think about how I got it, then I won't be able to leave the house tonight.

"Nobody," I answer. "It was an accident."

I close my eyes against the sudden flare of headlights and tires screeching in my ears.

"Jamie?"

Sucking in a much-needed gulp of air, I ground myself in the now. Anders is here and he smells amazing and his hands are warm and he looks gorgeous. "I have scars as well," Anders says. "Sometimes, if I press too hard on one, it aches. If my questions upset you, then... I apologize."

Forcing a smile, I say, "I'm fine." I pull out of his touch before I can stop myself. Guilt squeezes my chest. When I find the guts to glance over, hoping I haven't hurt him,

I find Anders frowning at me. "Really, I'm fine. Let's just have fun tonight, okay?" There's a desperate edge to my voice I can't swallow down fast enough.

I need tonight to not be about *that*.

"Let's get going, okay? We'll be late." I still need to get Jace over to Kate for his sleepover.

I've never been good about being vulnerable with anyone. A relationship is more than mushy words and hot sex. When things got real, I bailed and fast. If Anders could see who I truly am when my depression gets really bad, he'd run for the hills.

I zip up my leather jacket so Jace doesn't tease me mercilessly for what I'm wearing. Also, I don't want to scar my little brother. Knocking on Jace's door, I enter when his quiet voice invites me in. He sits on his bed, his knees to his chest. His scent is a whirlwind of anxiety, his little heart skipping in my ears. Kneeling on his bed, I give his knee a tap. "Hey, bud. You okay?"

Jace nods, blinking fast. "Yeah."

"Hey. Look at me." When he does, I squeeze his knee. "Are you feeling nervous about my going out tonight?"

His face crumples. "Will you drive?" When I nod, his lips tremble, and he wipes his eyes. My chest clutching with pity, I put my arm around his trembling shoulders.

"Deep breaths for me, kiddo. I'll be okay."

"Do you have to drive?" Tears leak from his glossy eyes.

"No, I can always take the train."

A sob escapes him. "But what if there's some bad guy on the train? My friends said somebody got shot in the subway last week. What if—" Croaky sobs heave his shoulders as he sucks in gulps of air.

"Oh, bud." I hold him close and kiss his soft hair. "That won't happen."

"How do you know?" Whimpering, he clutches at me.

I'm at a loss for words. Jace is right. How could I possibly be sure something bad won't happen? Life just isn't that simple. We both know how quickly things can change. Sorrow stings my eyes. If our parents were here, they'd know what to say to alleviate his anxiety.

If our parents were here, Jace wouldn't *have* anxiety.

Because of me, my brother is scarred for life.

"Is the lad okay?" Anders occupies the doorframe, head tilted and arms folded across his chest. "Are you?" he adds, the edges of his mouth creasing.

I try and smile, but I'm sure it's unconvincing. "Anders, I think I'm going to stay in tonight."

He dips his head. "Ah. What about Jess and Bailey?"

I sigh. "Guess I'll have to cancel."

Anders frowns thoughtfully. "I could go."

That doesn't sound like a good idea, especially after how nervous he was this morning. "I'm not sure. Won't you be overwhelmed?"

"Possibly, but... I want to make things right between myself and your companions."

I'm not sure if I'm on board, but the determined look in his eyes tells me he is. "All right. Have fun with Jess and Bailey. I'll call an Uber for you."

Anders nods stiffly. "I'll try." Brows furrowing, he adds, "What's an Uber?"

CHAPTER 10
ANDERS

My "Uber" ride is… uncomfortable. I keep my eyes on the driver the entire way there in case he tries anything. So far, things have been confusing but relatively peaceful in this timeline, but I know how swiftly things can go awry. When we stop outside the club, I allow myself to breathe more easily as I exit the car.

As I approach the club, my reservations only increase. The noise coming from beyond the doors makes me gnash my teeth. Already, I want to turn around and demand the driver take me back to my mate and our pup—Jamie and Jace. But it seemed important to Jamie that I bond with Jess and Bailey, and as I've learned, I am incapable of ignoring any request of his.

No. Not incapable. I simply don't want to.

Clenching my jaw, I make my way toward the club. The noise inside is worse than outside, so loud it throbs in my chest. Overhead, colors as bright as the northern lights swirl over the crowd of dancers. The air reeks of sweat and alcohol, clouding my senses. How can humans enjoy this?

I feel like prey with my senses so diluted, waiting to be ambushed.

Before I can panic, my gaze lands on Jess and Bailey sitting at the bar, enjoying drinks. My feet freeze in place as I grapple with sudden uncertainty. I'm not as eager as I thought to encounter the woman I shouted at this afternoon. The uncertainty eats away at me, and it's a feeling I loathe.

Just be yourself! Jamie had said before I left.

But when I'm myself, people tend to die. Or get hurt. Or despise me.

He'd frowned when I'd told him that.

But don't you have any friends? he'd asked, and the question had given me pause, making me cast my mind back.

Had I ever had friends? I remember aching for friends outside of my pack. Most people fawned all over Wulfric for being the Alpha's heir. There was no reason to bother with me. It used to upset me how Wulfric captivated others without even trying, simply for having something I didn't. All the other pups in the village wanted to be his friend, wanted the Alpha-heir's attention. Never mine.

I don't need friends. I earned the respect of others through my skills at arms and as a hunter. And of course, my prowess in the bedroom earned me many lovers, though none as appealing as Jamie.

"Boo!"

I jump out of my bloody skin.

Bailey claps a hand over their mouth. "Got you!"

Grumbling, I fold my arms. "I was only humoring you."

With a bark of laughter, Bailey tugs on my arms. "Come on! Sit down and have a drink before we die of old age waiting for you!"

"Do humans age that quickly?" I ask as Bailey pulls me over to the bar.

They must not have heard me over all the noise. "What do you want to drink?" Bailey asks, plopping down beside Jess, who has yet to acknowledge me.

I can't even read whatever is on the menu. "Uh... I'll have whatever you ordered."

While the bartender makes our drinks, I observe the room. People dance or cluster in groups, laughing loudly and yelling to hear one another over the music. It's so loud in here it's like a physical assault on my eardrums. Tension swells within me, making me curl my hands into fists.

"Bailey," Jess shouts past me, making me jump, "have you seen the *Red, White & Royal Blue* movie yet?"

Bailey groans. "I've been too scared to! Did it follow the book at all?"

"Alex and Henry's relationship was just like the book. So cute. The book is always better, though." Jess takes a swig of her beer.

Sipping their cocktail, Bailey says, "I wanted to do a reread before watching the movie, but my TBR is way too long."

"I feel that," Jess says. "I have, like, twenty books I haven't read, and I just keep adding to my hoard."

I have no idea what they're talking about, but I want to be able to return home and see Jamie smile when I tell him I bonded with his friends.

"What is... Red and Blue?" I ask.

Jess takes a sudden interest in her beer, but Bailey smiles. "It's a rom-com about the Prince of Wales and the US president's son falling in love. You should totally read it!"

My neck warms when I picture telling them I haven't a clue how to read. They'd laugh at me, no doubt. In the silence between us, the bartender hands me my drink. The glass is cold when I grip it, and there are chunks of something floating in the drink. I pick one out and gasp. It's cold as ice in my palm. I crunch on it. It *is* ice. Humans use ice to keep their drinks cool. That's... rather brilliant. Someone snickers. Both Jess and Bailey are watching me with amusement.

I spit the ice back into my cup, then take a sip. It's nothing like mead. There's a sweet, almost bubbly quality to the alcohol. It hits my stomach in a cold ball.

"So. What stories do you know?" I ask them.

Bailey shrugs. "I'll read pretty much anything as long as the author isn't a turd. I'm trying to write my own book."

"You're a skald?"

A confused look crosses Bailey's face.

Great. Have I used a word that doesn't exist in this time? "A, uh..." What's that word Jamie uses? "An author?"

Bailey grins. "I'm *trying* to be. Writing is hard as hell."

"What is your story about?"

After a gulp of their drink, Bailey explains. "It's... sort of a romance? I mean, there's a romantic subplot, but it's not the main focus. I really wanted to do a queer story about a nonbinary character whose experiences matched my own. I'm thinking I'll self-publish it when it's finished."

I only sort of understand what they're talking about. They use words I'm unfamiliar with, but I understand enough. "Storytelling is important. It's how we preserve our culture, our history, for the next generation."

"It is!" Bailey says. "I want to tell the kind of story I wish I had growing up in the South."

"Is the South dangerous?"

Bailey twists their fingers together on the bar top, anxiety oozing into their scent. "It can be. Nowhere is really safe if you're different."

"No, it isn't," I say, knowing all too well what it's like to be hunted simply for not being human. I wouldn't have imagined humans would feel the same. They are usually the ones harming my kind. "That's why you need a pack. People who can understand you."

Bailey's face brightens when they smile. "I know. I wish I'd found Jamie and Jess a lot sooner. Hey, bartender, another round!"

As we drink and chat, a tingling spreads through my limbs, and though the room tilts a little, I feel as if I could take on the world!

When the music gets louder, Bailey leaps from their seat. "Come on! Let's dance!" They grab my hand and Jess's and pull us toward the dance floor before I can protest. Somehow, my reservations have disappeared. My limbs tingle as I mimic Jess's and Bailey's ridiculous dance moves. I must look silly, but I don't care about anything.

Jess meets my gaze, and a laugh escapes her. "Nice moves, dude!"

The room gets warmer, making sweat drip down my body. At some point, the music went from being obnoxious to impossible to resist, moving through my body and making me sway. Jamie's packmates really aren't that bad.

After all the drinks I've had, the urge to make water is too uncomfortable to resist. "I'll be back!" I call to Jess and Bailey and dance my way back out the door. The frigid night wind lashes me as I hurry outside, weaving side to side. My feet carry me along the side of the building, where men and women mill about, smoking or talking.

Finding a secluded spot between two dumpsters, I fumble with the confusing zipper to my jeans and almost piss myself before I've got the damn thing down. A sigh of relief escapes me as I piss against the wall.

The tap of shoes on the pavement draws near, stopping right behind me. "Well, well. Anders, son of Erik," a cheery man's voice says.

My spine stiffens, and though I try to stop pissing long enough to turn around, I can't now that I've started. Damn it. I'm vulnerable. With a growl, I inhale, and my nose stings like I've been zapped by electricity crackling in the air. The hair on my body stands up straight. All ulfhednar know that scent.

A witch.

Shoving my prick back in my trousers, I zip up and whirl around, teeth bared. My heart sinks when I count four in total behind me. They're dressed normally without a staff in sight, but that doesn't mean they aren't a threat. They could be glamouring themselves to appear normal. Just my luck, it's a whole damn coven.

Damn, Loki must be having a laugh at my expense.

Curling my lip over my fangs, I growl, "What do you want?"

A man approaches, fair and blond. He wears dark jeans and a leather jacket. Though he has a slight build, the magic emanating from him is powerful. Underestimating him would be a bad idea. "We are enforcers of the Time Traveler Agency." I recognize his voice as the one who first spoke to me. "And we know you are not of this world, Anders."

Swallowing my unease at how he could possibly know that, I stare the witch down. "You're good at pointing out the obvious, aren't you?"

With a carefree smile, he lifts both hands. "Easy now. I have a flair for the dramatic. Forgive me." He clears his throat. "Let's start over, shall we? Blessings of Freya upon you. I'm Arlo, and I enforce the rules laid out by the Travelers Council."

As our eyes meet, my wolf stirs. My instincts tell me that this Arlo is important. That won't stop me from harming him if he threatens me.

"A pleasure," I say, not meaning it at all.

"You as well!" Arlo says, though I feel he means it more than I do. "You must pardon our sudden appearance. You see, when you passed through the portal, you were meant to come through the one in the Agency office. There you would have been set up with everything you need to thrive in this new world: a passport, ID, et cetera. However, it seems there was a slight malfunction, and so the TTA sent us to locate you."

That malfunction must have been Jamie. The portal let me out closest to where he'd be.

"I see. If that's all—" I try to walk away, but one of the witches thrusts out a meaty arm and slams his hand against the wall, cutting me off. A snarl rises in my throat. "If you mean to threaten me, I'd strongly advise against it."

Arlo has the gall to look offended. "I mean nothing of the sort. We only wished to welcome you to this timeline, get you documented, and remind you of the rules as a traveler of realms."

Kicking back my foot, I prop it on the wall, trying to project an aura of confidence. "Oh? And what are these rules?"

Clearing his throat softly, Arlo conjures a scroll with a simple flick of his finger. "There are rules you must abide by in order to preserve the peace and avoid discovery by the mundane among us." Unfurling the scroll, Arlo says, "One, you shall make any and all attempts to blend into your new surroundings."

Snorting, I motion to my outfit. "Done."

Glaring at me, Arlo goes on. "Two, you may not under any circumstances reveal your nature as either that of a traveler or ulfhednar to the mundane. Humans are distrusting of the paranormal, and so—"

Curling my lip, I snap, "I am aware of that!"

Arlo says, "Yes. Of course. We have your history with humans on your file."

They've been spying on me. How else can they possibly know about the humans who attacked my childhood village?

Arlo continues. "Exposing yourself to humans without the express permission of the Travelers Council is forbidden. And three—"

"And who are you to tell me what to do?" I counter, cutting him off.

"You are not just ulfhednar, Anders. You are of an Alpha bloodline, mateless, and at risk of going berserk."

My fingers curl. "You have no way of knowing—"

"I do, in fact. Wulfric gave us all the information on you when we approved your exile to this time."

Fury simmers low in my gut. They'd approved Wulfric banishing me. I'm here because of these spineless cravens! "You did this to me." The words escape me in a snarl.

"The Travelers Council allowed you to come here after Wulfric assured them you would adjust. We are here to ensure that you do just that. You cannot expose our world to the humans. It would bring ruin to us all, not to mention a headache of a PR mess for the Council to clean up," Arlo says.

My fingers twitch, and if I had my furs, I'd be sprouting claws. "And how will you ensure my cooperation, hmm?"

"We will observe you to make sure you are following the rules of the Council and that you are making efforts to claim a mate, either chosen or fated. At your earliest convenience, you should visit our New York branch of the TTA for documentation.

Sounds like a waste of time to me, especially since I won't be staying in this time much longer. "I have found my mate," I snap.

Arlo's shoulders relax, and he smiles. "You have? That's excellent!"

"But we're taking things slow. I will not rush him to accept our bond."

Arlo frowns. "I understand and appreciate that you are taking the well-being of your mate into consideration, truly. However, time is of the essence, and if the Council deems you are a threat to either yourself or others, then we have the authority to strip you of your furs and your inner wolf so you can never shift again."

His threat makes me bare my blunt teeth. "Try it, bastard!" A red haze falls over my eyes, and I charge. I'm not taking shit from him.

"Anders, wait! I just want to help!" Arlo says, holding up his hands, but he's shoved back by one of the other witches and into a portal that suddenly bursts into existence. "Do not harm him—" His voice cuts out as the portal closes.

Hands glowing with magic, the remaining witches assume a battle-ready stance as I rush at them.

I throw the first punch, my knuckles bouncing off bone that cracks under my fist. My opponent stumbles back, and I grin. I may not be able to shift, but I can still fight well even in this weakened form.

"Mr. Eriksson, stop!" A bearded caster thrusts out his hands, and a blast of wind slams into my ribs. The world spins around me as I tumble, lungs heaving for air. Before

I can stand, the thugs surround me. Snarling, I yank on someone's ankle and force them to the ground. I straddle them, fist ready to crack the craven's nose. A foot plows into my face, and blood bursts across my tongue when I chomp down on it. Another kick bruises my ribs, making pain spasm through my body.

Gods be damned. I can't do anything right in this world.

"Hey, assholes!"

The barrage of kicks and hits abruptly ceases, and my attackers yell out in pain and shock. My fury fades as surprise ripples through me. Through watery eyes, I stare between my attackers' parted ankles. Jess has wrestled one of the men away from me, and Bailey has managed to get a big, burly guy on his knees with his arm twisted behind his back.

The coven likely went down easily on purpose. I'd imagine harming humans goes against their code.

"I'd leave while you can still walk if I were you," Bailey says, smiling confidently as they grind their heel between their opponent's shoulder blades. "Jess, sweetums, can you call for one, two, three ambulances? Thank you!"

Jess whips out her phone.

The bearded caster stumbles to his feet and holds up his hands "I'm very sorry for the inconvenience!" He hurries off toward the main road. Bailey and Jess let his friends go, and they run off after him. Silence rings in my ears as I slump, cheek to the cold pavement.

"Come on up, tough guy." Jess holds out a hand and offers a smile.

I blink at her hand, a fresh wave of humiliation crashing over me.

"I'm fine." I rise without her help and straighten my shoulders. "I had everything under control."

Jess smirks. "Uh-huh. The blood pouring from your nose really screams, 'I got this.'"

I growl and wipe my nose.

"I think you look badass," Bailey chimes in, smiling sweetly as if they hadn't just pinned down a big brute of a guy. "Come on, big guy. Let's get you home to Jamie."

I hang my head and grunt, too worn down to muster any of my usual confidence.

Humans just came to my aid, and I let them help me, and now I'm going home to Jamie bloodied and bruised.

Odin's beard, can tonight get any worse?

Chapter 11

Jamie

"Those bastards did a number on you, huh, puppy dog?"

Anders grimaces at me as I hand him his furs. Jess and Bailey rode home with him but went their own separate ways at my apartment door.

I'm relieved they looked out for him, even if I want to beat up the assholes who hurt him. Or my wolf does. He's restless and wants to hunt down the witches or mages or whatever Anders called them. "Are these witches going to give you any more trouble?"

"Not if I stay on my best behavior." Anders shrugs on the black furs, and before my eyes, his broken nose stops flowing blood, and his bruises fade to fair skin.

"So, the rules are no exposing humans to the paranormal world, and you're to go to some agency or something?" My stomach flips. "Wait, but you exposed that you're ulfhednar to Jace and me. Can you get in trouble for that? Can we?"

"You and the lad are of an ulfhednar lineage. You should be fine. As for the agency, I'll go whenever I have time." He sets his nose with a nasty cracking sound that makes me wince. "I'm fine, pet."

He sure doesn't look fine. In fact, I've never seen him so downtrodden. Anders can barely meet my eyes and glowers down at the floor. I join him at the edge of the bed. As I recall those wounded puppy dog eyes, my heart sinks. I should have been there, but I couldn't leave Jace.

"Sorry I wasn't there." Before I can stop myself, I lean in and kiss his cheek.

Anders's fair skin colors adorably. "I should have been able to fight them off." He drops his gaze to the floor. "I failed to defend my honor. You must be ashamed of me."

Bumping my shoulder into his, I say, "Hey. I'm not ashamed of you. Why do you think that?"

Anders rolls his shoulders morosely but still doesn't meet my gaze.

"I'm not, Anders. I promise."

Those wary green eyes look at me at last, brightening with hope. "Truly?"

Ugh, my heart. I hate that he can even think that. "The opposite. I... I really like spending time with you, Anders."

Surprise softens Anders's sharp features, makes him look young and vulnerable. "You do?"

I laugh, then hop right up and straddle his knees. His pleased little growl makes me smile as I lace my hands behind his head. "I really do. My question is why don't you believe it?"

Anders wets his lips and looks behind me at something on the wall. Leaning in, he props his chin on my shoulder, wrapping those big, strong arms around my back. As he squeezes me to him, he mumbles, "Because most would rather have my brother than someone like me."

"What do you mean?"

"Someone who isn't good enough to be an Alpha." He says the words so softly I almost don't hear them. "Someone who couldn't even win a fight without his furs." Bitterness floods his voice. "Someone who acted the fool at your bookshop. How could you not be ashamed of me?"

I'm quiet as his words sink in. Anders gives off such a confident air to the point of arrogance, but beneath all that bluster is someone with deep insecurities, someone who doesn't feel like he's good enough. His jealousy toward Bailey this morning makes more sense.

"Hey..." I run my fingers through his hair. A pleased growl escapes him even as he jerks away from the touch. "Look at me, puppy dog." I take his face between my hands and force him to look at me. He scowls at me, but I can see the little cracks in his armor in those wounded eyes. Am I crazy for thinking he looks adorable when he's mad? Because he does. "I don't know who your brother is, and I don't care. I like *you*. And yeah, you got your ass whooped. So? Just means I can take care of you afterwards."

He glowers in the face of the sunny smile I give him. "Don't need anyone to take care of me. I can heal."

"Sure. But that doesn't mean you can't hurt." My own insecurity niggles at me, that maybe there's something wrong with *me* or otherwise he'd want me to care for him. Leaning all my weight to the side, I succeed in pulling him down to the mattress. I'm almost hanging off the edge, but Anders tugs me closer so I don't fall. Rubbing his hard chest, I say, "What's so great about your brother you think he could whisk me away?"

"Nothing... except everything," Anders admits.

"But I thought you hated him?"

"I do. He's a fool. He had everything handed to him, and he never deserved it, while I had to work twice as hard for anyone to give a damn."

"But there must be something you like about him. Otherwise, you wouldn't feel this way if you *really* believed you were better than him. You know?"

Anders gnashes his teeth and is quiet for nearly a minute. Finally, he exhales and says, "He's skilled. It seems once he sets his mind to something, he excels at it. Effortlessly. Mayhap because he's an Alpha, he's more determined to be the best he can be." Annoyance hardens his voice, but I'm happy he admitted to something. "And for whatever reason, everyone seems to like him without any extra effort on his part. Whereas I'm..."

"Prickly to anyone who isn't me?" I offer.

"Aye," he admits.

"*Well*," I say, drawing out the word, "maybe if you open up more to others and let them get to know all the other little shades of you, people would like you more? Give Jess and Bailey a chance."

Anders frowns. "If you met my brother, mayhap—"

"Nope." I swing my leg over his hips and crawl over him. My blood simmers as our bodies press together. "I can assure you I'd like you more. I don't think you understand, but I'm pretty obsessed with you, puppy dog."

A smirk lifts his lips. "Forsooth, I couldn't tell." Sarcasm laces his words.

"And so what if you made a few mistakes? Everyone does when they're learning. Besides, you made up with Jess, and Bailey likes you."

"They do not."

I scoff. "Trust me, if Bailey didn't like you, you'd know. They'll warm up to you in no time. Jess and Bailey are just protective of me, that's all."

Anders tilts his head, his hands rubbing up and down my back soothingly. "Why?"

I shrug, unsure how to get into it without killing the mood and bringing up bad memories. "We've all been through a lot, that's all."

A frown creases Anders's forehead. "Did someone hurt you?"

"No... Not someone. Just life, I guess." I push down the memories before they can surface. "Don't really wanna get into it. Anyway, I thought you did great on your first day. Did you almost murder Jess? Yeah, sure. Did you make a mess? A little. But come on, give yourself more credit. You're from a whole other time, having all these new experiences. You're doing amazing."

Anders huffs, but I can tell he's still unsatisfied.

I give his chest a pat. "How about we do something familiar to you? We could take our furs and go running somewhere."

Anders's eyes light up with interest. "You want to?"

"Yeah. You up for it?"

A smile spreads across Anders's face. "Sounds good."

After dropping Jace off at school the next day, I take Anders for a drive to a national park up in Yonkers. It's only a forty-five-minute drive, so I won't be late picking up Jace.

"Where are we going?" Anders asks.

"Somewhere I think you'll like."

Finally, I kill the engine at the base of a hiking trail. When I throw on my furs, I can hear for miles, smell all the colors of the woods with even more clarity than without them.

"This is... it's familiar," Anders says, pausing to take in a deep breath. "These woods remind me of home. I wouldn't have thought such unspoiled wilderness still remained in your time."

I smile sadly. "Trust me, if humans had their way, all these trees would be torn down. In this world, there isn't a lot of respect for nature, not unless we can profit from it in some way."

Anders growls his disapproval. "I know. Hunters burned the forests I hunted and played in as a pup."

"Thankfully, a lot of environmental activists fight to preserve forests like these from greedy developers."

Anders tilts his head thoughtfully. "Humans care about the forests?"

"Plenty of us do," I assure him.

He hums, boots crunching over frosty grass as we walk. "Then those few humans would have plenty in common with my pack, strange as it is to say. Why did you bring me here?"

I spin around to face him. "I want you to teach me how to be a wolf."

A curious smile hooks the corner of his mouth. "Oh? Why?"

"Why not! I've spent all my life totally oblivious to this side of myself."

Anders leans back against a tree, eyes bright with interest. "What would you like to know?"

"Anything, everything. I want to learn how to hunt. How to howl at the moon. I don't care. I want to know everything there is to know."

A raspy chuckle escapes Anders. "Fair enough."

"And in exchange... I can teach you how to be a part of my world. If you want." When his brows furrow, my heart sinks. I hope I haven't offended him. "What I mean is I can show you the ways of this world. Show you that it isn't as bad as you think it is. Sure, there are some crummy things about this time, I won't lie, but there's a lot of good too."

Anders scuffs the heel of his boot across the ground. "I find that hard to believe."

Going to him, I take his hands. They are rough with calluses, while mine are soft, aside from a few bandaged paper cuts. We're so different, the pair of us. "Our worlds couldn't be more different," I admit, brushing my thumb over the hardened palm of his hand, "but that doesn't mean they can't coexist or that you can't have a place here."

There's a light in Anders's eyes, a softness to his features, before he tugs out of my touch. "I told you, my time here is short-lived. I cannot afford to be idle, not while my brother still controls my pack."

"But it doesn't have to be that way. Puppy dog, come on, don't you get it?" I grip his shoulders. "You can find a new pack, a new home. Here." *I could be his new pack, but I'm too nervous to say that out loud.*

Anders scoffs, but he doesn't pull away. "How could I ever fit in here?"

"Easy!" I slap his shoulder. "You start small. We could buy you more clothes. Change your hairstyle to be more contemporary if you want. You work in a bookshop, so I could teach you how to read."

Those green eyes widen. "I... I couldn't." He takes a step back, withdrawing from me.

"Sure you can."

He shakes his head wildly. "No! It's impossible." His hands ball into fists. "I used to think there was nothing I could not accomplish. But now, here, in this place, I—" With a frustrated sigh, Anders paces away from me. "I'm not good at anything. All my skills are meaningless." Sighing, he hangs his head. This giant of a man suddenly seems so small in all his self-doubt. "There's no place in this world for me."

The bitter defeat in his voice makes my heart ache. "That's not true." Going to him, I turn him around to face me. "Go easy on yourself. Be patient. And if that's too hard, hey, I've got plenty of patience for the both of us. Just give reading a chance. I'll help you. You won't do this alone."

A sigh escapes Anders, his breath caressing my lips. "I will try it, pet, but I make no promises that I'll be any good.

However, if you'd like to learn the ways of the wolf, I'd be more than happy to teach you. That I can do easily."

My spirits soar. "Yes! Okay! Let's get started. Teach me all the wolfy things."

Anders pulls up his hood. The gaping wolf maw falls over his face, and fur erupts all over his body. Within seconds, he stands before me in his breathtaking wolf form. I'll never get used to seeing such a big, beautiful wolf up close.

On my knees, I ruffle his fluffy cheeks. "You are so beautiful."

He huffs, tongue lolling. He looks goofy and adorable. I know in this form he's a fearsome predator, but to me, he's just my sweet, grumpy, oversized puppy.

"Strange to hear you say that." His Nordic voice fills my mind.

"Why?" I stroke the tip of his big ear.

He flicks his ear, then growls. *"You were raised as a human. I'm amazed you weren't taught to hate and fear wolves. Every human I have known has only ever treated me like a savage beast."*

I sink my fingers into his thick, coarse fur, then lean in, bumping his cold nose against my forehead. "You're not a savage, Anders. You're just a big ol' puppy dog to me."

Growling, he nips my fingers, but our bond glows with relief. *"Shift. I smell a rabbit on the wind. We can hunt it together."*

I'm not sure I like the idea of hunting something cute and fluffy, but I still want to shift. Pulling up my furs, I let the shift roll over me, consuming me in dense fur. I stretch out on all fours with a wolfish grunt, muscles popping. Shifting to my wolf feels amazing. An animal's headspace is much simpler than a human's. All I want to do is hunt and run with my mate.

Anders rubs his body up against mine, panting. My heart sings to have him so near. He takes off into the woods, and I gallop at his heels. The musky odor of a rabbit's fur hits my nose. My mouth floods with saliva, but the human in me grimaces at the thought of eating live prey.

"Quiet," Anders instructs telepathically. *"The prey is just ahead, but we're downwind of it."* Beside me, Anders crouches so his belly is just brushing the grass. *"Get low."*

I have to fight the urge to crack a Lil Jon joke about windows, walls, and balls. It kills me, but he wouldn't get it anyway. Lowering myself to his level, I keep close as we prowl toward our prey.

"Be mindful of your footing." Anders brushes aside some twigs with his large paw and presses ahead. My mate moves with grace, shuffling around any twigs or piles of dead leaves.

Me? I walk right over the damn things and make a racket that startles the rabbit. The bunny bolts for the hills. The overwhelming urge to give chase possesses me, and I sprint after the rabbit with Anders close behind me.

Leaves spray behind us as we run, and the wind whips through my fur. It feels amazing. I'm so fast! I doubt anything could catch me. Pure power courses through my muscles as I run. Anders lurches ahead of me and cuts off the rabbit's path, forcing it to change direction and run straight at me. I open my jaws and snatch up the little bunny by the scruff of the neck. It squeaks and wriggles, but I'm careful not to bite down too hard and hurt it. Yes! I caught my first prey! I am the king of the forest, I am unstoppable, I am—crashing headlong into a tree. Ouch. Whining, I paw at my throbbing head.

Anders skids to a stop, tongue lolling out as his ribs heave. *"Are you hurt? You should have watched where you were going!"*

I thump my tail at him. *"I'm fine."* Oh shit. The bunny! I dropped the poor little guy. He's huddled a few feet away, pressed flat against the trunk of a tree and shaking violently. Oh no, I scared him. Whining pitifully, I crawl on my belly toward the rabbit. The poor little creature's heart is racing so fast I can see it pumping in its rib cage.

Growling, Anders licks between my ears where the throbbing is most painful. *"You're bleeding. Hold still. It should heal in seconds."*

I boop the bunny with the tip of my snout. *"Poor little thing. I scared him."*

Anders huffs. *"Poor little thing? It's food, pet. Put it out of its misery."*

I gasp. Well, if a wolf could gasp, that would be the sound I make. *"No!"* I flop dramatically onto my side and thrash around. *"I can't do it. He's too cute. He didn't do anything wrong."*

"It's not about right or wrong. It's about survival."

I whimper. *"But we have food at home. We don't need to hunt to survive. Can't we just let him go?"*

"Let it—" Anders shifts back to his human form and plops down on his butt in the leaves. "You want to let it go?"

I shift back and reach out to pet the rabbit's soft fur. He stays still, too scared to move, and lets me gently stroke him. "I caught him. That was the goal, right?"

Sighing, Anders combs his fingers through his hair. "If my pack could see me now... I'd never hear the end of this. Fine. Let him go."

I smile, relieved. "Thanks, puppy dog. Go on, little guy. Sorry for scaring you." I stand up and give the rabbit space. Anders follows me, and once my back is turned, I hear the rabbit scamper off into the woods. I take Anders's hand and squeeze it. "Pretty unconventional for a wolf, huh?"

"Aye. Very. I wouldn't have you any other way."

The admiration in his voice erases any doubts. Hand in hand, we walk back to the car.

Anders falls asleep in the passenger seat during the ride back into the city, clearly exhausted from last night. I don't have the heart to wake him. In sleep, all his defenses come down, and he's vulnerable and sweet. "Hey. Wakey, wakey. We're home."

Home. I wonder if he'll ever come to see my apartment as his home or if he'll always feel drawn to return to his time. I shove that thought away, not liking the way my insides twist at the idea of being abandoned.

Anders yawns, cracking his jaw. "Already? These cars of yours are faster than any horse."

We walk upstairs together.

"Want to shower?" I ask. I don't necessarily mean it in a flirty way, but when his eyes darken, my own desire wakes up within me.

"Oh, aye. I would indeed. Seeing you run and hunt was quite the spectacle."

With his hand in mine, he drags me to the bathroom. Once we're in the shower with the water cascading over us, he shoves me against the wall and claims my lips with eagerness that wakes me up, body and soul.

"I'm proud of you," he rumbles against my lips, his big hands running up and down my ribs before his fingers toy with my nipple rings. My cock twitches and fills, and all I want is more. "You make a fine wolf. Tell me what you need, and it will be done."

My mouth runs dry. I've never felt good about asking for what I need. I give and give until I have nothing left, and I've learned to live with going unsatisfied. I'm starting to suspect that's why so many of my relationships have ended badly.

"Jamie?"

I clear my throat, trying to find my voice. I don't want my relationship with Anders to meet that same fate. "I... I don't want you to hold back. Be rough with me."

A grin curls his lips. "How rough?"

"I don't know. Spank me. Pull my hair. Throw me around. Bite me. I don't care. I wanna see that animal in you come out."

Anders looks uncertain. "But what if I hurt you without meaning to?"

"Okay. If it's too much and I need you to stop without saying stop or no, I'll say matcha. Or if my mouth is full," I add, winking, "I'll pinch your thigh."

"Ah. I understand. You say matcha or pinch me, and I'll stop," he promises. "But until then?"

I grind against his hardening cock in invitation. "Don't hold back. No more puppy dog Anders. I wanna see bad dog Anders."

"Not a puppy," he growls before crushing his mouth to mine and devouring me. My lips tingle as he nips at them, and I moan into his mouth when he shoves his tongue inside mine. The taste of liquor and something uniquely Anders makes me whine with need. My whole body aches for my mate, for his cock, for his touch and attention. With a low, hungry groan, Anders thrusts against me. Our cocks grind together, stiff and aching, slick with water.

Anders starts kissing his way down my throat, nipping my skin and smoothing over his love bites with his tongue. I remember all too well what that tongue can do. I'm pliable and willing as I roll my head back, urging him to take more. Every part of me yearns to submit to him. I tip my head back, my instincts strong enough without my furs. A single word presses against my lips. I wonder how he'd react if I...

Growling low in his chest, Anders nips my collarbone.

"More," I pant. "Please, Alpha."

Anders freezes, his face hidden in my shoulder. My heart stops, and I worry I went too far.

"Call me that again," he commands, voice unexpectedly raw. Sliding his hand lower, he cups my aching cock and strokes it.

Arching up, I gasp, "Yes, Alpha. Give me more. Right there."

When Anders looks up, there's a mischievous smile on his face. "Are you telling an Alpha what to do, pet?"

I play along, wriggling my hips. "Yeah. So what?"

His eyes flare a wolfish yellow, and he snarls, showing his sharp teeth. A large hand curls around my throat and squeezes. A gasp escapes me. His grip is strong enough to surprise me but not choke me. He very well could if he wanted to, but I'm not scared of him. I know he won't hurt me. I trust him, and fuck, that's so hot.

"I am your Alpha, pet. *You* serve *me*. Understood?"

My cock throbs, my body aching to submit and serve him. Instead, I smirk and arch a brow at Anders. "Oh yeah? Make me."

Anders curls his lip, jaw tight. I am still getting to know him, but he's moody enough that I can differentiate between real anger and the faux outrage on his face. With one hand, he forces me to my knees. His thick, meaty cock makes my mouth water. "Shut your loose mouth and service your Alpha."

My legs practically gape open at the demand, but I won't make this too easy for him. My mate likes a challenge, after all. "And how am I supposed to service you if my mouth is shut, *Alpha*?"

Those eyes flash dangerously, and then his fingers are in my hair and tugging, *hard*. I gasp from the pain, but it only fuels my lust. Anders yanks on my hair, shoving my face in his crotch. The musky male scent of him makes my cock throb.

"I will not ask again. Swallow my prick until you're gagging on it. I want to feel it buried down your throat." He grasps his cock, smacking it against my cheek. "Are my instructions clear?"

"Yes." I groan, damn near drooling with the need to suck him off.

"Yes, what?" he snarls, tugging my hair.

"Y-yes, Alpha."

"Good, pet," he rumbles, loosening his grip on my hair and stroking his fingers over my scalp.

I wrap my lips around the blunt head of his cock and suck until my cheeks hollow, bobbing my head. Anders sighs with bliss and grips the back of my head, urging me on. He's one hell of a mouthful, so thick and wide. I want him in my ass, stretching me, filling me full to bursting.

Anders guides me, urging me to take him deeper, faster. His harsh grip on my hair prevents me from pulling off his cock. I'm trapped, and I love every second of it. Honestly, he could be rougher with me—I wouldn't mind. I take in a deep breath through my nose and dive in, swallowing every inch of him until my nose is buried in his groin. I gag and pull off, but the second I've got my breath back, I swallow him down.

With a deep moan of approval, Anders rocks his hips, pumping in and out of my mouth. "Good, pet. So good to your Alpha. How much more can you take?"

"More," I pant, kissing the head of his dick. "Use me, Alpha."

And oh, he does. He grips my head in his hands and angles my face upward. Through streaming eyes, I watch as Anders smiles arrogantly, eyes dark with longing. He holds my face steady and thrusts deep, fucking my mouth. "Gods," he says, groaning, "look at you. You were meant to serve. Why else would you look so good on your knees? Such a good little pet for your Alpha's cock."

His words stoke a fire in me only he can extinguish. I love being on my knees for him, love his hands on me, commanding and yet protective, love the way he uses me and gives me so much at the same time.

I go slack between his hands and let him use me, let him take everything he needs. It's fulfilling in a way nothing else is, submitting to him, giving him pleasure. The room fills with the sloppy sounds of my sucking, Anders's grunts and pants, and the water from the shower spattering on the porcelain.

"Almost there, pet," Anders says, voice rough and breathy as he pumps his hips faster and faster. "You'll take every drop. Swallow it down and thank your Alpha, won't you?"

I moan my enthusiasm, drunk off the taste of his cock.

Suddenly, he yanks me off his cock by the hair. I whimper my disappointment, trying to lunge back in for a taste. Anders fists his cock and strokes it, his chest rising and falling quickly. "Open for me. Stick out your tongue."

Panting, I obey. My heart races as I await his climax, hungering to taste him, to please him. Anders tangles his fingers in my hair and strokes his cock with his other hand. With an animalistic grunt, he throws his head back and snarls as he comes. Thick, hot ribbons of cum streak my cheeks, and I catch some on my tongue.

Anders pants above me, eyes wide and dark. "Good. So good. My perfect mate."

His praise makes my heart sing. Anders swipes his thumb through the mess of cum on my face, then rubs it over my lips. I open for him and suck on his thumb, moaning as the taste of him bursts across my tongue. His touch is gentle as it weaves through my hair, his eyes soft and glowing with reverence.

"You've earned a reward for pleasing me so thoroughly." Leaning down, he claims my lips, then helps me stand. We dry ourselves fast and, effortlessly, Anders carries me from the bathroom to the bedroom. Once we're in my bedroom, my back hits the mattress, and Anders looms over me, powerful and all-consuming. My body hums with need, and I'm practically panting, out of my mind with want.

"It's your turn, pet."

Anders flips me onto my stomach and rumbles out a pleased noise. Grasping my cheeks, he spreads me open. His claws dimple my ass, and his body vibrates with a low growl, causing a shiver to run down my spine. I feel like prey, caught and ripe for devouring by a hungry wolf. I lift my hips, offering myself.

Anders's growling only gets louder. His breath fans across my lower back, and when he puts his teeth to the meat of my ass, his fangs prick my skin. Wrapping a hand around my cock, Anders bites down on my ass but doesn't break the skin. The wet warmth of his tongue laps over my hole, making my knees quiver. Whimpering, I push my hips back, urging him on.

He licks into me while he pumps my cock, reducing me to a writhing mess beneath him. That damn tongue. It puts the steamiest sex scene in any romance novel I've read to shame. It is surprisingly long, thrusting into me like a small, hot, wet cock. The slurping sounds escaping Anders as he devours me make my face burn hot. When he stops licking at me, I groan my disappointment. The combination of his hand and that sinful tongue is almost enough to drive me over the edge.

Anders sucks on his fingers, then presses them against my entrance, then inside. The stretch and sensation of fullness has me rocking my hips back on his fingers as he presses them in deep, then draws them back out.

"Alpha," I whine.

"Oh?" He nips my ass cheek. "Just what is it that you need? Tell me."

"N-need you inside me. Now. Please."

With a wolfish growl, he tugs me up by my hips so I'm on my hands and knees. Propping himself up on one knee, he positions himself. His pelvis bumps my ass, his cock rubbing right between my cheeks. The drawer opens, and the lube cap snicks. Then his blunt, slick head is pressing into me. The stretch has my eyes closing in bliss, and my gasp fills the room as he sinks in. He works me open, rocking his hips back and forth.

"Gods. Feels like I've died and gone to Valhalla itself when I'm inside you."

We both groan as he takes me deeper, faster. He wraps his hand around my throat, angling my head to the side. Our lips collide as he pounds into me, and we swallow each other's desperate grunts and moans.

His thrusts are so forceful I can't hold myself up and collapse into the bed. When he grabs my wrists and pins them down, there's nothing for me to do but let myself be taken, hard and fast. I don't have to think, don't have to worry. I don't need to be in control. I can just be his.

My orgasm erupts from me, turning me into a moaning, babbling mess as I streak the sheets with my cum. I'm about to collapse, but Anders wraps his arm around me and hauls me up and against his body.

"Not done with you," he growls into my ear. "You don't get to rest, pet, not until I've filled your tight little hole with my seed." He traps me against him while he continues to move, pounding into me. Amazingly, my cock stiffens again. Being a paranormal creature definitely has its perks. Hello, no refractory period.

I grind down on his hips, whimpering as the need to come again possesses me, turning me into some feral, sex-crazed beast.

"Shameless little wench," Anders says harshly, wrapping a hand around my cock and pumping fast. My toes curl as he strokes me to the hard, frantic smack of his hips. His other palm smacks against my ass, coaxing a shout from my lips. "So insatiable. Do I have to loosen this tight little hole all night before you're finally satisfied?"

He swirls his hips, rubbing against all the right spots, then tugs on my nipple rings, sparking pleasure all throughout my body. Shoving me back to my hands and knees, he lies atop me, pinning my body between his and the bed. I tear at the sheets, crying out as he fastens his teeth into my shoulder, biting down on his marks. "Mine, all mine. Say it."

"Yours, Alpha. Yours! Want your cum. Fill me up. Please."

Anders's hoarse shout fills the room as his release paints my insides, leaving me a hot, sticky mess. His knot keeps it all inside, and I feel so full, wrecked, owned by his cock and his cum. His, completely. I clench around Anders once again as he wrings another explosive orgasm out of me. It feels like it never ends.

We catch our breath. Bliss spreads throughout my body. "Hey, let's start teaching you to read today."

Anders stiffens behind me, and not in the good way. "I... I'm not sure I can learn how."

I twist my body around to look at him and find him frowning as he traces a pattern into my shoulder with a blunt fingernail. "I'm a very good teacher. We'll start small and simple, then work our way up."

Anders drops a kiss to my bare shoulder. "Fine. But I warned you."

I chuckle and squeeze his fingers. "You've got this."

I can't wait to help Anders learn more about my world. I want to see him open up and bloom like a flower under the sunlight.

Who knows? Maybe he'll decide my time isn't as bad as he thought.

Maybe... he'll stay. I sure hope so.

Because it's getting harder to imagine being alone again.

CHAPTER 12
ANDERS

SOMETHING ABOUT JAMIE SULLIVAN must have me enthralled. Why else would I agree to learn how to read instead of obtaining his necklace? I must be truly mad, and yet I can't bring myself to care. Instead, I only want to spend more and more time with him, in and out of bed. I've never yearned to know anyone inside and out. If teaching me to read makes my mate happy, then I will devote myself to my studies.

When I'm with Jamie, I don't feel like the man who wasn't good enough to be Alpha. I'm not *an* Alpha, but I'm *Jamie's* Alpha. Somehow, that feels like enough. Although I'm realizing I don't quite know who I am or what my place is in Jamie's world, I want to find out. I want to see the person I can become and if I can be worthy of Jamie's affections and boundless patience.

Before the shop opens for the day, Jamie drives me to the bookshop after dropping Jace off for school. He flicks on the lights. The tables are empty, and the only sounds to penetrate the silence are the occasional rumble of a car that passes by.

Jamie sighs beside me. "I love coming here before everyone else."

"I can see the appeal," I say, following him inside.

"It's like my own little corner of the world. Just me and my books, no responsibilities or obligations." Jamie roams the shelves, caressing the spines of the books with a fondness that makes me chuckle.

"Was owning a bookshop something you always wanted?" I hunger to know everything about him until I know him even better than I know myself.

Jamie stops by a section that's more colorful than the rest of the store. There are pictures of animals, toys on the rug, chairs small enough for young children to sit in. "Not always, but after my parents passed, we lived with my grandma for a few years. Life was... hard, for a while." His smile falls from his face, and for a moment, I glimpse the man behind the smiles and sunny disposition.

Jamie is still hurting, still missing his family. He won't say it aloud, but I feel it all the same. How he can still smile and carry on with his life when his hurt goes so deep, I am unsure. After I lost my parents, I lost myself as well. Grief turned to rage that shaped who I am today.

"It still hurts you."

Jamie clears his throat. "I mean, yeah. Of course it does. Reading helped me forget or helped me put words to everything I was feeling through characters going through the same shit as I was. Books are amazing like that; they're portals to other people and other worlds, other experiences. They remind us we're not alone."

When Jamie sits on the rug, I join him. "You are stronger than you think you are, Jamie, son of Sullivan."

Jamie laughs softly, ducking his head. "Not really. Most days, I'm barely holding myself together."

Sliding a finger beneath his chin, I lift his face toward mine. "After I lost my father, it... changed me." There's an ache in my throat that hasn't been there in years. I clear it harshly, then make myself break eye contact, uncomfortable by how weak I feel. "This darkness, this anger, woke up inside me and consumed me."

"That's normal." Jamie leans his cheek on my shoulder, his hair tickling my neck.

"I let it warp me, the way flame warps a blade. My anger turned me into a weapon against my brother, my own family." It's the first time I've truly realized this.

Jamie couldn't be more different than me. Soft where I'm hard. Kind where I'm cruel. Trusting where I'm closed off. He's a far better person than me, but I want to be worthy of him.

"It's not too late, you know. You could still make amends with them."

Is it possible? Could my brothers forgive me if I proved myself worthy of their forgiveness? A flicker of hope blooms within me, hope I didn't even know was there. A hope for a second chance with the only family I have. Could I—

No. Never. Not after how badly I hurt Wulfric's mate. Not after how I continuously challenged Wulfric over the years.

The hope curdles and dies before I give it the chance to bloom.

"What is this book?" The book in his lap is thin and has a colorful, eye-catching picture on the cover. I'd say it's a happy, hopeful story just based on the artwork. "Is that a duck?"

"It's a book about our alphabet. There are twenty-six letters that make up our alphabet. They form all sorts of words. Once you memorize them, reading will be a lot easier." He grabs some blocks from a toy bin and lays them out. "If you prefer a more hands-on approach, you can use these blocks."

"That's a lot of letters." It sounds like a daunting task. "How can I possibly memorize all of them?"

"Well, how did you learn to fight with a sword?"

"I practiced from the moment I was old enough for several hours a day."

"See? That's how. You just need to apply that dedication to reading. You can do this. I'll help you."

I did promise to give this a chance, so I move to sit behind Jamie, giving him room to recline against my chest. "Then let's begin."

Jamie leans back against me, opens the book, and begins our lesson.

Throughout the week, Jamie proves himself to be a dedicated teacher. Every morning, we have breakfast with Jace, Jamie drops him off at school, and we head to the bookshop before it opens, where he teaches me the alphabet. It's frustrating. There are so many damned letters that I'm confident only Odin himself could memorize them with ease, and only because he's our god of wisdom.

I can never remember which order the damn letters go in either. I can't believe they have children learning these skills at such a young age. Still, I am determined. This will be the one thing I get right in this new world. I have always been a swift and dedicated learner.

And if learning to read makes Jamie happy, that can only bring us closer together. I'll be able to understand his obsession with those romance novels he loves to read so much.

But aside from my cunning and dedication, there's another thing I'm known for: my lack of patience.

"Snakes feast on your entrails!" I roar, chucking the blocks across the bookshop.

Jamie comes out of the kitchen with our muffins. "That was a creative insult."

"This is simply impossible! I give up!"

"Whoa, whoa, hold up a second." Jamie sets the pastries on our table and sits across from me. "You were doing great. What got you so pissed?"

With a scowl, I lean back against the window. The glass is cold and streaked with rain on the outside. "I can never remember what comes after *E*!" I don't struggle with any other letter as much as I do with that gods damned... whatever letter is after *E*. "It's just one letter. How in Odin's beard am I supposed to learn to read if I can't remember one stupid letter?"

"The letter is—"

"No, don't tell me!"

"Okay." Jamie takes a big bite of his muffin.

I think. And think. And think. Until my damn brain starts to hurt.

Jamie snorts, and I open my eyes to glare at him, but he's the picture of innocence.

"Can I give you a hint?"

I exhale, chest deflating. "Aye. I suppose." I spit the words, disgraced.

"It's an animal."

"That's helpful. Only millions of those."

He rolls his eyes. "Someone is so saucy today. It's an animal that lives in the water. It has scales."

"*F*!" I blurt out, slamming my fist on the table. "Fish! *F* is for fish!"

"Heck yeah!"

I groan and fall back into my seat. "Why is this so difficult?"

Jamie hums thoughtfully, ever patient. "Hmm. It would help you to have a visual connection with the letter. Like how you know *E* is for elephant."

I nod. "Those big creatures with the trunk and the tusks, right?"

"Yeah, exactly. So you need a visual representation of the letter *F*."

"Visuals aren't working. I need something else."

Jamie tilts his head, a sly little smile blooming over his face. "There's a lot of words that start with *F*. I can think of a few that might stand out to you."

Leaning on the table, I focus all my attention on him. "Hit me."

He grins, and I wonder what he's planning. Jamie pushes his chair back and walks around the table. Before I can blink, he's in my lap, knees on either side of my thighs. "Fondling."

The scent of his lust makes my prick twitch in my jeans. "Oh? What does that mean?" Just because I can understand his language doesn't mean every word is familiar to me.

"It means this." He slides my hand down his back and settles it over his ass. I squeeze before I can stop myself, loving the way he feels in my hand.

I swallow hard. "Keep this up, pet, and we'll give anyone who walks past this window a show."

Jamie's phone rings, making us both jump and Jamie curse. "Shit. It's Jace's principal!" He scrambles off my lap. "Hi, Mrs. Leroy, how are you? What?" Jamie's mouth goes slack. Grimacing, he shakes his head in disbelief. "I am so sorry. I will be there as soon as I can!" Tapping frantically, he ends the call, then checks the time. "Damn it!"

I sit up and go to his side. "What is it?"

"Jace started a fight at school!"

My heart sinks. Fury swells within me like a rising tide. "Is the lad hurt?" Nobody hurts my pup. Granted, the lad isn't *really* mine, but—

"No, he's fine, but I don't understand!" Jamie stomps to the door. "Why would he do this?"

Before he can storm out, I grab the knob. "Send one of those messages with your phone to Jess and Bailey. Mayhap they can handle the store. Let us worry about Jace."

Jamie's eyes widen. "No, no. This isn't your problem. You don't have to worry about this."

I flinch, surprising even myself with how much his dismissal hurts.

"Hey, no, wait, that's not what I meant…" Jamie grips my arms and squeezes. "I just… I don't want to burden you. Jace is my brother, my responsibility."

Feeling a bit better, I reach out and lift his chin to meet my eyes. "And you're mine."

Jamie's throat bobs, color brightening his cheeks. "Y-yes, but—"

My wolf growls low, pleased he accepted my claim. When I brush my thumb over his bottom lip, Jamie's breath catches. "Then so is the pup. You are my mate, Jamie, and what's yours is mine now."

Until we part ways, everything Jamie has, all he is, belongs to me.

CHAPTER 13

JAMIE

WHAT'S YOURS IS MINE now.

Those words refuse to leave my mind as I drive to Jace's school.

It's been so difficult trying to find someone I can trust with Jace. Not too many guys are enthusiastic about sharing me with my little brother. But Anders just accepted that Jace and I come as a package. Since we met, he's been so good with my brother, patient and kind like he's known Jace forever.

Like we're a family.

Swallowing around the lump in my throat, I grip the wheel tightly. That's a dangerous line of thinking. Anders isn't staying. He has goals, and I'm not part of them. Once the year is over, Anders will choose revenge over Jace and me and return to his timeline. I'll have to move on without him. This isn't a relationship—it's just sex. That's all. I can't afford to get attached.

"I don't understand why he would start a fight." I bite my nail while I wait for the light to change. "He never acts out like this."

"Does he have enemies at school?" Anders's big body is tense, a muscle flickering in his jaw.

I totally don't feel mushy over how protective he is of Jace already. Not at all. "Not that I know of." Did some kid start a fight? If someone is bullying my little brother, there's going to be hell to pay. "What if he's being bullied and I've just been so busy with the shop that I missed the signs?" The idea that I've been unintentionally neglectful makes my knuckles whiten around the steering wheel.

"Then we will deal with it," Anders growls, and the fact that he looks ready to charge into a fight on Jace's behalf soothes me.

We. We will deal with it.

For the first time in so long, I'm not in this alone.

My heart's ready to beat out of my chest as I jog to the principal's office. Throwing open the door, I find her behind her desk. Jace is hunched in a chair and scowling. There's a Band-Aid on his cheek, which is already bruising purple.

"Jace!" I kneel beside his chair. "Are you okay?"

Lips folded tight together, Jace glowers at the floor.

"Please have a seat, Mr. Sullivan. Kevin and his parents will be here at any moment."

Oh, great. I have to speak with angry parents.

She directs a smile at Anders. "And you are?"

"My boyfriend," I blurt. I need Anders in the room for this.

"Aye," Anders agrees, making my cheeks warm as he comes up behind my chair and grips the top of it, looming over me like a big, protective guard dog. Instantly, a comforting sense of safety envelops me like a blanket—until the door bangs open and a man and woman storm in with a scowling, red-faced little boy.

"Mr. and Mrs. Davidson, please have a—"

"I want that boy expelled!" Mr. Davidson booms, pointing at Jace. I have the sudden urge to bite his damn finger off. "He's a violent, out-of-control hooligan!"

Outrage flares in me.

"I am not. He's a bully! He started it first!" Jace snaps, leaping out of his seat.

"Easy, lad." Anders grips Jace's shoulders.

Shushing both my guys reassuringly, I ball my hands into fists so I don't explode at Davidson as I turn to face him. "I understand you're upset, Mr. Davidson, but can someone please explain what happened? I'm sure we can work this out."

Mrs. Davidson throws me a scathing look. "That boy attacked my child completely unprovoked!"

"I didn't!" Jace erupts, and Anders urges him to sit down. "He deserved it anyway!"

"Jace, that's enough!" I say, shocked. "Is this true?" I ask the principal, hoping for a more measured response to cool my boiling blood.

"The schoolyard monitor pulled them apart when they started fighting, but she wasn't sure who started it, and we have mixed reports from the other children present. Regardless of who started it, we have a zero-tolerance policy for violence at this school. Both Jace and Kevin are suspended for a week. I expect better behavior when they return to class."

My heart sinks into my stomach. How am I going to look after Jace *and* manage the store at the same time? Anger rises in me.

"What?" Kevin barks. "But he started it!"

Jace stays silent, arms folded and lower lip jutting out.

"I understand," I say, trying to contain my frustration. "I'm sorry for the inconvenience this caused."

"That's it?" Mrs. Davidson sneers. "That boy should never be allowed to come back!" She side-eyes Anders. "Then again, with a father who looks like *that*, it's no wonder the boy's a savage."

A low snarl escapes Anders, making both the Davidsons jump. "That's enough."

I grip Jace's arm. "Let's go home."

He rips his arm away and storms out into the hallway, his rejection like a blow to my chest. "Jace!" Anders and

I pursue him into the hall, and Mr. Davidson and his fuming son are just behind us.

Anders rounds on Mr. Davidson. "Control your runt," he growls, and Mr. Davidson blanches. "If he lays a hand on Jace again, there will be consequences."

"Leave them alone," I grumble. "They're not worth it." Anger simmering low in my gut, I follow Jace outside. As I walk, I take deep, steadying breaths. Getting mad at Jace won't help the situation at all. He's an empathetic kid, so he probably feels bad enough that his behavior has caused trouble for me.

Jace is already slouching in the back seat, arms wrapped around his chest and face hidden from view. I get in without a word and pull on my seat belt. Once Anders is buckled in, I drive us home, stealing glances at Jace in the mirror. Tears have dripped onto his shirt, and the sight makes my chest tighten.

Fuck. What a shitty day this has turned out to be. I'm dreading going upstairs when we park outside the apartment. All through the drive, I tried to think about what to do. Do I punish Jace? Is the suspension punishment enough? What do I say? I wish my parents were here to tell me what to do.

Once we're upstairs, I turn to Jace. "Go to your room. I'll be there in a moment."

Jace throws his backpack on the floor and storms into his bedroom, slamming the door. Blowing out a breath, I go into the kitchen and pour a tall, cold glass of water. I drain the whole glass in a few gulps and try to gather my thoughts. I never got into fights as a kid, so I have no frame of reference to draw from.

"Did you fight a lot as a kid?" I ask Anders.

His mustache lifts in a smile. "Oh, aye." He sounds proud of himself.

"And what did your parents do?"

"That depends. If I won, they were very proud. If I lost, they told me I brought shame on my ancestors and the family name."

"Not sure that's what Jace needs to hear right now..."

"Go easy on the lad. Hear his side of the story first."

Right. That will make it easier to decide how to approach this. Girding myself, I knock on Jace's door. When I don't get a response, I ease it open just enough to peer inside. The lamp is on, and Jace is sitting on his bed with his knees to his chest, flipping through the pages of a book. The sour odor of anger still permeates from him, though.

Clearing my throat softly, I say, "Hey. Can we talk?"

Jace shrugs, white-knuckling the corners of his book.

Dropping onto the edge of his bed, I count the loose threads in the carpet, trying to piece together the perfect thing to say. My parents wouldn't have had to try. They always knew how to calm us boys when we got upset. I'm nothing compared to them. Jace would be better off with anyone other than me.

Clearing the despair from my throat, I say, "Jace... can you tell me what happened?"

He doesn't even look at me.

"Hey." At a loss, I try and take the book away. "Jace. Talk to me."

Jace slaps the book down on his bed. Man, where did he get all this attitude from? "Talk about what? I got into a fight. The end."

My molars squeak together as I grind down. "No, it isn't 'the end.' Stop being a pain. You owe me an explanation."

"If you're so sick of me, just drop me off at an orphanage," Jace snaps.

"Tempting!" I bark back, way beyond talking now.

"You only care about me when I'm upset anyway."

I flinch from his words. "What? That is *not* true." Is it? His accusation hits me like a cannonball, blowing a hole straight through any confidence I had.

"Yes, it is!" Jace's shout fills the room, making me wince. "You're always busy all the time!"

Guilt twists my stomach into knots. Is this how he really feels? In my own hurt, I lash out. "And you thought I wasn't busy enough, so you got yourself suspended! Is that it? Why are you such a freaking brat?"

"I wish Mom and Dad were here instead of you!" he screams, tears coursing down his cheeks.

An ache spreads through me, like I've been punched in the stomach. I wish that too, so fucking much. I miss them. I need them here helping me, telling me what to do. Throat thick, I choke out, "So do I."

I wish I'd died in their place.

Instead of coming to an understanding, we've ripped the scabs off wounds that have never healed, and we're bleeding all over again. Incapable of speaking, I stumble from the room and slam the door before I say something I'll regret. Jace's sobs come from behind the door, making my heart break.

Tears try to dampen my cheeks, but I can't. I can't break. If I break, I don't know how I'll put myself back together. Jace needs me to be strong for him. Furiously scrubbing my eyes, I ignore Anders and head to the front door.

"Where are you going?" Anders asks.

"A walk." I sniff hard, shouldering my bag. "I'll be back in a bit, just... need to clear my head."

"Aren't you hungry? You didn't eat a big breakfast. I could cook us something."

A bitter laugh punches out of me. "You don't even know how to use the stove."

Anders is quiet behind me, and the scent of his hurt makes me want to hit myself. "Aye... that's true."

I want to scream, to fall apart in his arms, to rage and cry. Instead, I let the door slam behind me. At the end of the day, the only one who can take care of this family is me.

No matter how wonderful Anders is.

CHAPTER 14

ANDERS

Silence rings in my ears as I watch Jamie walk out on me.

Within my soul, my wolf howls in dismay.

Our mate doesn't trust us to care and provide for him, and the realization hurts worse than a cut from any sword or fang. Jamie has been doing everything on his own for so long. It doesn't take any kind of magic to understand that. What must I do to show him he can trust me?

Balling my hands into fists, I march into the kitchen and throw open that giant ice-coffin thing. There's not much inside to work with, though there's some broccoli and a package of steak. Perfect. I can work with that. When I turn to the stove and all its dials, I lose my confidence. Scowling, I toss the food on the counter.

If we were all wolves, we could just eat the steak raw, but the lad could get sick. My wolf whimpers inside as the quiet sobs and sniffles reach my ears. I've never heard either of them so angry at each other. The stress they're both under is something I'll never understand.

If I could just find a way to ease their burdens...

Unable to listen to the lad cry, I go and knock on his door.

"Go away, Jamie!"

"It's Anders. Are you hungry?"

The boy sniffles. "Sort of."

"Would you like steak, lad?"

"I guess..."

"Then come out here and show me how to make it."

The door opens, and Jace comes out, face sticky with tears and snot.

"Wash your face, then get in here."

Nodding glumly, he goes into the bathroom, returning moments later with his face still splotchy but clean. "What do you need help with?" he asks, rubbing his eyes.

Surveying the beast of a contraption before me, I say, "How in Hel's name do you work this thing?"

The boy manages a laugh, face brightening as he grabs a big pan and hefts it up onto the stove. He flicks the knob, and I jump back when bright blue flame bursts to life beneath the pan.

"Ah. That was... simple."

"It's not too hard. And you can adjust the temperature too, see?" He rotates the knob, reducing the flame's brightness. While I wait for the pan to heat, I stare uselessly at the broccoli.

"Need a knife? They're in here." Jace slides open a drawer built into the counter, revealing many knives of various lengths and blade types.

Picking up a knife that looks suitable for chopping vegetables, I set to work. "Put another pan on the stove, lad." Once that is done, I throw the chopped broccoli in and turn on the heat. I also toss in some diced onions.

"You should put this on too." Jace holds up a bottle of something. "It's soy sauce. It'll make it taste better."

Opening the bottle, I give the contents a sniff and recoil. It smells salty, but I'll trust the boy's judgment. Once I've poured a little of the contents over the vegetables, I watch the steak sizzle in the pan. "Who did that to your face?" I ask, motioning at the bandage on his cheek.

Jace's nose wrinkles in anger. "Kevin. He's a jerk. He's always teasing me."

A growl rumbles up from my chest. "Why?"

Bobbing his shoulders, Jace sighs. "Don't know. I never did anything to him."

"Children can be cruel." There's a sour taste in my mouth. "Especially when another child has something they do not."

A memory bursts into my mind of me shoving Wulfric to the ground and laughing with the boys I'd thought were my friends as he'd cried.

"Were you bullied too?" Jace asks.

I rotate my jaw, muscles popping. I don't have the heart to tell him I was just like the boy who bullied him… still am, in some ways. "I can tell you that the whelp's behavior has nothing to do with you. So, you had enough and hit him, yes?"

"I tried." Jace glowers at his fists. "I suck at fighting back. He's way bigger and stronger than I am."

An idea pops into my head. Turning my back on the stove, I hold up my hand, palm facing him. "Hit it."

Jace's eyes go round with surprise. "What?"

"You want to learn how to defend yourself or not? Hit it."

Holding up his fist like he's only just noticing it for the first time, he smacks his knuckles against my palm. It's like a punch from a puffin.

"Again," I growl.

"But what if I—"

"You won't hurt me."

He hits my fist again, leaving behind a dull ache.

"Again!" I snarl.

With a frustrated shout, Jace pounds my palm with his fist, making vibrations tingle up my arm.

"Good. Try that the next time someone bullies you, and they should leave you alone." Returning to the stove, I stir the broccoli. "Why not simply tell Jamie you're being bullied?"

Lips wobbling, Jace hangs his head. "He has enough going on." Despite the wetness in his eyes, his glare is fiery. "And you can't tell him, okay? You can't. I want to be a man and deal with it on my own! Like Jamie does."

"But you don't have to, lad. You're part of a pack, and pack means you're never alone."

Jace's mouth lifts. "Really? I'm your pack?"

A chuckle bubbles up from my chest. It's rusty, but it feels good to laugh. Tousling his mop of hair, I say, "Aye, lad. You and Jamie."

Jace flashes his teeth in a radiant grin. "Does this mean I can shift?"

"Not yet." Another laugh bursts out of me when he pouts. "Lad, you ought to apologize for what you said."

Color crawls up Jace's ears as he drops his chin to his chest. "What did I say?"

"That comment about wishing your parents were here instead."

Jace balls his hands into fists. "I'm not sorry. I *did* mean that."

The steak hisses as I flip it, and I wince as hot grease spatters my arm. "He is doing the best he can!"

My own words slap me in the face, and all the anger flows out of me. As I stare into Jace's seething face, it's like a mirror into my own anger at *my* brother. My brother, who I criticized endlessly, who I challenged at every opportunity.

Wasn't Wulfric also doing the best he could, as an Alpha to our pack, as a brother to my siblings and me? I remember how hard our father worked for our pack, constantly tending to the needs of others, often at the expense of his own. I remember Wulfric surrounded by our people during one of our meetings, everyone vying for his attention. All the times I'd mocked him in front of our people, challenged him—humiliated him.

There's a sour feeling in my stomach, and I realize it's *shame*. I was... horrible to him. I was so consumed by my own jealousy for everything he had that I lacked that I didn't see, didn't *care* to see, the immense burden being an Alpha at such a young age put on him. I took it all out on him.

I wish Wulfric were here now so I could say how sorry I am.

Clearing the emotion from my throat, I say, "Jamie is struggling too. Just... try to understand that he is doing the best he can. Be frustrated, but do not be cruel or say things you'll regret. Otherwise, you may push him away and lose him for good." I dump the steak on a plate.

Jace's face has gone pale, his eyes bright with worry. "I... I didn't mean it. He knows that, right?"

"Hard to say unless you tell him yourself." Cutting the steak into strips, I divide the pieces between three plates, then add some broccoli. "Come, let's eat."

Just as we've set the table, the lock clicks in the front door. Jamie's sweet scent makes my wolf howl in delight as he walks in. Parsing through his aroma, I detect notes of apprehension, guilt, and sadness. Mustering up a smile that doesn't reach his eyes, Jamie holds up a grocery bag. "I bought some ice cream. Anders, you'll love this stuff. It's just what a bad day calls for." His smile wobbles when Jace approaches slowly, head down.

The lad's shoulders heave as a choked noise bursts from him, and he throws his arms around Jamie's waist and hides his face in his stomach. "Please don't leave me, Jamie. I'm sorry. I'm so sorry."

Tears flood Jamie's eyes, and he wraps his brother in his arms, holding him tight. "Never. I'll never leave you, kiddo. I promise. It's okay. We can do some fun stuff this weekend together, just us. Okay?"

Jace bobs his head, still clinging to Jamie.

My eyes sting, and I look away, surprised by how emotional I'm getting... and by how much I suddenly wish I could say similar words to all my brothers.

"I'm sorry. I'm sorry. Please, take me back. Please, let me be your pack again."

But I know in my heart, it will never happen.

"Something smells good!" Jamie's smile is genuine as he guides Jace to the table. "That looks so tasty! Who made this?"

I motion at Jace. "Your lad did. He's a talented cook."

Jace laughs, wiping his eyes and sniffling. "Yeah. Totally made all of this."

Eyes soft and tender, Jamie meets my gaze. "Thank you." His words send a shiver of delight down my spine. "Let's eat before it gets cold." We gather around the table and tuck in. Jamie's eyes widen. "This steak is so undercooked it should be mooing."

I moan around a buttery-soft mouthful. "Just the way I like it."

Jace pretends to tear into his steak like a wild animal, making us both laugh.

Later that evening, Jace insists we read together, so we meet in his room. Jamie cracks open a book, and once Jace is under the covers, he begins to read. It's a story about an ugly duckling, different from all the others, who struggles to find acceptance—until, in the end, he finally finds a family who loves and accepts him.

To my surprise, my eyes get misty, and I feign interest in the floor so nobody notices.

Yawning, Jamie leads the way to our room. "Thank you for the meal."

Running my hand down his back, I guide him inside. "It was my pleasure."

"Anders." Gripping my arms, Jamie suddenly presses me against the door. Desire roars through my blood as his lean body blankets mine. His pink tongue peeks out, gliding over his bottom lip. "I mean, I..." Those blue eyes stray from mine, suddenly damp. "I've never had someone take care of us like that before. It means a lot to me, so..." Blinking fast, he glances at my mouth.

The urge to close the space between our lips burns within me. If I do not taste him now, the desire will surely consume me from the inside out.

"I'm sorry things were such a mess today." Jamie's voice shakes. "I know we're a burden, and nothing I do is good enough. I'm trying, but it's hard and things are messy, and I'm sorry—"

Cupping Jamie's stubbled cheek, I murmur, "You are not a burden. Neither is the lad. You could never be."

Jamie's lips quiver like he's about to cry until he lunges in and claims my mouth. As he clutches my face, his lips gliding over mine, the world around me ceases to exist. My wolf howls in unity within my soul, like all is right in the world at last. I adore how sweet he tastes, the tender desperation in his touch, and how perfectly his lips fit against mine.

I don't think I could ever leave him behind. I should pull away. I've got to remember my goals. This isn't my time, it's not where I belong, but as I part my lips and let Jamie's tongue dance with mine, none of that matters.

With a carnal growl, I grip the back of his thighs as he jumps. His legs wrap around my waist, and I can feel how hard he is against my stomach. I pull on his hair and bring his lips crashing down to mine. Careful not to drop him, I carry him to the bed.

Jamie laughs as I toss him onto it, bouncing on the mattress.

I'm already tearing off my clothes. Naked, I step over my discarded clothes and prowl toward the bed. I pounce, caging him between my body and the mattress. Jamie's breath hitches around a moan as I lick and suck on the fair skin of his throat. I rock my hips, grinding my bare cock against his jeans.

"Clothes off, pet. Now. Before I rip them to shreds."

Panting, Jamie undresses until he's naked beneath me. I twist and tug on his nipple rings, making him arch and gasp. Rolling my hips, I grind against his cock. Jamie moans breathlessly, reaching between our bodies to stroke us both in his hand.

"Fuck. Get the lube. Hurry up. Need you inside me. Now."

I yank open the drawer so violently the whole thing almost falls out. Grabbing the lube, I spurt a copious amount into my hand. Wrapping my slick fingers around our cocks, I stroke in earnest, groaning as we glide together, smooth and fast.

Once I'm slick enough, I grab for his knees, but Jamie suddenly flips us so he's the one on top. My feet touch the cool floorboards as Jamie straddles my lap. Reaching behind himself, he inserts two slick fingers into his own ass and moans.

"Not fair, pet," I growl, caressing his stretched hole with a lubed finger. I think I'll die here and now unless I get inside him soon.

Jamie bites his lip with a whimper as I push inside. My finger brushes two of his. Fuck. He's so tight. "Ready for my cock?"

"Yes," Jamie gasps. "Been ready all day."

"Then have me," I growl against his lips, damn near feral as he tightens around our fingers.

Jamie withdraws his fingers, and I do the same, already missing his heat—until he sinks down onto me. Never in my life have I known such bliss. Every time we make love, I'm closer to Valhalla's glory than the last. We both sigh, breaths mingling, and then I claim his lips in deep, hungry kisses as he begins to ride. His arms wind around me, holding on tight.

"You are worthy, James Sullivan," I rasp against his mouth as I move with him, lips brushing with every word. "Of everything. The loyalty of your friends. Your grandmother's trust. My body. My heart. My soul. Don't you dare doubt that. Am I clear?"

"Yeah," Jamie says, breathless as he rides my cock faster and faster. "Yes. Anders. Yes."

I snap my hips faster, pounding into the blissful heat of his body until Jamie's mouth slackens and he cries out, hoarse and jubilant. Wrapping my arms around his shoulders, I hold on tight as the bed creaks, the mattress dipping beneath our frenzied movements.

"And if anyone is ever fool enough to make you question how worthy you are, I'll burn their world to the ground."

There's nothing I wouldn't do for him. And I don't know when this happened. No one will ever hurt my mate.

I snarl my gratification as the musky scent of Jamie's seed fills the air, spilling hot against my chest and stomach. Growling a strangled version of his name, I pound into his clenching heat and claim my own release deep inside him.

Jamie clears his throat. "You, uh... you really meant that?"

"Yes."

"I didn't even specify—"

I kiss him, stroking my fingers through his hair. "Yes, pet. Yes to all of it. I never say things I don't mean. For better or worse."

Jamie smiles, soft and tired. "Thanks. I needed to hear that. All of it." His voice wavers and he coughs, clearly trying to hide his emotions.

I smirk. "I know. I have a way with words."

"Dick." Jamie smacks my ass.

Closing my eyes, I nuzzle into Jamie's neck.

Mayhap like that ugly duckling, I can find where I belong too.

CHAPTER 15

JAMIE

EARLY THE NEXT MORNING, I find Anders going through the bathroom cabinet. "Where is your razor? I wish to shave my beard."

"Shave it?" I ask, walking around in front of him to admire the beard in question. It's long and dense with little silver hairs popping out here and there. He must have lived a hard life for his hair to already be going gray. Reaching out, I play with his wet beard, twirling it around my fingers. "But it's so nice."

"I've been growing it out since I was a lad, but it's time for a change. I... I would like to fit in more."

"Really?" Hope flares warm and bright in my chest. It almost sounds like he wants to stay here in this time.

Anders's big hands grip my hips, and he pushes me back against the sink. I sit on it, his thighs between my knees. "Aye." Anders frowns, lowering his gaze. "I'm going to be here for a while. I should blend in more with my environment."

For a while. I try and hide my disappointment by looking at the floor. "Okay." I twist around to open the mirror behind me, trying to fight down my disappointment. I find the shaving cream, my best razor, and some fresh blades. I fit the razor with the blade, then grab my brush and the cream. I squirt some into my palms.

Anders sniffs my hands. "Smells good."

"I'm going to give this a trim first," I warn him, but he still jumps when I switch on my electric clippers. Anders eyes them with suspicion.

"Okay?" I ask. If he's uncomfortable, I'll stop.

Anders swallows. "I..." He glances at me, and I'm shaken to the core by the vulnerability in his eyes.

"I won't hurt you, Anders. I promise. If you tell me to stop, I will."

Anders holds my gaze, and after a moment's hesitation, he nods.

My heart does flips in my chest as I lift the clippers toward his beard. Trust doesn't come easily to Anders, yet here he is, trusting me not to hurt him. I won't let him down.

Slowly and carefully, I shave off his beard. Anders flinches at first, shoulders drawn up to his ears. I ask him questions to help him relax, small things like what his village is like, if it ever warms up where he's from. Gradually, Anders relaxes.

Once I've finished using the clippers, I lather shaving cream into his stubble. Those green eyes never stray from my face. His big hands knead at my thighs while I massage the cream in. Beneath the rough hair, his jawline is sharp and angular. I can picture the exact shape of his face, handsome but sharp and severe. There's nothing sharp about his gaze, though. No, he looks at me with pure indulgence, like I'm all that exists as he trusts me to press a blade to his skin without doing him harm.

It's... intimate. Touching his face. Caring for him like this. Doing something soft and domestic together like shaving. I like it. I like it too much, especially knowing what time we have together is brief.

"Ready?" I ask, my voice a whisper, our breath mingling. Anders's throat bobs when he swallows, and then he nods. I gently press the blade to his skin and glide it through the hair. Anders's eyes widen, but he stays still and patient while I work. I stop once in a while to rinse the blade under the tap, then continue.

My wolf is in harmony with his, and a calm like nothing I've ever felt guides my hand in slow, gentle motions. Slowly, his face reveals itself to me. He looks shockingly young, cheekbones high and flat, jaw as chiseled as I knew it would be. There's a scar on his chin where hair doesn't grow, and I wonder where he got it and how. I wonder at all of him, wishing I had time to learn all there is to know about Anders and the world he comes from.

"Where'd you get the scar?" I ask. He's got lots of them; I've seen them when we make love.

"Hunters. Ulfhednar heal our wounds, but cuts made by a silver blade never fade."

I think back to our talk in the diner. So much of his anger toward his brother sounded like fear to me. He's lost his parents, and he's scared that unless he returns home, he'll lose more of his family.

My fingers slip. I wince when a few drops of blood well to the surface of Anders's cheek. "I'm so sorry." The wound heals in seconds before my eyes. "Did that hurt?"

Anders shrugs. "I doubt there's anything you could do that would hurt me, pet, even if you tried. You have a kind soul. I've always thought of kindness as a weakness, but you have defied my expectations. There is nothing weak about you. I'm glad your life has been easier than mine. My wolf does not like the idea of you knowing the hardships that I have."

It's like he read my thoughts. I don't know how to tell him I have known plenty of hardships. Sure, we had sex, and we're stuck together for now, but it doesn't make talking about the past any easier. Maybe I've never been cut by a blade, but I've known pain that stabs just as deeply. Pain I've learned to hide behind a smile, laughter, books, and coffee.

I cup his cheek and angle his head, shaving with care beneath his nose. He closes his eyes, a low rumbling in his chest that speaks to my wolf. I can feel how pleased he is, how content... How he trusts me not to hurt him. It makes my heart fluttery and light.

In a few minutes, Anders's face is clean-shaven. He wipes away the remnants of the cream with a towel and considers himself in the mirror, running a hand over his smooth jaw.

"Okay?" I ask.

Anders's brow furrows. "It's... different. But I like it."

I exhale my relief. "Really?"

"Aye. Feels like I can be a new person. Someone else."

I'd like nothing more than for Anders to find a place here, maybe even with me, but I shove that thought away. Anders has made it clear his place here is tempo-rary.

Closing my eyes, I try desperately to ignore the howl of my wolf, begging for him to stay.

After shutting down my computer, I stretch out my back as I leave the office, passing through the empty kitchen. Beyond the kitchen, the café is wonderfully busy. Every table is full. People work on their laptops, read while they sip their coffee, and chat with their friends. I can't help but feel warm with pride. My gran created a space where people can come together.

Since Jace is suspended, he's hanging out at the store this week. He's also been helpful and brought people their pastries and drinks for us. I'd love for him to work in the shop once he's older. I think he could be a natural.

I go to help fulfill drink orders behind the counter, and I spot a face I haven't seen in a while. It's Kieran Grove and one of my regulars, Amanda. I almost don't recognize Kieran; he's grown out a beard as red as his hair. Hell, he almost looks like a Viking warrior.

"Hey, Kieran!" I wave at him. "The usual?" He always has an iced matcha latte.

"Yes, please," he calls. After he pays, I get his drink ready. It's nice to see him and Amanda again. The last time I saw them, they'd been planning a trip to Iceland together after Kieran's jerk of an ex dumped him. I hope they had fun.

I deliver Kieran's drink, and by the time I'm back behind the counter, Kieran is talking animatedly to Amanda about something.

"Jamie, sugar-bear," Bailey says as they prepare an espresso, "how about you and Jace come over to my place? It's time for our annual LOTR marathon."

"Oh yeah! I'd totally forgotten. I did promise Jace we should do something fun this weekend. Should we watch *The Hobbit* trilogy too?" Obviously not in the same night. Those movies are long as fuck.

Bailey laughs. "Those movies are goofy as hell, but why not?"

Maybe the second trilogy isn't a masterpiece, but it's still quality entertainment.

Bailey grins impishly. "You should have Anders cosplay as Thorin."

"Holy shit. I never noticed the similarities!" Maybe Anders is too tall to play the dwarf Thorin, but now that I think about it, he looks a *lot* like Richard Armitage. Cue the drooling. Yummy. "Maybe I can dress up as Bilbo, and we can be BagginShield." It's the ship name for Bilbo and Thorin. They were a popular ship on Tumblr back in the day, even though they were never canonized as a queer couple.

"BagginShield is cute," Jess interjects, "but nothing will ever top the epic romance that is Sam and Frodo."

"Never! Sam and Frodo will live forever!"

We laugh, and for the next hour, I fantasize about introducing Anders to some of my favorite films and hobbies.

"Tyr's balls! It's you!" Anders's voice snarls.

I jolt out of my thoughts. Anders looms over Amanda and Kieran's table, body taut with tension, and anger is rolling off him in waves as he glares at Kieran. What is going on? How does Anders know Kieran? The fear blanching Kieran's face makes my stomach lurch.

"Well, well. Seems like Loki is having a laugh at my expense today. What happened? Did my brother get tired of his new pet and send you packing? Need a consolatory belly rub? Oh, how about a little scratchy behind your ears?" Anders sneers.

What gives? I've never seen Anders be so nasty before. It's not a side of him that I like.

I rush out from behind the counter as Kieran and Amanda say something to him.

"Whoa, whoa, whoa!" I flash an easygoing smile and get between them. I elbow Anders in the ribs. "I sincerely apologize for my new employee. He's *supposed* to be stocking the dark romance section. Aren't you, puppy dog?"

Anders's whole face goes red. "I can't kill them?"

What? I hide my shock behind a smile. "No!" I hiss, whipping around toward him.

Anders growls. "Can I maim them? Just a little bit."

What the fuck? I bat my eyelashes. "No."

Anders deflates. "Fine." My big, bad Viking ulfhednar warrior is practically pouting as he stomps back to the dark romance section.

What the *hell*, Anders? I'm going to give him so much shit for bothering customers. After apologizing to Amanda and Kieran, I seek out my asshole mate and find him grumbling as he stocks the shelves. I pick up a book and smack him gently on the head with it.

"Ow," he snaps.

"What in the fuck, Anders?"

He recoils from my harsh tone.

"You can't antagonize customers like that. I don't care what beef you have with them. Which, by the way, what is your problem with Kieran? He's a nice guy."

Anders's face flushes red with rage. What did I say? "He's not!" he snarls, lurching to his feet. "He's the human who seduced my brother, the human who threatens the future of our pack!"

Oh. Well, that explains his attitude toward Kieran, even if it's still unacceptable. I just saw a whole other side to him, a side I'm not sure I like. "Anders, you're better than that." *Isn't he?* I wonder, as I remember the fear that flashed across Kieran's face. Anders wouldn't have...

"What did you do to him?"

Anders's anger falters, his shoulders dropping from where they'd hunched around his ears. "I..." His voice becomes softer, smaller, and he breaks eye contact with me. "Leave it, pet. Don't ask me again."

"Why? What happened that's so bad you won't even tell me?" I grip his arm.

"Because if you knew, you'd bloody hate me!" Anders's expression shutters, but not before I see the fear in his eyes. "Never ask me again." And he turns and shoves past a few shoppers as he ducks into the bathroom.

I can't believe he shut me out like that. What did he do to Kieran that's so bad he thinks I'd hate him? Anxiety makes my stomach churn.

In preparation for our movie night, I dress myself up as a hobbit. Okay, so maybe my hobbit is more on the twink side, but I hear Tolkien had a lot of queer friends, so I'm sure he'd be down with it.

"Jamie, hurry up!" Jace calls from the living room.

I twirl in front of the mirror so my cloak can spin dramatically around my ankles. Looks good. Now I just hope it won't get caught in the subway doors. It'll be easier to beat the traffic if we take the train to Bailey's place in Queens.

In the living room, Jace has dressed up as an elf and is playing pretend with his plastic bow. I'm disappointed to find that Anders refused to dress up in the costume I loaned him, but that's okay. He can be boring. I'll love him anyway.

"What are you wearing?" Anders gives me a double take.

"I'm Bilbo! Or I guess his gay cousin Dildo." I spin my cloak around. "Cool, huh? Now, let's go on an adventure!" I say in a terrible British accent and take Anders's hand, but I can't help feeling a twinge of disappointment when he doesn't hold on tight like he usually does.

Something has been eating at him ever since his encounter with Kieran. Maybe seeing him just brought up some bad memories. I wish I could do something to help.

"Jace, excited to watch the movies?" I ask once we're on the train.

He grins, swaying side to side with the train's movements. "The first trilogy is the best. The other one is just goofy."

From where he stands, gripping the pole over our heads, Anders leans down and asks quietly, "What is a movie?"

Oh, right. This will be his first time seeing a movie. He's in for a treat. "It's like a story, but you can see it." I don't know how to describe it. "None of it is real, but it's acted out. Actors memorize their lines off a script, which is the story. Then they act it out as their characters. It's like... playing pretend when you were a kid."

"Ah." He still looks confused.

"You'll see for yourself. Trust me, you'll love it."

When we arrive at Bailey's apartment, we're buzzed in. Bailey answers the front door dressed up as an elf—pointed ears, medieval dress, and all. They look stunning. "Welcome, ring-bearers!"

Anders looks them up and down. "Bailey? Why are you dressed like that?"

Bailey clears their throat. "You are mistaken, Master Human. I am Legolas."

Jace gawks. "Hey, no fair! I'm Legolas!"

Bailey stares intently off into the distance, clearly seeing something we can't. "Inside, quickly! There are orcs coming!"

"What?" Anders squawks as Bailey tugs us inside.

Jess and Bailey have gone all out, even cooking LOTR-inspired food. Anders picks up a piece of lembas bread, the elven bread that can fill the stomach of a grown man with a single bite. He sniffs and takes a nibble.

Jess wears a red wig and a fake beard, clearly cosplaying as Gimli, the dwarven member of the Fellowship of the Ring. "Hey, guys." She waves.

Bailey rolls their eyes. "Jess, come on, get in character!"

Jess coughs and deepens her voice. "Greetings, Master Elves, Master Hobbit. We have food and drink aplenty, even for elves, I suppose." She glares at Jace.

Jace holds his head high. "I suppose I can tolerate your presence, dwarf. But only for the sake of the greater good!"

Jess touches the fake axe in her belt. "Keep your weapons stowed, elf, and so shall I."

Jace huffs. "Agreed!" They both *hmph!* and stalk dramatically away from each other.

Anders shoots me a confused look. "What is going on? Why is Jess armed? I thought she and Jace were friends!"

I snort, realizing how bewildering this must be for him. "We're LARPing. Playing characters," I explain.

"Why?"

"Because it's fun!" Grabbing a couple of handfuls of the lembas bread for myself, I go and sit on the couch. "I haven't eaten since second breakfast!" I declare in my god-awful accent, plopping down on the sofa.

Jess turns on the TV and opens a streaming channel. "Urgh! I hate these confounded magical objects! If only Gandalf were here. There we go." She locates the film collection. "Shall we watch the extended edition?"

"Let's just watch the regular editions," I suggest in my normal voice.

Bailey dims the lights, then bounds over to sit next to Jess, who puts an arm around them. Anders squeezes in between Jess and me while Jace is squished to my left. Anders gasps as the prologue plays out across the screen. I bite back a laugh at his wide, astounded eyes as the forces of the Dark Lord Sauron clash with the heroes. Anders gets up and cautiously approaches the TV, only to jump as the fighting gets more intense.

"Anders, sit down. I can't see!" Jess says.

I'm trying hard not to laugh as Anders reaches out and pokes the television screen before jerking his hand back. "Incredible!"

Jace covers his mouth, shoulders shaking with giggles.

"He's just never seen such a high-quality TV before," I say, laughing nervously, then wildly motion him over.

Anders drops back down beside me, his whole body tense as he watches the fighting. "They're trapped in that box. What happens if they get out?"

"It's a TV," I whisper. "And it's not real. I promise."

Anders's face goes pale as a character dies in the battle against Sauron. "Y-you're sure?"

I take his hand and squeeze. "I promise, puppy dog. It's all make-believe."

He grips my hand tight. "O-oh. All right then." Anders relaxes more once all the fighting has stopped. He has lots of questions. "Where is this place? It's beautiful."

"They filmed a lot of the movie in New Zealand," I whisper, handing him some bread.

"Why is the little fellow so short? He doesn't look like a child." He points at Frodo.

I chuckle. "He's not actually short. Special effects make him look short."

Anders loves the scene with the fireworks. I almost like watching him more than the movie as he gasps in awe and astonishment, earning a few amused looks from Jess and Bailey.

He'll fit in with my friends just fine.

Chapter 16
Anders

My encounter with Kieran Grove replayed in my head the rest of yesterday.

Fears I thought I'd buried clawed their way to the surface. Why was Kieran here? What has happened to my village since I've been gone?

I can't sleep, tossing and turning. I dread what my village and the island itself will look like when I return. Will Kieran have invited hunters into our home? They will burn the forests. Hunt the game and starve my family. Burn them with fire and silver. Is Wulfric still alive? What about my brothers and my aunt?

Oh gods. I've let myself become so complacent.

I have to go back. Soon. I must assess the situation and plan a course of action. If humans have descended upon my pack, then I will do whatever I can to aid them. If Wulfric has let the humans take over, then I must challenge him. I'll have no choice, though the prospect of facing my brother in combat doesn't fill me with the thrill it once did.

When I open my eyes, morning has come. Jamie's side of the bed is empty but warm. I roll over and face the ceiling. My chest is heavy. I know what I must ask of him. I only pray he won't be upset.

The apartment smells like coffee and pancakes. I love pancakes. Jamie is humming in the kitchen. "Morning," Jamie chirps. He has bags under his eyes. "Did you like the movie?" He hands me a plate of oatmeal pancakes.

We finished the first movie, and Bailey and Jess told me there were two more. "It was... interesting." Once I'd realized the people in the box, the TV, weren't going to come out and lop my head off, I'd relaxed.

I take a big bite of my pancake and moan. They're so soft and fluffy. My mate is an amazing cook. I drizzle some maple syrup over the cakes for extra sweetness, then add a splash to my coffee.

"You and your sweet tooth," Jamie says, voice soft and fond. "I'm guessing you didn't have a good time. Your face did that thing that makes you look constipated."

"They're fine people. For humans. But I admit I still don't trust them, or any human for that matter."

Jamie's face falls. "Anders."

"You grew up among humans, Jamie. I grew up being hunted by them. No matter how kind they may seem, once they learn what you are, your friends will turn against you."

Jamie recoils. "What? No. They'd never."

I sigh. "It's a fact. They can never know what we are."

Jamie folds his arms. "I don't believe you. Sure, maybe some humans would be jerks about it, but Jess and Bailey are good. They'd never hate us just for being different."

"It's not about being different," I snap, needing him to understand. "They will only ever see us as monsters, Jamie."

But my stubborn mate only shakes his head. "You don't know that, Anders. You can't just make snap judgments like that."

"It's a judgment based on a lifetime's worth of the cruelty of humans."

"What is with you? You've been acting grouchy and paranoid ever since you saw Kieran."

I shove aside my plate, my appetite diminished. "For damn good reason."

"Oh? Tell me, then! Kieran's a good guy."

I snort. "Hardly. He has my brother charmed, but I never liked him. He's going to trick them all into thinking he's one of them, and then he'll betray them."

Jamie groans and leans on the counter, tugging his fingers through his hair. "Anders, you're better than this. You're a good person."

Am I really? I'm good to him. I would never dream of being cruel to Jamie. "That isn't true. Others would tell you I've been the villain in their story. My brother. Kieran.

Anyone who has threatened my pack. Certainly the lovers I've kicked out of my bed."

Jamie swallows, his heart racing faster in my ears. "Are you going to be the villain in mine?"

I meet his gaze sharply, alarmed he'd ever think that I'd hurt him.

"Am I going to lose you to this obsession for revenge?"

The barstool creaks as I rise. Jamie takes a step back against the wall as I cage him in. Reaching out, I take his chin in my hand and make him meet my gaze. I need him close, need him to understand. "The only time I'll ever be the villain in your story, James Sullivan, is when you need me to be. Say the word, and I'll unleash Hel herself upon your foes." My gaze lands on the necklace against his chest. "Jamie, I need to check in on my pack. I need to be sure Kieran isn't planning anything."

Jamie's eyes widen. "Anders, I don't like this."

"I won't do anything rash. If it's as I've feared and the pack is in chaos, I would need to plan my next move."

Jamie closes his hand around the necklace. "And you'd come back?"

I hesitate, suddenly finding it near impossible to refuse him. It wasn't long ago I would have thanked him for his hospitality and left without a second thought. Now...

"You want me to come back?"

Jamie's lips part, but he takes a moment to reply. "I mean, sure, but only if you want to. Your home is there.

Your family. Everything that's familiar to you. Why would you want to come back to New York, of all places?" Jamie laughs softly, but his wounded eyes contradict his attempt at humor.

"I wouldn't be coming back to New York, Jamie. I'd be coming back to *you*. Wherever you may be. In the past, present, future. It does not matter to me." Jamie tries to look away, but I capture his face in my hands. "Never doubt the way that I feel for you. You are mine, and I am yours. I crossed time and space to find you, and I'll be damned before I let you go. Trust in our bond. Trust me and the depth of my feelings for you. Can you do that?"

I've never meant any words more. For so long, I lived in the darkness of my brother's shadow, never feeling good enough. When Jamie came into my life, he brought the sunshine with him. Day by day, he's challenging my deeply held beliefs. He's changing me into someone else, someone far better than the monster I was before. My world is a brighter, better place because of knowing him.

"Now, answer me. Do you want me to come back?"

"Yes. Of course I do." Jamie squeezes my hands.

A smile spreads across my face, but it trembles. Jamie wants me to stay, but what if my brothers need me? Torn in two, I grip his hands like he's an anchor in stormy seas. "I will see how the village fares, and then I will return with news. How does that sound?"

Jamie holds my gaze and nods. "O-okay, Anders. I will. Just don't take too long, okay?"

I kiss his fingertips. "I won't, not longer than a few hours. I swear this to you."

With trembling fingers, Jamie removes the necklace and hands it to me. "Take good care of it."

"You have my word." I pocket the necklace.

"What?" a wavering voice whispers behind me.

When I turn, Jace has come out of the bathroom, hair shiny and damp. His eyes are wide and glistening, his little mouth slack. "You're... leaving? But what about my school presentation? You promised you'd help me."

The hurt in his voice twists like a knife in my chest. Going to him, I kneel so I can look him in the eyes. His fists are clenched, his lip trembling as he glares at the floor. "It is only temporary. I will return in time for your presentation, lad. I promise."

"Yeah, right." Jace pushes me away, and I'm surprised by the ache that throbs in my chest. "What's the matter with us? Everyone always leaves!" Rubbing his eyes, he runs into the bedroom and slams the door.

Swallowing what feels like an egg in my throat, I hang my head. "What does he mean?"

Jamie sighs behind me. Turning, I find him hugging himself, eyes downcast. "Before you... nobody I dated stuck around. I'd be careful to really get to know a guy before introducing him to Jace, but no matter how sure I was or how great things were going, the relationship would fall apart. Jace really liked my last boyfriend, Tim. He was a great guy, but things didn't work out. Jace was crushed."

A growl rises in me at the thought of Jamie with someone else, someone who hurt him and the lad. Who wouldn't cherish this little pack?

Rising, I go to him and envelop him in my arms. "I will come back to you and the boy. I swear it on my life." Jamie throws his trembling arms around me, crushing me to him.

"You'd better."

Jamie drives us to the piers. He's unusually quiet. I don't know what more I can say to ease his doubts. I will have to prove my devotion by returning to him as swiftly as I can.

Once we're at the piers, we walk along the docks together. The sun rises over the water, and seagulls cry out as they chase the dawn. It's hard to believe I once found this timeline so intimidating. Jamie's present is as beautiful as my past, just in different ways.

He laughs softly. "I can't believe I punched you in the face."

A smile tugs at my mouth. "I can. It hurt. I knew right away how strong you were. The Norns chose well when they brought us together."

"Here we are..." Jamie stops before the railing. A security guard unlocks a gate leading to a long stretch of dock that sways side to side. Boats are moored along it. "Looks like the marina is open. You can rent a boat," Jamie suggests.

I make to walk away, but Jamie grips my hand tightly. Clearing his throat, he lets go. My hand still tingles from his touch as Jamie chips in for a rowboat. The dock rocks beneath us, and I seize Jamie's hand so he doesn't lose his balance. I don't know what to say. Jamie won't meet my gaze. He's clearly unhappy with me.

"Ah. Here she is." The boat looks nothing like the one I rode in on but similar enough that I shouldn't have any trouble. Jamie's hand flinches in mine. "Do you want to come with me?" I ask, turning to face him.

Jamie shakes his head. "Jace needs me. I don't want to risk, I don't know, getting stuck in the past."

I have yet to hear of such a thing, but I suppose anything is possible. "That makes sense..." My reluctance to part from him slips into my voice before I can shore up my heart's defenses.

"Just, you know... be safe. And come back to us. Don't go rushing off to challenge Wulfric. Okay?" His voice wobbles.

"Oh, pet." I pull him into my arms, my heart quivering when he practically throws himself on me. "I will. I promise." I plant a kiss on the top of his silver locks. He shivers against me, his hands gripping me tight.

I can't help but lean down and kiss him. As our lips meet, I realize how much I'll miss him, even if I'll only be gone for a few hours at most. He's become a part of me down to the marrow of my bones. "I'll see you soon," I vow to him, then step into the boat.

"Yeah. See you." Jamie tries to smile, but it doesn't touch his eyes.

I want to climb off the damn boat and go back to him, but I steel myself and grip the oars tightly. The necklace around my neck begins to quiver against my chest. I row toward the horizon and think of the island of Ulfheim. I picture my brothers and my aunt. As I will it, a tear appears in the fabric of this realm. Through the tear is an island shrouded in early morning mist. My heart soars. Ulfheim is close. I only hope my family is all right.

I make myself row until my arms are burning. The waves toss me about as the portal sucks me in ever closer. The tip of the boat enters the portal. Almost there. I look back at Jamie. He's watching me leave.

"Jamie," I call out before I can stop myself, "I will—"

Then, everything is gone.

My stomach turns over as I pass from one time and into another. The waves carry me to Ulfheim's shores. My heart races as I grow closer until finally my boat bumps over the rocky shore. I jump out, boots splashing in the frigid water, and drag the boat the rest of the way to shore.

I breathe in deep, filling my lungs with the clean ocean air. I am home. At last. Oh, how I've missed this place. Bending down, I scoop up a handful of stones that pile on the shore. I should take one with me, just so I have a tiny piece of the island.

Distant howls make my heart lurch. That's my pack. They must be going for the first morning hunt. My brother Gunnar would be leading them. He's always been the best hunter out of all of us. If I'm swift, I can catch up and observe them. As long as I stay downwind of the pack, they shouldn't be able to scent me.

I drop to all fours as my furs consume me. My wolf longs to cry out to his pack, but I keep my song locked inside. They can't know I'm here, not yet. I take off, leaving the beach behind as I run. As the wind whips through my fur, memories rush through my mind. I remember running with my father and brothers. Racing Lyall to the village. Mocking Wulfric as we walked back into the village together after a hunt.

I follow the scents of the pack to the tundra where the reindeer will be grazing at this hour. I keep to the cover of the trees as I pursue the pack. The trees clear, opening to a vast field. Leaning out from behind the cover of a tree trunk, I watch and wait.

One by one, the pack emerges from the trees below the hill, stalking toward the grazing reindeer. A gray wolf marches beside an enormous black wolf. The gray wolf is Gunnar. The black one is Wulfric. My fur bristles with fury as a familiar white wolf comes to stand beside Wulfric. Kieran. He may act like he's one of us, but it's a trick. I know it.

All my fury evaporates when another white wolf, larger than Kieran, comes bounding up to his side and playfully nips his ear. Lyall. My twin. Gods, how I have missed him. A whine pulls from my throat, and my wolf tries to reach across the bonds between us to connect with our pack. Lyall's bond is the only one that hasn't been broken, but it hangs by a single thread.

Lyall's ear twitches. He looks toward me, and I lurch back behind the tree. Heart pounding, I stay still for a few seconds. Did he see me? A secret part of me almost hopes he did. I miss talking to him, running and playing with him.

Slowly, I poke my head around the tree. A growl escapes me when Kieran pounces on Lyall, and the two try to play, only to be interrupted by Wulfric's commanding bark. Probably telling them to cut it out and focus.

How is this possible, I wonder with dismay. Kieran is an outsider, born a human, yet they are treating him like they've known him all their lives! Meanwhile, they exiled me, their own flesh and blood. No. This must be a trick.

Kieran is plotting something, I know it. He's a human. All they do is scheme and betray us. They despise our kind. At any minute while they are distracted with the hunt, he'll put his fangs in their necks. He's probably got a whole clan of hunters just waiting for an opportune time to strike.

Heart racing, I watch and wait to be proven right.

The hunt begins. The wolves split up and circle the herd, forcing the reindeer to form their own inner circle to protect the most vulnerable of the herd. A chase ensues. Wulfric leads the charge when an opening appears in the herd's defenses. The pack rushes in, nipping at hooves, dodging the swipe of antlers, yelping as they get trampled, although their healing kicks in to repair any damage.

After some time, the pack brings down a sickly male with broken antlers. Wulfric shifts to his human form. "We are victorious, brothers and sisters!" he cries, and the pack howls their delight.

Kieran shifts and runs, leaping into Wulfric's arms. I tense. This is it. He'll produce a dagger made of silver and stab my brother. I know it!

But... it doesn't happen. Instead, Wulfric captures Kieran's lips in a kiss. When they break apart, Kieran is smiling at him in a way that sends a pang of yearning through me. His smile, the light in his eyes... it reminds me of Jamie. It's the way he looks at me.

I always thought my fool brother Wulfric was being bewitched by Kieran. But it seems as if the feeling is *mutual*. They care for each other the way a mated pair does. But how can this be? I thought Kieran was only using my brother to survive the pack's mistrust of humans. Somehow, he ended up falling for Wulfric.

Stunned, I can only watch as the pack trusses the reindeer to a horse and begins the trip back to the village. My stomach churns, and my paws feel unsteady. No. No, I refuse to accept that I was wrong all this time about Kieran. Revenge has been the sole thing that has kept me going. If I let go of that, then what purpose will I have?

The village. I must get there. I must see that it is still standing.

Keeping low, I follow the pack as they leave the tundra, which gives way to a road covered in hoof prints, wagon wheel tracks, and paw prints. I stay within the trees and always downwind. Most of the pack has shifted to human form, including Gunnar, Wulfric, and Kieran.

I don't see Lyall among them. Where has he run off to?

"That was an impressive kill, Kieran," Gunnar is saying.

Kieran grimaces. "I'm not sure I'll ever be down with hunting cute animals. It's kinda gross."

"Even so, you make a fine wolf, little rabbit." Wulfric drapes an arm around Kieran's shoulders and steers him close.

Gunnar grunts. "Aye, suppose you do." His voice has a strange, growly quality to it.

Kieran arches a brow at him. "Are you okay, Gunnar?"

Gunnar coughs, but even that sounds more like a bark. "I'm fine."

Damn it. I know exactly what is happening. My fool brother has refused to find his fated mate, and the berserker is trying to come out. Gunnar had his chosen mate, a wolf named Leif. After his death, Gunnar has had no interest in pursuing someone new. I know I mocked him a time or two for his devotion. Leif was only a chosen mate. Now that I've found Jamie, I can't imagine ever moving on if I lost him, even if he hadn't been the one fated for me.

Guilt churns in my stomach.

The thatched rooftops and stone chimney stacks come into view, and my heart flips. We're almost home. Gods, how I have missed the village. I quicken my pace as much as I can while staying downwind of the pack. When the village of Ulfheim appears, a lump rises in my throat. There's the butcher's hut, the smells of fresh meat wafting out the door. The bakery doors burst open, and the baker's wife runs out to greet the pack, a basket of fresh rolls in her arms. The horses whicker from the stables, the scent of manure and fresh hay carrying on the breeze. Children shriek as they run through the muddy roads, throwing snowballs at each other.

"Alpha-Mate!" a little girl shouts, running up to Kieran. I recognize her as the daughter of a farmer.

Kieran kneels down to hug her. "Hey, kiddo. How's your archery?"

"Kieran," a boy shouts. "Can you teach me to play the lyre? You're the best in the whole village!"

"Enough, children," Wulfric gently scolds. "Your Alpha-Mate is a very busy man."

They all love Kieran. Somehow, this human has become a trusted, beloved member of the community. The village is whole, thriving, and happy. The sight fills me with sweet relief, and yet... something isn't sitting right with me.

"Welcome home, lads!" A whine of yearning escapes me as Helga rushes out the door of Wulfric and Kieran's home. She gives them hugs, then kisses Gunnar's cheek.

Gods. I wish I could go and greet her. I can't even remember the last time she kissed my cheek or looked at me with anything other than disappointment and frustration.

"Where's Lyall run off to?" she asks.

There's a twinge of something in my chest. Jealousy.

"Probably off chasing his own tail," Gunnar grumbles.

"Come on inside. Let's get that reindeer ready for butchering." Helga hefts the whole reindeer over her shoulder with strength no ordinary small woman her age should be capable of.

I want to shift and cry out for her to wait. I miss her. I miss Gunnar and Lyall. I want to wrestle with them, shift and hunt with them. I want to hug my aunt, the woman who became a second mother to me after losing my own.

All four of them go into the house together. The door slams, concealing them from view, and despite my furs, a shudder runs down my spine. Before I can stop myself, I dash from the trees and approach the house from the back.

The thralls that used to be present in the gardens are not there anymore, so nobody notices my arrival. I put my paws up on the windowsill and peer inside. I have a view of the four of them as they gather around the table. Helga pours homemade mead into wooden mugs, and they sit together, warmed by the fire and by the company of pack. Gunnar barks a rare laugh, his smile softening the hard lines on his face. Helga pats Kieran's hand as he regales them with an exaggerated tale of their hunt.

And Wulfric... Wulfric only has eyes for his mate. I barely recognize my little brother as he smiles, his eyes aglow with tenderness.

Why? Why do they look so *damn* happy? Why are they carrying on as if I never existed?

Helga suddenly frowns. "Is it not strange? How different things are without Anders?"

My heart leaps. At last, they've mentioned me. They haven't forgotten about me! I could weep from relief.

Wulfric's smile falls off his face. "Aye. I know what you mean. Things are... quieter."

Gunnar hums thoughtfully. "It's strange. I've barely noticed his absence until you brought him up."

Wulfric grimaces. "It's for the best that he's gone. Things are peaceful at last. I never have to worry about him challenging me or blaming me for every single little thing wrong in his life. If I could, I'd exile him again."

"He wasn't a great guy," Kieran says, squeezing Wulfric's hand. "Let's not talk about him anymore, okay?"

"Fine by me," Wulfric growls.

And that's that. They move on to other things, and I'm forgotten about.

Can I even blame Wulfric for hating me so?

I brought this huge, powerful man to his knees, crippled by the cruel words I'd spewed at him.

If I'd been on that beach when the hunters came, our father would still be here.

Wulfric had collapsed, curled in on himself, like he was back on that beach. I'd done that to him, and I'd felt justified in breaking him down to nothing. Because as long as I blamed Wulfric for our father's death, I couldn't blame myself for not being there. It was his fault, not mine. *Not mine.*

A void yawns within my chest.

My pack is so much happier without me, and I can't even fault them for it. I slide down from the window and shift back. I struggle to breathe around the ache in my throat. My eyes burn and prickle with unshed tears. I draw my knees to my chest and try to breathe, but everything hurts too damn much.

I've pushed away my only family, and I have no one to blame but myself. I can never ask them for forgiveness, not after how cruel I was. I was so focused on everything I'd lost that I ceased to care about the people in my life who were still there. And now, I've lost them forever. They don't miss me. They don't even care. And how can I blame them when I was nothing but cruel, self-absorbed, and bitter?

"A-Anders?" A hushed voice chokes out my name.

I lurch away from the window, horrified to be caught in such a moment of weakness. I scrub frantically at my eyes, and my breath catches as Lyall comes into focus. His mane of golden hair blows in the wind, and his eyes are wide.

"I knew it was you," Lyall croaks, voice shaking. "Gods. Brother, what are you doing here?"

I could cry. At least someone hasn't forgotten about me. Before I can stop myself, I've wrenched my twin into a bone-breaking hug. Despite my inner turmoil, I manage a smile. "It's good to see you too." I hold him until I'm sure my tears won't fall. Then I pull away to cup the back of his neck. The frayed bond between us glows with tentative hope.

Lyall grins, eyes wet, and claps me on the back. "I've missed you. What are you doing skulking around like a thief?" His smile wavers. He steps away from me. "You haven't come back to cause trouble, have you?"

I shake my hand. "Not here." Gripping his arm, I steer him from the house and into the trees. "No, just to check in on everyone. How are you?" I swing my arm around his shoulder and give him a shake.

Lyall chuckles. "I'm well. And you?"

I take a moment with my reply, parsing through my heartache to the memories of this morning with Jamie. "I found my mate."

Lyall whips around to face me. "Truly? That's amazing, brother! How did you meet him?"

"The moment I was exiled. He's from the future, but he's ulfhednar, like us."

"What's it like, living among humans?" Lyall asks as we walk, our feet carrying us back toward the shore where I arrived.

"It's... not what I expected."

Lyall elbows me. "They're not all bad, are they?"

"Not all of them," I admit grudgingly. "I'm a ways off from trusting them completely, but they have yet to betray me. How have things been in the village?"

We leave the village behind as Lyall catches me up on recent events. A few of the villagers got mated. Trade is prosperous. No hunters have prowled our shores. All seems well.

"Everyone seems happier without me," I say, casting my gaze to the road.

Lyall sighs beside me. "Anders..."

"Do not lie to me. I've seen for myself how at ease Wulfric is."

"It's true, people are at ease knowing nobody will challenge our Alpha." Lyall knocks his shoulder into mine, making me smile half-heartedly. "But if you're truly sorry, then apologize. Prove you've changed. Mayhap you'll be allowed back."

"You think I have changed?"

Lyall grins. "You didn't kick in the door and challenge Wulfric to a duel. So yes, I think you have. That mate of yours has been good for you, it seems."

Could I earn my pack's forgiveness? Hope blooms in my chest. "How?"

"I can't tell you that. You're smart. You can think of something."

We arrive back at my boat. "Thank you for coming to see me," I tell him.

"Of course. You'll be coming back, won't you?"

I don't know how to answer his question. I want to return, but only when I'm sure I can right the wrongs I've committed against my family. "I hope so."

Lyall pulls me into a hug. Closing my eyes tight, I bask in the warm glow of my pack. Gods, how am I only just realizing now how much I have missed being among the pack that raised me? I want to find a way to make things right. I just don't know how, and I'm scared nothing I do will ever repair the damage I've done.

"Safe travels, brother." Lyall's voice is raspy and full of emotion. "Odin guide you."

"Farewell." I squeeze him tight, then step out of his arms. He smiles, though his eyes are damp, and I turn away before he can see how saying goodbye has torn a hole in my heart.

Turning my back on the home I've lost, I look to the future.

Chapter 17

Jamie

The café buzzes with activity, but I can't focus on any of my duties. So far, I've spilled someone's drink, given someone the wrong order, and handed someone a croissant when they asked for a cheese Danish. So my day is going just great.

I miss Anders, and he's only been gone two hours.

He promised me he would come back, but my stomach churns with doubt. I should have been more cautious, tried harder to protect myself. If Anders doesn't come back, I can't imagine ever giving someone else my heart again.

Fact is, I don't know why he'd want to return when he has a family in his past. His whole world is there, where everything is familiar. Why would he want to come back to the future? To me and my broken little family?

"Is Anders coming back?" Jace has stuck to my side behind the counter all morning. When he isn't bringing people their orders, he picks at his fingernails in that nervous way he does.

I make the corners of my mouth twitch up. "Yeah. Sure he will."

"Does he not like us?"

Hurt twists in my chest. Kneeling before my brother, I flick some hair out of his face. "He likes you just fine, bud. He'll come back, and tomorrow, you'll do your presentation with him."

"Promise?"

I kiss his forehead. "Yeah."

The bell jingles. Plastering a fake smile on my face, I turn around. "Welcome."

A man I don't recognize steps into the shop. We get our fair share of newcomers to the store, but most are Brooklyn natives. Honestly, he looks like he should be browsing the aisles of a high-end clothing store with the threads he's got on. I bet his trousers, sleek shoes, leather jacket, and cashmere sweater cost more than my rent. His golden hair is gelled back except for a few strands that flop over his forehead. As his brown eyes meet mine, my wolf lurches within my soul.

There's something off about his scent. It almost... burns my nose. I don't like it, and neither does Wolf Jamie. It makes me want to sneeze. Whoever this guy is, he isn't human. Grabbing Jace's shoulder, I say without taking my eyes off this guy, "Jace, go into the kitchen and stay there until I come for you."

Wide-eyed, he nods and rushes away to do as he's told.

The guy with the odd scent leans on the counter, propping his chin in his hand. He flashes perfect teeth in a smile. "Aww. You hurt my feelings, wolfy," he says in a British accent.

My heart skips. Yup, definitely not human if he can tell what I am at a glance.

"Didn't anyone ever tell you witches don't actually eat children? This isn't *Hansel and Gretel*."

Shit. A witch. Could he be one of the witches that attacked Anders? My apprehension shifts to boiling rage that has me fighting down a snarl.

"Hello. I'm Arlo. Is Anders in?"

"None of your business." The words come out sharp as a knife. "Are you one of the witches that hurt him? Get out of my store."

Arlo's eyes widen, and he holds up his hands. "I didn't raise a hand against him, and I'm terribly sorry that the situation escalated the way it did."

"Your buddies broke his nose."

Arlo winces. "Again, I do apologize. Being ulfhednar, I assume he healed quickly once he put on his furs?"

I'm surprised he's saying all this at a normal volume, and I look around to make sure nobody is listening in.

"Relax, darling. I've got a compulsion globe around us. They think we're talking about football."

"Oh. That's good, I guess?" I'm not sure I like the fact he's just cast some weird spell on us. I didn't even see or hear it happen. "So what is it you want?"

"Anders has yet to visit the Agency to receive the documentation he needs in this timeline."

"We've been busy."

He nods understandingly. "I'm sure, but it's important if he plans to live here permanently. More importantly..." Arlo leans on the counter, closing the distance between us. "Has he taken you as his mate yet?"

Heat rushes to my cheeks. "Again, that's not your business."

"I'm aware it's a personal question, but it is imperative that he claims you. Quickly."

"I know about the berserker stuff, but he's been good so far. We're taking things slow. He won't hurt me."

Arlo shakes his head, brows furrowing. "I wish you both had that luxury, Jamie. I do. But the fact is that while you are surely safe around him as his mate, what about those around you? An unmated wolf from an Alpha bloodline is territorial. If he perceives there is a threat against you or your relationship, it might be enough to push him over the edge."

My mouth runs dry as I remember the day Anders saw Bailey hug and kiss me. "We've got things under control."

"I should hope so." Arlo's voice is grave. "I will be observing you both closely, Jamie. If I see signs that Anders's condition is worsening, then I will have to act."

"I won't let you hurt him."

"I won't. But my superiors are the ones who make the final decision. Convince him to claim you, Jamie. Please. You will be sparing yourself so much pain and hardship." He touches my arm, squeezing. The sadness in his eyes makes me freeze before I can pull away. "I know the pain of losing the one you love to their berserker's rage. It's something I wouldn't wish upon anyone."

With a last squeeze of my arm, Arlo turns and walks out of the shop.

What the hell was that all about? His last words make me shiver with unease.

How can I convince Anders to claim me when he has plans for a future I'm not a part of? And even if Anders saw a future with me, how could I saddle Anders with someone like me? It wouldn't be fair to bind him to my messy, broken family. To me with all my baggage.

Who in their right mind would want to be stuck with me for all eternity?

The bond connecting me to Anders lights up in my chest, flooding my insides with soothing warmth. The breath catches in my lungs. "Anders," I whisper, my heart soaring as I realize he's back. I whirl toward the door and run, startling people out of my path with my sudden movement. The doors fly open as I hurtle out onto the sidewalk. It's started snowing, and there's a thin coating sticking to the sidewalk. My frantic breaths plume in the air as I look around. He's probably at the piers. I need to get there.

Shooting Jess a text to hold down the fort until I'm back, I get in my car and drive as fast as I safely can without getting ticketed. I'm only wearing my sweater, but I'll brave the cold if it means I can see Anders again. I can't believe he came back. He's here, really here. He chose me.

My heart's in my throat as I park the car and step out of it. "Anders?" I don't have to look long. As if on their own, my eyes ping to Anders's familiar profile. He's staring out across the water, hunched over where he's leaning on the railing. My heart and soul would know him anywhere.

I come to stand within reach of him. "You... you're back," I say a bit breathlessly, my voice shaky. My joy mixes with trepidation. Whatever happened in the past, it's upset him. Anders doesn't even react to the sound of my voice. Snow gathers on his black wolf furs around his shoulders. It's like he's a statue. Slowly, I walk around him and stand by the railing.

A jolt of horror goes through me when I see how puffy his eyes are, red-rimmed and bloodshot. Holy shit. Anders looks like he's been crying, or trying not to. He's so strong, so against showing any kind of emotion he considers weak. Whatever happened, it must have been bad.

"Oh, puppy dog." I want to hold him so badly, but I don't know if he'll let me. "What happened? Can you tell me?"

Anders's jaw trembles. He opens his mouth but closes it quickly without making a sound. Slumping, he rests his elbows on the icy railing. "Don't know where to start. Mayhap I should not have returned here. But how could I have stayed?" He's speaking more to himself.

"Of course you should have returned. I'm happy you came back." Relieved, in fact. I squeeze his cold hand, trying to warm him up. "What happened to your village? Was it as bad as you thought?"

A bitter laugh escapes Anders, and he hangs his head, hiding his face. "No."

"But that's good, isn't it?"

Anders doesn't respond for almost a minute. "I saw my family."

I don't know how to react. I figure if it was a happy reunion, Anders wouldn't be drowning in heartbreak right now. "H-how did it go?" I ask, but I think I can guess.

"I don't know if I can even call them family anymore. Not after what I've—" His voice chokes off, and he jerks his hand out of my grasp, folding his hands close to his chest like he's curling in on himself. "Gods. I was wrong. So wrong." Regret floods his voice.

"About? You can tell me."

Anders grinds his teeth, then exhales harshly. "Why not? What does it matter? I've already lost everyone I cared about. I don't deserve to keep you."

His words hurt like a punch to my solar plexus. "Hey." My voice is small, but I fight through the fear that he's about to push me away for good. I step in close, touching my shoulder to his. His furs are damp, the wetness seeping through my sweater and making me shiver, but I need to be close to him. "You haven't lost me. Whatever is going on, just tell me, and I promise I'll listen. I won't judge you. We can work through this."

Anders's shoulders rise and fall shakily. Sniffing, he finally looks up and out over the gray water of the river. Shrugging off his furs, he wraps them around my shoulders. "We'll be here a while, then."

I huddle into his furs for warmth while Anders gathers his thoughts.

"You know my brother and I never got along. I challenged his authority, frequently and aggressively. Because I was jealous, yes, but also because I blamed him. I've blamed him all his life. First, because Mother died giving birth to him. Then after Father was killed." Anders drops his gaze to our feet, and I can almost taste his shame. "None of it was his fault. I was cruel to him, and it wasn't fair. I have always known this. I never wanted to admit how wrong I was, not even to myself. But if I had someone to push all my blame onto, then I could not blame myself."

"But why would you be responsible?" I ask.

Anders closes his eyes tightly. "Because I was not there to save our father. When the hunters stormed our shores, another group took our village by surprise. They bound me with silver. Carved into my flesh."

"God. Anders, I'm so sorry."

He just shakes his head. "What for? You weren't responsible."

"I know, I just... I'm sorry you went through that."

Anders shivers and looks away out over the water. He's gripping the railing so hard his knuckles have whitened. "Everything changed when Kieran Grove arrived in our time. I hated him instantly because he was a human, and they'd hurt our kind before. But that wasn't all. I think... I think I was jealous of what he and Wulfric had. It wasn't enough my brother was an Alpha, that everyone fawned over him since birth, but he'd found his fated mate."

"And you'd never had anyone fawn over you?"

He scoffs. "One person. A farm boy I was sweet on. The first person I'd felt any romantic feelings for." Giving his head a shake, he says, "I'd rather not get into that. Not right now."

I want to hear that story, but it can wait. "So, what happened with Kieran?"

Anders exhales roughly.

"Anders?"

He twists his fingers together, and when he speaks, it's so soft I almost miss it. "You won't be able to look at me."

My heart races faster. I'm afraid of what he'll tell me. It sounds bad if it's tearing him up this much. "Tell me." I put my hand on his shoulder.

A shaky breath escapes him as he slumps, his eyes closing like he's the one who can't stand to look at me. "Kieran started making plans to change our way of life. Wanted to free our thralls. Wulfric allowed it. I thought if he would allow such a drastic change, then there was no telling what else Kieran could make him do. I was furious. Scared he'd bring ruin upon us, that I'd lose what was left of my family to humans once more. So I—" Anders's voice breaks, and he looks away. "I-I had Kieran beaten to within an inch of his life." The words leave him in a breathless whisper. "Didn't even have the stones to challenge him myself."

"Anders," I murmur, horrified.

He flinches. "Wulfric challenged me. I lost the will to fight and surrendered. Let myself be exiled. All this time, I was so sure I was right to hate Kieran. But when I returned to the village, nothing had changed for the worse. Kieran was one of them. Wulfric was happier than I've ever seen him. They were so much happier without me, and I couldn't even fault them for it. I divided our pack. I dishonored the memory of my parents. What I did was unforgiveable, and now, I've lost them. I pushed away everyone I've ever loved, and I don't know how I can make it right."

The words pour out of him as tears spill from his eyes. He hunches over the railing, making himself look so much smaller than he usually is. His pain and remorse threaten to drown me. My own tears prick my eyes. I can't stand to see him like this.

It's true—what he did was terrible, and I don't blame his family for being angry with him and hurt by his actions. It's not my place to forgive him because I'm not the wounded party here. But as someone who wasn't harmed by his behavior, I can look at his actions without emotion clouding my judgment.

What Anders did was wrong, but his actions didn't happen in a vacuum. His fear of humans was born from the trauma of losing his father and being tortured by hunters. Instead of owning up to his feelings of guilt and grief, he lashed out at others.

Now, here he is, allowing himself to feel his grief and guilt while acknowledging his mistakes. More than that, deeply regretting them.

While Anders sniffs and wipes his eyes, I put my arm around his shoulders. Anders stiffens, his eyes going wide. "Aren't you angry? How can you stand to touch me? I'm... I'm a despicable craven."

I snort. "Puppy dog, you'd sound more convincing if your nose wasn't blocked up."

"Jamie." Anders's voice is a growl. "Quit mocking me. If you're disgusted with me, then just let me go."

"Okay. First of all"—I yank on his chin and make him look at me—"I am not letting you go. Not ever. I'm in this with you for life. Second of all, why would I hate you?"

He rolls his shoulders and tries to look away, but I keep a firm hold of his chin. "How can you *not*?"

"Because I don't look at you and see the same man who bullied his brother and hurt his mate. Anders, can't you see? The man you were is not the man you are now."

Anders's breath hitches, and those watery green eyes fill with something that looks, and feels in our bond, a lot like hope. "You... you think so? Truly?"

I run my fingers over his jawline. "I *know* it. An awful, irredeemable person wouldn't be beating themselves up as much as you are over this. This is seriously eating away at you. Maybe you should just apologize to your brothers and Kieran, just so they know."

"They won't forgive me."

"Maybe, maybe not. That's not what matters. What's important is that you make sure they know how sorry you are."

Anders sighs softly, touching his forehead to mine. He lingers there a moment, thumb brushing over my cheekbone. "I want to do this. But not yet. I need to figure out the right things to say."

"Okay. How about we head home? It's freezing."

"But the shop—"

I wave a hand. "It's okay. It's really slow today, so Jess can handle things. Let's just swing by to grab Jace."

"If you're sure..." Anders straightens, one arm going around my shoulder.

Once we're home, I make us both a mug of hot chocolate and take the drinks into the bedroom. In the quiet, I can hear Jace cursing through the bedroom wall at his Nintendo Switch. Anders lies in bed, eyes closed. I almost think he's sleeping until he sits up, accepting his hot drink with a rumble of thanks. Before I can walk around the other side of the bed, Anders wraps an arm around my waist and tugs.

I end up in his lap, adjusting myself into a comfortable spot against his chest so I don't spill my drink. Settling, I rest my head against his pecs. They make perfect pillows. Anders keeps one arm around me and presses something against my stomach.

"Here." He drops my gran's necklace into my lap. "Thank you for entrusting it to me."

I lift his hand to my lips and kiss his fingers. "Thank you for giving it back."

Damn. I can't believe he's really here. I honestly thought I'd never see him again. Somehow, Anders has become such an intrinsic part of my life. But does he feel the same? It's so hard to imagine he cares for me the way I do for him.

"Thank you for coming home." I wince. "Sorry. I know this isn't your *home* home."

Anders's hand freezes where he is caressing my stomach. "And why wouldn't I have come back to you?"

My cheeks warm. I really didn't want to out my insecurities like this. "It just doesn't make sense to me." I clear my throat. "I forgot to put marshmallows in my hot chocolate." I try to stand, but Anders yanks me back down.

"Tell me," he commands, voice rough and low.

Oh no. Here goes... In a rush, I say, "Because everything important to you is in the past."

Anders's chest rises and falls on a slow exhale, like he's trying for patience. "Have I not made it clear how important you and the lad are to me?"

"N-no. You have." My mouth is dry. I take a sip of hot chocolate, then set the drink on the nightstand. "If... if your brothers had asked you to stay, would you have?"

Anders doesn't answer right away. He takes a slurp of his drink, puts it down, then wraps his arms tight around me. "I am unsure."

It's not the ringing endorsement I wanted, but hey, I should be grateful he didn't say yes. "Oh."

He sighs. "Do not sound so disappointed, pet. I only meant—" He bites off his words with a frustrated growl. "I only meant that when I was exiled, I had a goal. Return home, overthrow my brother, and lead his pack. Meeting you, the one I was fated for, that was never part of my plans."

"And what's your plan now? Do you still want to return home, after everything?"

I feel Anders nuzzle his nose into my hair. He breathes in deep and exhales, his breath warm against my scalp. "I have no plan, pet. From the moment I met you, nothing has worked out the way I wanted—and I wouldn't have it any other way. I don't know where I fit anymore. Where it is that I can call home. All I do know is that I want to be wherever you are, James Sullivan."

His words make my heart sing. "Sounds good to me."

"Could we continue my reading lessons?" Anders asks.

I grin. "Sure. Actually, there's a book I wanted to introduce you to. It's a Viking romance by my favorite author." I grab the dog-eared book from my nightstand. I've reread this whole series dozens of times. "It's my go-to comfort read."

Anders squints at the title. "Th... the Viking's—what is that word?"

I try not to laugh at his bad pronunciation. "It's called *The Viking's Irish Lad*. It's the first in a gay historical romance series by L. A. Richardson. He writes some of the best romances I've ever read, but his historical stuff is just amazing! They're so well researched, spicy, and heartwarming."

"What do you mean by spicy?" he asks, leaning down to give the book a sniff, like he thinks it will smell of paprika or something.

"You know. Lots of fucking."

Anders smirks. "Oh. And you like these fucking books?"

I return his smirk with a lecherous smile. "Oh yeah. You will too. I'll read it to you. You can tell me how accurate it is."

Anders settles back against the pillows, and I begin to read. I'm so familiar with the story that I know it almost word for word. Anders listens, but sometimes he interrupts to ask about a new word that's caught his eye. By chapter two, the Irish lad has been captured by the sexy alphahole Viking chieftain. Anders decides to try reading a bit. He's slow, and he mispronounces a lot of words, but I'm amazed by what a fast learner he is, and when his face lights up when he pronounces a word right, my heart feels light and warm.

I want more days like this. Just the two of us, curled up together and enjoying a book. Anders fits so perfectly into my life despite all our differences that it's getting impossible to imagine being without him.

I've liked a lot of guys before, but I never loved them.

Not like I love Anders.

"Jamie, tomorrow, do you think we could—"

It's like a chunk of ice drops into my stomach. Tomorrow. Shit. What's the date?

"Jamie, what is it?" Anders sounds startled when I suddenly lean over him and grab for my phone. I open my calendar app, and my worst fears are confirmed.

Tomorrow is the worst day of my life. The one I dread the most every year.

How could I forget? I've been so distracted that it completely slipped my mind.

Trying to fight down the urge to bolt from the bed, I curl onto my side away from him.

"Jamie? Are you well?"

I nod, trying to breathe. "Just... just tired. Keep reading. Please."

"Very well." Anders continues to read. He stumbles over words but keeps on going, then pauses with a frustrated sigh. "What in Tyr's balls? Jamie, what is this word? Jamie?"

I screw my eyes shut.

How am I going to get through tomorrow without falling apart?

CHAPTER 18

ANDERS

WHEN I WAKE WITH Jamie curled up beside me, all I want to do is lie in bed all day with him and never leave. I may have lost my pack, but if I hadn't been exiled, I might never have met him.

Leaning in, I nuzzle my nose into his neck and breathe in his scent. Waves of calm wash over me, and my wolf, though dormant without my furs, rumbles in satisfaction. Our mate is perfect. It shames me that I ever thought of leaving him. I must make things right.

I will claim him. Soon.

"Pet? Wake up. Jace will need breakfast soon."

Jamie's back is to me. In the quiet, I realize his breathing is uneven, and his body is far too tense. He's awake, so why isn't he leaping out of bed with his usual energy? His scent shifts, and sadness clouds his sweetness.

"I, uh... just need a minute, okay?" His voice is shaky and subdued.

"What's happened?" I touch his shoulder. "Jamie, what's—"

He twists his shoulder, jerking out of my touch. The ache of his rejection feels like someone struck me in the chest. "Sorry." Jamie's voice shakes, and he sinks deeper beneath his blankets until just the top of his head is visible. "Need space."

I don't understand. Have I done something wrong? I don't even know what to say. "Aye." At a loss, I get out of bed. The cold floor gives my bare feet a shock. Outside the bedroom, the cold has spread throughout the apartment.

In the kitchen, I make us some coffee, preparing Jamie's the way I know he likes. Surely he'll want coffee. I can't fathom what's come over him.

Jace shuffles into the kitchen. "Morning," he chirps.

"Morning," I say, tousling his hair. "Orange juice?"

"Yes, please." Jace hops up onto a barstool at the counter.

I pour my coffee into my mug, add sugar, then bring both our drinks to the counter.

Jace takes a big, refreshing sip. "What was it like going back to the past?"

Before I can answer, the bedroom door slams open. Both of us fall silent. Jamie crosses the room, head down, and goes into the bathroom without acknowledging either of us. The shower starts running. The ball of dread in my chest only expands, threatening to morph into a void that sucks me in.

Jace hangs his head, sighing.

"Not you too. What's wrong?" I ask.

Worrying his lip, Jace says, "I don't wanna talk about it. Sorry."

What would Jamie keep from me? We tell each other everything. Don't we?

Unless... has Jamie had enough of me? He was so happy to see me yesterday. Clearly, he's keeping something from me, but if I weren't pleasing him, he would tell me. Right? Deep within me, my berserker howls in fury and despair, sharpening my fangs and claws even without my furs. Something is wrong with our mate. I'm going to find whoever hurt him and make sure they don't live another day.

I've lost my pack, and that was hard enough. But I can't lose Jamie. To distract myself, I go to the kitchen and gather ingredients for a cheese and bologna sandwich, helping myself to a few pieces of bologna.

"Can I help?" Jace pulls a step stool up to the counter beside me.

"Sure." I move over to give him more room to assemble his sandwich.

Jace says, "Don't forget you're helping me with my presentation today."

A piece of bologna goes down my throat wrong. Coughing, I sputter, "Hel below! W-what exactly must I do?"

Jace grabs a jar of mayo and slathers some on both slices of bread. "Just tell them stories about cool stuff from your time. What kind of books do you like, Anders?"

I tilt my shoulder. "I enjoy all kinds of stories, but my favorite have dragons, gods, and epic battles."

Jace smiles. "Yeah, those stories are awesome. I always loved reading comics with my mom." There's an odd crack in his voice, sadness souring his scent.

Jace's words inspire a memory of my own. "My father used to take me on walks in the woods. We'd hunt together," I continue, handing him some bologna, "and he taught me everything I know about surviving in the wilderness."

"What about your mom? What'd she teach you?"

My chest tightens painfully. "She passed when I was very young. I don't remember much of her, except that she was kind and loving."

Jace clears his throat and looks away, the scent of sadness wafting from him.

A similar sadness to Jace's rushes through the bond connecting me to Jamie. It's heavier, like storm clouds. I wish I could go to him and offer him comfort, but in the mood he's in, I worry he'd reject me.

Tossing some cheese in my mouth, I say between chews, "I wasn't an especially good hunter, but when I caught my first prey, my father was so proud." Knowing I'd pleased him remains my happiest, most cherished memory. "He supported me in everything I wished to do, without judgment."

Jace smiles sadly. "That's what parents do. It's how you know."

"Know?"

He shrugs, staring down at the counter. "That they loved us."

My father loved me.

This simple truth, buried underneath all my feelings of jealousy, grief, and rage, is like a ray of dawn breaking through a long, dark night.

Of course he loved me.

Even if I wasn't an Alpha, even if I'd gotten jealous when he'd spent time in the woods training Wulfric. I'd drowned in bitter feelings of envy for so long, I'd forgotten such an important fact. My father had loved me for who I was and all I wasn't.

Emotion clogs my throat. I used to get so mad I'd lash out at my father for spending time with Wulfric. I'd accuse him of playing favorites. The shame burns me to my marrow, and I have to close my eyes to force the memories away. I wasted my father's final years being so angry and bitter, and I hate myself for it.

I loved him. So much.

Had I ever told him? Had he known?

"Are you okay?"

When I open my eyes, they're misty and hot with un-shed tears.

Jace's eyes widen. "I'm sorry! I didn't mean to make you sad."

"I'm fine, lad." I cough and duck my head to discreetly wipe my eyes on my sleeve. Ever since I arrived in this timeline, I've become a soft, weak mess.

"I miss my parents too. All the time," Jace admits. "Especially today."

"What does that mean?"

But Jace shakes his head. "Don't wanna talk about it."

I let it go, wrap his sandwich in foil, and hand it to him.

The bathroom door opens. Jamie's hair is still wet. Why didn't he bother to dry it? He'll freeze outside. Then I see his eyes, bloodshot and wet, and my heart stops.

Jamie smiles, but it doesn't reach his eyes. "Sorry for taking too long." He dumps his coffee into his thermos. "Let's get going." He isn't fooling anyone with that fake casual tone.

It's obvious to anyone that he was crying, or trying very hard not to. Is that why he spent so long in the shower? The sadness coming from his bond wasn't especially heightened. Unless, mayhap, he was trying to hold back his tears?

By the gods. What has happened to him?

Rushing to the door, Jace grabs Jamie's coat and hands it to him. "Come on, get your coat on."

Jamie shrugs it on, sniffling. "Thanks. I'm super excited for your presentation, bud."

"No," I say, standing so swiftly my knee knocks into the table. "You can't go anywhere today, Jamie. Not like this."

He stiffens, brows furrowing. "I'll be fine." Finally, there's something other than forced cheer in his voice. He's pissed that I haven't fallen for his act.

I barely strangle the snarl rising to my lips. "You're staying home, Jamie. Do not make me chain you to the bed. You are in no state to—"

Jamie crosses his arms. "You're my boyfriend, Anders. Not my—my father." His voice catches, and the firm set of his lips trembles. "You don't tell me what I can and can't do."

Jace looks worriedly between us. "Come on, guys, please don't fight!"

I want to swing Jamie over my shoulder, carry him into our room, and lock him in until he tells me what in Hel's name is going on.

"Anders." Jamie's shaky voice snaps me out of my rage. "I'm okay. Let's just go." And without another word, he throws open the door and storms out.

It feels like there are worms writhing in my gut as we arrive at the school. Jace insisted I get changed into my gear from my timeline, and he's also wearing a tunic and a horned helmet. The armor feels heavier than it used to. I've become accustomed to the clothing of this time. "Ready, lad?"

Jace grins. "Yeah, let's do this!" He leaps from the car and rushes toward the building. Chuckling at his enthusiasm, I follow with Jamie beside me. "Hurry up, guys!" Jace waves us over.

Jamie offers a quiet smile. "Coming, bud!" Once Jace disappears through the door, the smile falls off his face. Before I can take his hand and offer comfort to my mate, Jamie quickens his pace. I follow him through the halls, which are bustling with parents and their children. Inside Jace's classroom, he runs up to greet his friends, most of whom are wearing unique costumes.

What was I nervous for? I can speak in front of pups.

Jamie gives Jace an encouraging pat on the shoulder, then goes to stand in the back. I follow as the woman I assume is the teacher stands before the class, welcoming everyone before the presentations begin. It takes a long time to get to Jace's. Many students tell stories, some about these people called cowboys or astronauts who walked on the moon itself, and images flash across a big white board to accompany their stories.

"Next, Jace Sullivan!"

He leaps up and waves wildly at us, making me chuckle.

Clearing his throat, Jace addresses the class, reading from a paper he holds. "Today, I want to talk about these really fascinating people called Vikings. But I won't do it alone. Please welcome Anders, a real, live Viking!"

Heat rushes up my neck when all the children look at me, excited whispers filling the room. Waving awkwardly, I go up to stand next to Jace. "Greetings, everyone. Blessings of Odin upon you."

Practically bouncing on the balls of his feet, Jace says, "Vikings were seafaring warriors who traveled all around the world. Anders, where's a really cool place you visited?"

When everyone looks at me, I suddenly don't know what to say. "Well, I, uh—"

Someone yawns loudly. "Boring! That's not a real Viking. They're all dead. This is *stupid*." Damn it. That's the obnoxious boy who bullied Jace. I'd recognize the little shit anywhere.

Jace flinches, crumpling the paper in his fists.

"Kevin!" the teacher reprimands. "If you're going to be rude, you need to go and wait outside. Mr. and Mrs. Davidson, please tell him not to be disruptive."

Kevin's parents go and whisper to their bratty child. Kevin stomps his foot. "But this is stupid! Why couldn't I go before *him*?" He glares at Jace. The poor lad is red-faced, tears bright in his eyes.

"I raided the shores of Francia." The class loses interest in Kevin's antics and turns their attention to me, just like I'd hoped. "I've sailed endless blue seas, roamed scorching deserts, and fought many foes."

Jace looks up, wide-eyed with intrigue. "Really?"

"Tell us more!" a little lass calls.

My confidence grows as I answer questions and tell the pups all about my time. Even the adults look fascinated. Jamie is finally smiling as he watches me. I get so carried away with my stories that the teacher clears her throat and says, "Thank you so much, Anders and Jace. Unfortunately, we are out of time, but this was wonderful!"

The class claps for us as Jace and I go and stand next to Jamie. Jamie squeezes my hand and bumps his shoulder against mine. *Thank you*, he mouths, appreciation softening his face.

I squeeze back. "My pleasure," I whisper.

Anything to make the lad happy.

Anything for Jamie.

After a brief lunch break for the kids, the presentations resume.

"Finally!" Kevin barks, stomping up to the front of the class. Jamie's hand tenses in mine, and I stroke his knuckles soothingly. To the class, Kevin announces, "I'm going to be doing a presentation on the history... of snails!"

"What are snails?" I whisper to Jamie.

Haughtily clearing his throat, Kevin begins to drone on about snails while images flash on the white board. It turns out snails happen to be small creatures of some kind with a hard shell. While at first I'm interested in learning about these strange little things for the first time, ten minutes later, I'm yawning so hard my jaw pops.

A girl suddenly exclaims, "This is boring! Bring back the Viking!"

Kevin's face goes red.

"Yeah," chimes in a boy with glasses, "I wanna hear more about epic battles!"

"That's enough," the teacher says. "Let Kevin continue."

Kevin throws down his papers and storms from the classroom, slamming the door behind him. His parents rush after him, leaving the teacher to approach the children who upset Kevin and reprimand them.

Jace frowns. "That was mean..."

"The little lout deserves it," I grumble, and Jamie elbows me.

"Don't be rude, puppy dog."

Jace furrows his brow as he suddenly rushes out of the classroom, making Jamie and me rush after him. Outside, Kevin is sniffling as his parents escort him to their car. Kevin's mother gets in the driver's seat while his father sits beside her.

Before Kevin can get in, Jace calls out, "Hey, Kevin!"

Kevin's shoulders hunch up toward his ears, his fists clenching. He glares at Jace through wet red eyes. "What do you want?"

Jace hesitates, worrying his lower lip. "I... I liked your presentation. I didn't know anything about snails until today. It was interesting."

Pride glows warm in my chest. Jace is a kind lad. I can't say I would have been as kind to the boys who'd picked on me as a pup. It's good that he's already so much better than I am.

"Shut up," Kevin snaps, making Jace jump. "I don't care what you think! What, you think you're special just 'cause *some* people liked your presentation? You're so annoying. I bet your mom and dad died just to get away from you."

Jamie squeezes my hand so tightly it aches.

Jace stumbles back, eyes big and round. "Wha... what?"

"Hey," I snarl, dropping Jamie's hand and making for the brat, but Kevin slams the car door behind him. All I can do is watch the boy who just hurt Jace get away. Damn it. I feel so bloody helpless. If he weren't a child, I would have butchered him where he stood for such a callous remark. I'm almost afraid to turn around and see the devastation that's surely on Jace's face.

Quiet sobs reach my ears, making me wince.

"Jace," Jamie says, voice soft and devastated.

Tears cascade down Jace's face, his lips trembling violently. The poor lad's tears make my heart break. I long to go to him and hold him close, but Jamie is there, pulling him in for a much-needed hug as he breaks down. "I... I m-miss Mom and Dad!" Jace wails, hiding his face in Jamie's stomach.

"I know." Jamie's voice cracks, his eyes damp before he tucks his chin to his chest, hiding his face from my view.

Unable to bear it a second longer, I go to my hurting family and envelop them both in my arms, squeezing tight. I wish I knew the right thing to say, the perfect words to take all their pain away. Mayhap if I were Wulfric... but I'm not. All I can do is hold them, and if that's what they need, I'll give it to them, no questions asked.

Jamie helps me get a distraught Jace into the car. During the drive home, the lad cries on and off, and the sound of his sorrow tears into me with claw and fang. I'm almost relieved when Jace falls asleep, surely overcome by the toll such heavy emotions took on his little body. Suddenly, Jamie pulls us over, even though we're nowhere near home yet. His sadness floods the car, so overwhelming it feels as if I will drown in it.

"Once we're home, can you take him upstairs?" Jamie asks, scrubbing a hand over his exhausted face. "I need to head to the shop and cover the lunch shift."

Shocked, I say, "You can't work today. You're miserable, pet. Stay home."

"Anders, damn it, would you just stop! I can take care of myself. I've done it for fucking years. I don't n-need your—" Jamie's tone is sharp, but the crack in his voice gives away just how much today is weighing on him. A shuddery gasp falls from his lips. "Fuck. I'm so sorry, Anders. I just... fuck!" He wrenches off his seat belt and lurches from the car.

"Jamie, wait," I hiss, fighting with my damned seat belt until the stupid thing comes off. Closing the door quietly so I don't wake Jace, I walk around to the driver's side of the car and freeze. Jamie is hiding his face in his hands, but his heaving shoulders betray his anguish.

"I miss them so much." He gulps in a breath. "If—if they were here, they could comfort Jace. They knew how to comfort him, and make him laugh, and how to take care of him, and I'm just—" Suddenly, he slams a fist on the hood of the car. Tears dampen his puffy cheeks, and his nose is bright red.

"Pet." My own voice shakes as I reach for him. "You are amazing with the lad. You—"

"Just stop, Anders!" Jamie's voice is sharp and pleading. "I don't deserve Jace. I... I don't even deserve to be alive when my parents aren't. I d-don't deserve you." His voice thickens, and he lifts both hands, curling them in his hair. A strangled noise escapes him that cracks my heart in two.

All I can do is shake my head. "That's enough. I won't stand here and listen to you talk this way about yourself. Jamie, you're... you're the best person I know. You've made this time feel more like home than anywhere else."

Gods. No one I have ever known has stirred up such feelings within me. The moment I met him, I knew he was mine, but that was the extent of it. All my life, I wanted to be an Alpha, like my father and my brother. But with Jamie, I finally feel like I am good enough. I may not be an Alpha in the official sense, but I'm Jamie's. His. And somehow, that's become more important than anything else.

I just want to be a man who can make him happy, a man deserving of him.

Gripping his hands, I tug them gently from his hair and turn him toward me. His jaw is tightly clenched, his lips pressed so firmly together they've turned white. Pulling him close, I wrap my arms around him and hold him to me.

"Sorry." Jamie's voice shakes. His arms twitch like he wants to hold me back, but they remain pinned to his sides. "Fuck. I'm such a mess."

Kissing his hair, I murmur, "You care deeply. There is no shame in having a big heart."

"I'm... I'm so ashamed of myself." He hides his face in my chest.

"Ashamed? Why?" I comb my fingers through his hair.

"Never wanted anyone to see me like this."

I press my lips to his temple. "Even the sun has days where it doesn't want to shine, pet. That doesn't make you undeserving of love." I need to get him home, away from the demands of the world. Nobody will ask for anything from him today, or I'll bite their damn head off. "Get us home."

"What?" Jamie looks up, wide-eyed. "I can't! I have to—"

A growl from me silences him as I slide my palm over the nape of his neck, gently squeezing. "Listen to your Alpha. Get us home so I can care for you the way you deserve. Understood?"

Calm settles over Jamie. With a shuddery exhale that sounds a lot like a wolfish whimper, he tips his head back to show his throat. "Y-Yes, Alpha."

I watch him until he's made it to the car. My mate has no idea how to put himself first, and that is going to change. I'm going to get him home and care for him in every way I can.

I won't leave Jamie's side until I know he's okay.

CHAPTER 19

JAMIE

OH GOD. I CAN'T believe Anders saw me break down. I never wanted him to see this side of me. Anders deserves Fun Jamie. Sunshine Jamie. The Jamie who is on top of his game and confident. Not messy, sad, depressed Jamie.

I haven't let myself drown in the past in a long time.

Ever since my parents died, I've tried so hard to be strong. I locked my guilt and my heartache in a box and buried it. But every year on my birthday, if I'm not careful, the box opens, and I can lose myself in memories of that awful day.

I jump when Anders suddenly climbs into the car. "Take us home, pet."

My hands are shaky as I grip the wheel. It took me a long time to get over my fear of driving. I only started driving again two years ago and finally felt confident behind the wheel. Today, I wish I could hand the wheel to Anders.

Come on, Jamie. That's ridiculous. Just drive.

"Are we going?" Anders asks.

Hands shaking, I turn the ignition key and step on the gas.

Suddenly, I'm eighteen again. My mom is in the seat beside me, and Dad's in the back.

Mom and Dad are laughing. I don't remember why. Then, she screams, and—

"Jamie." A big hand cups the back of my neck.

I gasp as his touch yanks me from memories of the worst day of my life.

"Don't think. Just drive." The deep, low growl of his voice speaks to my wolf, even without my furs. "Get us home, and I will take care of you."

I angle my head on instinct, showing my throat. My wolf's instincts are telling me to submit, to obey. In sub-mission to my Alpha, I will find peace. "Yes, Alpha," I whisper.

Don't think. Just do what Alpha says, my wolf's instincts whisper. *Please him.*

Squeezing the wheel tight, I drive us from the parking space. Thoughts try to creep in. I grind my teeth, trying to keep them out. Please. I just want my head to be clear. I don't want to think. When my Alpha's hand glides over my thigh to squeeze my knee, I find myself relaxing back into the seat. Alpha's touch feels so good.

I don't understand what's going on. Anders has said himself he isn't an Alpha, so I'm not sure why my body is reacting to him like this. It doesn't feel like a heat. I'm not burning up with desire and need. Anders's presence has an almost catatonic effect on me. My wolf wants me to trust him, to let him take care of us. So I will.

I've tried so hard to take care of myself. To be a fortress. Now, my fortress is crumbling. Can I trust Anders to help keep me together? Do I even deserve to ask that of him?

Before I know it, we've arrived safely at my apartment. Anders carries Jace, who is still asleep. Once we're in the apartment, Anders tells me to wait while he puts Jace to bed. I obey my Alpha and remain by the door, feeling like an empty shell until he returns. He insists on taking off my coat and tugging off my boots. My stomach gives a loud growl, displeased we didn't eat breakfast. Anders's eyes narrow. "When is the last time you ate?"

I cast my mind back, but everything is a blur. Fuck. I wish I'd died instead that day. I should have. Jace would be much happier with his parents. A lump rises in my throat.

"Pet." Anders tips my chin up. "Answer my question."

"I don't think I ate today."

Anders takes my hand and steers me to the sofa. "Sit." I do as he says. Anders leaves, and when he comes back, he's carrying my grandmother's furs. "Wear these."

"Why?" I ask.

"On my worst days, my favorite thing to do is shed my skin and live as a wolf for a few hours. An animal's headspace is simpler than that of our human form. Try it. I will make us some food."

I shrug them on, concentrating on the sensation of the furs, on my bond with Anders. All the distressing thoughts of the day begin to blur as I change shape. Fur envelops me, and I stretch out on all fours. The sofa is soft beneath my paws. My mate's scent fills the air, so sweet I want to roll around in it. My stomach growls. I am hungry. Want to eat. Hunt. But first, sleepy... I squeak out a yawn, the muscles in my jaw popping. Closing my eyes, I lay my head on my paws. Sleep first, then food.

Mate chuckles. "Good, pet. You rest. I will get us some food."

He touches me between my ears. Mate's hand is warm and soft. My ears flick. He laughs, and my tail thumps at the sound.

I sleep.

"Jamie? I made... well, it's something, at least."

When I open my eyes, I realize I've shifted back to my human form at some point. Anders was right—shifting did help. The disaster that was this morning feels distant, like it happened to someone else. Still upsetting, but my head isn't fogged anymore.

The room smells like steak, and my stomach roars.

Anders joins me on the couch just as I sit up. Wrapping an arm around me, he scoots close so our thighs are touching. In his lap, he balances a plate full of thinly cut pieces of the sirloin I bought.

"Wow, that looks great!" My mate sure can sear up a decent steak dinner.

Anders huffs. "Wanted to go hunting, but there's nothing to hunt around here, so I had to use your stove. It's not as fresh as it would be if I'd caught it myself, but this still counts as hunting," he says, glaring at me, daring me to challenge him.

"Hey, I didn't say anything."

With a pleased little smile, he picks up a bite-sized piece of steak. I open my mouth and let him feed me. It tastes really good. The outside is a nice brown, and the inside is buttery soft and juicy. I moan my approval as I chew.

"More?" Anders grabs another piece.

I frown. "What about Jace?"

"I brought him a plate. He's watching television in his room. He is safe. Eat, pet."

I should go check on him... but the scent of the steak is too tempting to resist. When I part my lips, Anders feeds me another bite. Once I've swallowed, I say, "What about you?"

"I ate some while I cooked. Don't worry about me. Eat."

My cheeks flush. I feel bad for letting him take care of me like this. "Anders—"

A low growl rumbles in his chest. Sighing, I eat another bite. Okay, it's not exactly torture to let my hot boyfriend nurture me. Have I ever let anyone look after me like this? I search my memories but come up empty-handed. I always took care of the guys I dated—bought them dinner, took them out, let them spill their sorrows to me. I never asked for anything in return. I've never let myself be this vulnerable with another person before.

Anders's forest-green gaze never strays from me. He's utterly attentive as he nourishes my body with his home-cooked meal and my battered soul with the warmth of his body blanketed against mine.

Fuck. What have I done to deserve this? Nothing.

"Think I'm full," I say, unable to eat any more with this painful lump in my throat. I want to go bury myself under my blankets and just lie there, not even to sleep.

Anders puts the plate on the coffee table and licks his fingers clean of any steak residue. Closing my eyes, I lean back against his arm, and he tucks his other arm around my waist. Leaning in, he touches his forehead to mine.

"Why didn't you tell me it was your birthday today?"

My eyes snap open. Wetting my lips, I drop my gaze to my lap. "How'd you know?"

"The lad mentioned it when I brought him dinner. He said that you don't usually celebrate. Is that true?"

I nod.

"Why don't you let anyone celebrate?"

Screwing my eyes shut against the rising tide of painful memories, I say, "Because it's not a day worth celebrating."

Anders runs his hand up and down my thigh. "Why would you think that?"

I really don't want to do this... but I have to. I've told my friends, but I've never told any of the guys I've dated. Never trusted anyone enough to let them see me at my lowest.

I've never loved a man enough to open up like this.

Not like I love him.

"When I turned eighteen..." I pause to take in a breath. Reaching out, I touch Anders's face, running my thumb over his cheekbone. Touching him grounds me, reminds me I'm not alone. "My parents wanted to take me out to dinner at our favorite restaurant to celebrate. Jace had a cold, so he had to stay home. Dad let me drive his car. I was so excited because I'd just earned my license. My parents were proud of me, I think. Well, Mom was a little nervous. She kept reminding me to keep my eyes on the road. I did."

I swallow hard.

"The light was yellow. I usually stop for those, just to be safe, but we were running late for dinner. I thought I had time to make it. It was dumb. It was just some stupid dinner reservations. I should have waited, I—"

"Pet. What happened next?" Anders squeezes my shoulder.

"Th-this drunk guy in a pickup truck came in barreling in from my right just as I reached the intersection."

I'll never forget the way mom screamed seconds before he slammed into her side of the vehicle. Glass had exploded around us, metal shrieking as it bent and snapped. The collision knocked my head into the window, and I passed out.

When I woke up, my normal life was gone. I was in a hospital bed, hooked up to tubes and wires. I had a concussion. Broken ribs. A jagged scar across my hip where shrapnel had sliced into me.

The doctor came in and told me the words that tore my world to shreds.

Mr. Sullivan, I'm so sorry. Both your parents were killed.

She told me my mom died the moment the car struck her side of the vehicle. It was quick. Painless. My father clung on just long enough to get to the hospital but died before they could treat his wounds.

I didn't feel anything. It didn't make sense. Couldn't be real. My parents were alive; they were just too hurt to come and see me. I demanded to see them. I had to. I knew they were alive. I clung onto my denial with everything I had. When Gran showed up with Jace, their eyes were red and wet, faces blotchy from crying.

Gran said, *I'm sorry. I'm so sorry. They're gone, both of them.*

How could this have happened? Why my family? Why not someone else's?

I should have been more careful. This was all my fault. If I'd just waited, if I'd insisted we stay home, if I had done *anything* differently that night, they would still be here.

By the time I finish speaking, tears soak my cheeks. I've never been able to tell this story without crying, so I stopped telling it. I've been torn open all over again, and I don't know how to put myself back together. The dark despair of that horrible night fastens its hooks in me and tugs, dragging me down.

Then Anders's arms are around me, holding me to his chest. His big, warm hands run up and down my back. My face is mashed against his shoulder, and he's all I can feel and touch and smell. He kisses my hair, then the shell of my ear, and whispers, "It wasn't your fault, Jamie. It wasn't."

I break apart. For the first time in so many years, I break down in gut-wrenching sobs that leave me utterly defenseless. All I can do is cling to him as he strokes my back and whispers sweet words I don't deserve.

When there are no more tears left for me to cry, I lie against his wet chest, too drained to move. I hate that Anders had to see me like this. "Sorry," I croak. "I'll get you a new shirt."

He sits up, still holding me close. "Let's bathe. I'll get the water running."

Anders goes into the bathroom and turns on the faucet in the tub. To keep myself busy, I eat the rest of the steak, and the plate is clean when Anders returns. "Come on. The water isn't too hot."

I only grunt, feeling like my limbs are made of gelatin as he helps me stand up. In the bathroom, I go to peel off his shirt, but Anders bats my hands away. He strips me of my shirt, tossing it over the towel rack, then unbuttons my jeans. When I step out of them, Anders pulls down my underwear.

"Your turn." I help him undress, cheeks warming as I throw his snotty, tear-soaked shirt on the ground. "We'll have to burn that."

"Why?" He snorts. "Just wash it. Tears and snot are hardly the worst thing I've had on me."

Once Anders is naked, I dip my toe in the water. It's warm but not scalding. He gets in first, then urges me to join him. We sink into the water together, my back to his chest. The warm water eases all the aches and pains of the day, on the outside anyway. But it's Anders's powerful body behind me and his tender touch as he rubs a soapy cloth over my skin that helps heal all the cracks in my heart.

"Thanks for not running for the hills." I give his hand a squeeze.

I can practically see his bewildered expression. "Running from what?"

"Me. Most of the guys I've dated in the past didn't want to stick around when I get... like I was today. Sad. Closed off. I don't blame them."

"Those men you dated before," Anders says with a growly undercurrent in his voice, "are they still alive?"

Snorting, I pinch his thigh. "Stop it. Besides, they're ancient history."

Grumbling, Anders shifts behind me. His soft cock rubs along the cleft of my buttocks. I'm way too drained for sex; otherwise, I'd love to take advantage of our nakedness. But just sitting like this, naked and enjoying each other's company, is nice. Really nice.

"I don't like the idea of anyone mistreating you."

Smiling, I caress his arm. "They weren't bad. I pushed people away to keep myself safe. You're the only guy who pushed back and fought for me." My voice wavers. "Thank you."

Anders sticks out his chest with a pleased rumble. "If there's anything I am good at, it is fighting. I will always fight for you, Jamie."

I lift his hand and kiss his fingers to give myself time for the lump in my throat to go away. Finally, I say, "You must have some crappy relationships under your belt too. Spill it."

"Only one."

Now I'm curious.

I shift between his thighs so I can get a better look at him. "Who?" I play with his wet, curly chest hair while he composes a reply.

"A farmer from my village."

Anders combs wet fingers through my hair. His jaw tightens, a muscle ticking under the skin. "You really liked him, huh?"

"Aye, that I did. He was the first lad I was sweet on. My first kiss in the tundra's hot springs. His name was Jorik. He noticed me rather than Wulfric. Everyone wanted Wulfric, clamored to be his chosen mate the moment he came of age to be mated. He rejected all of them, of course. Wanted to wait for his fated mate to come along. I thought Jorik was impervious to Wulfric's Alpha status. Had no idea he'd been playing the pair of us. Not until I found him in the stables with Wulfric."

"Did Wulfric know you liked him?"

"Of course he did. We were young and foolish and enjoyed being cruel to each other. In the end, Jorik left us both and rode out of the village with his true fated mate."

Anders's tone is casual, but I hate that he was used like that and hurt by his brother. "Sorry that happened to you."

"I was a fool to think anyone would care for me when they could have Alpha Wulfric. It's what I deserved."

The water ripples in the bath as I turn around. "Don't." I lace my fingers at the back of his neck. "You may not be an Alpha, not by birth. But you're *my* Alpha."

Anders's breath catches. "Say it again?" His voice is soft, plaintive.

Leaning in, I brush the words against his lips. "My Alpha."

Anders lunges in for a kiss that leaves me breathless, and before my eyes, the gruff and guarded man I've come to know melts against me with each tender kiss.

"Yours," he whispers. "Yours, always."

Chapter 20
Anders

"I would like to celebrate your birthday," I tell Jamie over breakfast.

Jamie pauses in the middle of buttering his toast. "You don't have to." He shakes his head and spoons some jam onto his toast. He cuts the toast in half and hands it to Jace and me.

I take a bite, the sweet jam and salty butter a delectable combination, even if I hate the seedy bread. "I never said I *had* to. I want to celebrate you. I'd like it if you would let me."

"Why?" Jamie asks, pushing his eggs around his plate.

This man... "Because I care for you, why else? Or do people in this time not celebrate birthdays after they've already happened?"

Jamie shrugs, staring down at his plate. "It could be a belated birthday celebration, I guess."

"Belated?"

"Kind of like a late celebration."

I nod, chewing some eggs. That works just fine. "We could do it this evening."

"If you want."

"I do. Very much."

Jamie sighs, then smiles a little as he kicks my foot under the table. "All right, if it would make you happy."

The things I would do to see him smile like that again... I want him happy. Need him to know how deeply I cherish him. His happiness is my happiness, and when he's sad, the world is a darker place. I quickly look down at my plate, alarmed by the intensity of my feelings. During this celebration, I want to finally ask him to let me claim him.

Jace says, "Speaking of birthdays, my friend Natalie is having a slumber party at her house tonight. Can I go? Please? A lot of my friends will be there." He gives Jamie big, pleading eyes.

"What time is the party?"

"It starts at five."

"Okay, that works. While you're at your party, Anders and I can have ours." Jamie teases my foot beneath the table, brushing his toes along my sole. "Come on, we need to shower, then get to work." He springs to his feet and carries his empty plate to the sink. "Jace, hurry up, bud. Brush your teeth and grab your backpack! We've got a big day ahead of us!"

Once we're all ready, we leave the apartment and get in the car. I rest my hand on Jamie's thigh as he drives. He isn't gripping the wheel like he'll drown if he lets go, and his scent and posture are relaxed. I hated seeing him so distraught last night. I've never felt like an Alpha before, not until my mate opened up his wounded heart and gave me the privilege of caring for him. That's what an Alpha is. It's what they do; they care for the ones they love. They don't use power and authority to control them.

Wulfric has made a far better Alpha than I ever would have.

I wish I could tell him that, that I could let him know how truly sorry I am for dividing our pack.

We drop Jace off for his classes, then drive to the bookshop.

"Morning, everyone!" Jamie says as we enter the shop.

Bailey waves. "Hey! Feeling better?"

"Much," Jamie says.

"Hey, Anders, give me a hand!" Jess calls out.

I follow her voice to the back of the store, where she is assembling a new shelf that just arrived.

She's sitting on the floor, examining two pieces of the shelf in front of her. "Okay. I think these parts go here. Can you hand me a nail?"

Sitting beside her, I hand her the supplies she asks for. "Have you celebrated a birthday before?"

She arches a pierced brow, a teasing smile hooking the corner of her mouth. "Uh, yeah?"

"I want to do something special for Jamie tonight." I already know I'll ask to claim him, but as for everything else... "No one else is as special to me as he is. I want things to be perfect tonight. Since you and Bailey are together, I thought you'd have some advice."

Jess's smile morphs into a grin. "That's so sweet. It's great Jamie's finally found someone who values him. I'll tell you what. Bailey and I were planning to buy this special-edition book by his favorite author."

"That L. A. Richardson person?"

"Yeah. He's having a signing today. It conflicts with Jamie's schedule, but what if you go during your lunch break?"

That *is* a good idea. "I'll do it. Where is the signing?" Jess pulls a pen and notepad from her apron's pocket. She scribbles briefly, then hands it to me. "It's a big bookstore across the street from Union Square." She shows me a picture of the place on her phone. "You can't miss it. But it's in Manhattan, so you'd have to take the train around the corner."

I lift my shoulder. "Easy enough."

When I return to Jamie, he's grinning. "Look what Bailey gave me!" He holds up a card of some kind.

"A scrap of paper?"

Jamie giggles. "No, puppy dog. It's a gift card for my favorite restaurant. I've gotta take you sometime!"

"How about tonight after work?" I run my hand down his side to squeeze his waist. "We can celebrate your birthday there."

Happiness curls Jamie's mouth. "That sounds great. I'd love that."

Touching my forehead to his, I inhale his sweet scent.

Nothing will stop me from giving Jamie the best night of his life.

Nothing except the slowest damn train in all the nine realms.

We've been stuck in a tunnel for what feels like an age, and it's hot as the fires of bloody Muspelheim. Sweat trickles down my body and soaks into my shirt. Gods, I hope I arrive in time. I've got to get Jamie a gift. It's the least I can do to show how much my mate means to me, aside from claiming him, of course.

Finally, the train lurches to life, and after several stops, I get out at Union Square. The bookstore looms over the park, making it easy to find. It's massive inside and packed with people. Fortunately, a security guard directs me to the third floor; otherwise, I'd have no idea where to look.

I ride some weird contraption that's like stairs, but they move, so you don't have to climb them. I get on one going in the wrong direction, so I end up walking in place for nearly a minute before I figure out how to get on the other one. This world is so damn confusing.

Just as I step off the contraption, I jump out of the path of a crowd of people, chattering excitedly as they carry copies of the same book. It looks like there is a Viking on the cover. Oh gods, please don't let me be too late.

Staff are stacking chairs and sweeping a section of the store. There's a sign nearby promoting the event from what little I can read. L. A. Richardson's name is on the sign, and so is a picture of his book. Disappointment has me slumping against a shelf. I'm too late. This would have been the perfect gift for Jamie, everything I needed to help show my devotion.

Now what will I do?

"Excuse me, are you okay?"

The man before me looks just like the picture on the sign, a short man with a round stomach and glasses perched on his nose.

Hope flares within me. The author is still here! Mayhap there is a chance I can still get Jamie his gift. "L. A. Richardson?"

He smiles. "That's me. My event just ended, but I'm more than happy to sign something for you if you'd like."

I shake my head. "I need a copy of one of your books. The special one."

The author's smile falls off his face. "I'm so sorry. I just sold my last copy."

No, no, no! This is all going wrong.

"If you sign up for my mailing list, you'll be kept updated about all my upcoming events and—"

"My ma—*boyfriend* is a huge fan of your stories, Mr. Richardson. He owns a bookshop and has a whole shelf dedicated to your works."

"Wow! That's so sweet," Richardson says, and his face lights up with delight. "I would love to do a reading at his shop."

That would be even better than a signed copy! A chance to meet his favorite author in person would make Jamie so happy.

"That would be most excellent! He loves everything you've written. He and I were reading through your latest historical series. It's good, very good. The spicy scenes, as Jamie calls them, are exquisitely detailed."

Richardson flushes with pride. "I do love those Vikings."

Clearing my throat, I ask, "Have you experienced the kind of love you write about?"

He laughs. "Me? Gosh. No. These are fantasies of mine, nothing more. I'm no lad, but who do you think the Irish lad is supposed to represent?" He points to himself.

"I have found the kind of love in your books," I tell him. "The passion you describe, the intensity of the characters' feelings... You describe word for word every way in which I feel for Jamie."

"Aww. That's wonderful to hear."

A smile tugs at my lips as I think of my mate. The sunshine in his smile that burns so bright it hides all that darkness inside. How resilient he is, despite all his losses. The way he let me take care of him when he needed it most.

"Jamie went through a lot when he was younger. He lost his family, and for a long time, he was in a dark place. It was your books that helped him escape, your books that brought a light into that darkness. Your characters are dear to him. Their adventures and romantic conquests bring him joy. He is without a doubt your biggest, most loyal fan. Meeting you would make him happy beyond words. His happiness is my happiness. Do this for me, and I would be in your debt."

The author is quiet for a moment, drinking in my words. "Wow. That's so nice to hear. I spend so much time drowning in self-doubt and imposter syndrome. It's easy to forget I have real, true fans out there." He sits up straighter, determination in his eyes. "All right. How about this: I can show up and do a reading for Jamie this afternoon. Is 4:00 p.m. enough time to get things ready? I don't need anything fancy, just a quiet place to sit and read to him."

I sigh in relief. Jamie will be delighted. "Yes, thank you."

I can't wait to see Jamie's face. He'll be thrilled!

With my task complete, I pull out the phone Jess loaned me in case I ran into any trouble. It's a confusing device. Jess looked at me like I had five heads when I told her I had no clue how to use this. She gave up trying to explain how it worked and just said, "Hold that little button on the side and say, 'Call Bailey,' if you need anything."

Holding the button, I say, "Call Bailey."

A monotone feminine voice says, "Calling Bailey."

I almost drop the thing. It talks! Is there a person trapped in here? Mayhap a faerie? I shake the phone. A dwarven smith is the only one who could have forged such a thing.

"Hey, Anders! Have any luck getting the book?"

Oh gods. Bailey is trapped in there too!

"Even better! The author has agreed to do a reading at 4:00 p.m. The store must be ready by then."

"Wow! That's amazing." Bailey laughs. "Then it's time for the next stage of the plan. See you later."

"Bailey, wait! Are you trapped in this dwarven construct? Do you need help getting out?"

"Huh?"

When I return to the shop, I have to knock to be let in. Jamie has gone to take Jace to his friend's party. Jess and Bailey have temporarily closed the store and are bustling about. Jess is stringing up lights while Bailey is stacking a table full of snacks and drinks and carefully sets a cake in the center.

"You work quickly," I say.

"Babe, dim the lights!" Jess calls from up on the ladder.

Bailey lowers the lights and flicks another switch. I gasp when the strings of lights come on, twinkling like stars. It truly is beautiful. Jamie will love it.

Someone knocks, and Bailey rushes to answer. It's Richardson, carrying something inside a paper bag. "Wow! This looks great. I've been wanting to come to this shop for a while." He introduces himself to Bailey and Jess, waves at me, and lets Jess show him where he'll be sitting.

My stomach feels like bugs are flying around inside. I hope Jamie will be pleased.

Bailey checks their phone. "Okay, he should be back any minute! Places, everyone!"

Gulping, I say, "Places? What does that mean? Where is my place?"

Bailey rolls their eyes with a smile. "I don't know! Just be there to welcome him when he comes in!"

Marching to the door, I await Jamie's arrival.

A car pulls up outside, and a door slams. Jamie's scent whispers under the door, making my wolf stir within my chest. The knob turns but doesn't open. "What the..." Jamie mumbles.

A key turns in the lock.

My heart's about to burst.

The door opens... and there he is. Jamie freezes in the doorway, lips parting, eyes going wide.

My knees are shaking as I walk toward him. *Please, let him be happy with this...*

"What..." he whispers, shaking his head in disbelief. "This is... Oh my god, Anders. Did you do this?"

I shake my head. "Not alone."

"It was his idea," Bailey chimes in, making my face flush.

"All of it was," Jess says, swinging an arm around Bailey's shoulders.

A smile lights up Jamie's face. "This is... wow. This is beautiful, Anders. I—oh my god." He lurches to a stop, voice going all high and squeaky. I grin when Richardson rises and walks toward Jamie.

"Hi, Jamie. I'm—"

Jamie covers his mouth, his chest rising and falling quickly. "Oh my god. You're L. A. Richardson. But—what—how—"

"Anders showed up at my signing and insisted I come and read for you." He holds out his hand. Jamie grabs it and shakes. Oh gods, he's practically panting, and there are tears in his eyes. "Thank you so much for supporting my books. It... it means the world to me."

"I love your books so much," Jamie gushes, the words coming out in a breathless rush along with a sudden stream of tears. "T-they saved my life."

Richardson smiles. "Want a hug?"

"Please," Jamie squeaks.

He pulls Jamie into a tight hug. "Now, shall we?"

"Yes!" Jamie practically bounces on the balls of his feet, clapping his hands together.

Richardson takes a seat on the couch and says, "Have you read my latest book?"

"No. I didn't even preorder. I wanted to get a copy from you in person at the reading," Jamie says, dashing away his happy tears as he sits in an armchair across from him.

"Well, how about this. I'll read you the first three chapters, and then you can have my copy."

An inhuman noise escapes Jamie. "No! No, I'm happy to pay for it! I want to support your work."

Richardson laughs. "Your support of my books means more to me than money." He opens the book. "Ready?"

Jamie looks over his shoulder, and our eyes meet. "Come and listen," he says.

Heart soaring, I go and sit on the arm of his chair.

When Jamie leans his head against my side, fingers curling around my wrist, my wolf howls in delight.

"Thank you," Jamie whispers, squeezing tight.

"Anything for you," I murmur into his hair.

For the man I love, there is nothing I would not give.

Chapter 21

Jamie

I will never forget this evening for as long as I live. How could I? My favorite author read me three amazing chapters of his new book in my favorite series. The shop looks more beautiful than I've ever seen it, transformed into a fairyland by the strings of lights swaying overhead. And Anders orchestrated all of this… for me. I can't believe it. Nobody has ever done something like this for me. I want to speak to him as soon as possible, alone.

When Richardson finishes reading, Jess, Bailey, and I clap for him. He left off on such a good cliff-hanger, I have to know what happens next. Richardson produces a pen from his pocket and signs the inside of the book, then hands it to me. I make an embarrassing squeaky sound, but I don't care.

Oh my god! I can't believe I'm holding a book he signed for me. I must protect this copy at all costs. "Thank you so much!" I hug it to my chest.

"It was a pleasure. Meeting you has kick-started my motivation to finish the next book, so thank *you*."

Cracking open the paperback, I take another look at my favorite author's perfect signature. Tonight has been so unreal, and I have my amazing boyfriend to thank for that. Unable to hold back, I rush over and throw my arms around Anders, squeezing tightly. "Thank you so much." Emotion thickens my voice, and I hide my face in his chest.

Nobody has ever done something like this for me—I haven't *let* anyone put me first like this. Not until Anders came along.

He puts his arms around me, squeezing back. "The night isn't over, pet."

Astonished, I jerk my head up to face him. "What?"

When he bares his teeth in a grin, my stomach swoops. "I haven't celebrated you properly yet. Dinner, remember? And then there's something I must ask of you."

My heart lurches with both nerves and excitement. "You're making me a little nervous, puppy dog." I check my phone. "The restaurant gets really busy soon. We should go over and grab a table."

"Aye, will do." Anders waves at Jess and Bailey, and we head to the car.

Taking his hand, I kiss his fingertips. "I'm a lucky guy."

"Makes both of us," Anders rumbles, and I think my heart will overflow with all the emotions he stirs within me.

We arrive at the restaurant just before peak hours, and since the patio has heat lamps and blankets, we decide to sit outdoors. Anders snatches up the menu and peruses it with a confidence he didn't have only a month ago. A rush of affection sweeps over me. He's different. Softer, more sure of himself. He's blossoming before my eyes, and I can't wait to show him even more of this world, experiencing it with him as if for the first time.

Somehow, before I was even aware of it, I fell so hard for Anders. My wolf's instincts are singing through my heart, telling me this man is my forever.

But does he feel the same? Nerves make my stomach flip.

Anders coughs. "Ready to order?"

There's a trip in his heartbeat. He's nervous too, and that makes me even more nervous. "Y-yeah!" I haven't even been looking at the menu, my eyes glazing over, only seeing the font.

"How is Jace doing?"

"He's having fun." I'd texted him before the reading. Shoot. I should probably check in again. "Do you mind if I call him, just to say good night?"

Anders's soft smile is pure indulgence. "Of course. Can I speak to him too?"

God, what have I done to deserve a guy like him? Before Anders, nobody had been so supportive and loving toward Jace. He understands how important my brother is to me and cares for him like I do. I call Jace, tapping to put us on speakerphone. It rings and rings, then goes to voicemail. Anxiety grips my stomach. "Maybe he's in bed." That's the most logical answer, of course, but my brain tries to tug me down paths better left unknown. Like *why* he isn't answering.

Our server stops by our table. "Ready to order?"

"I'll have the... err..." Anders squints at the menu. "The filet mignon." He butchers the pronunciation, but I'm pleased his reading skills have improved.

"And for you, sir?"

I order some pasta, then try and call Jace once we're alone. Still no answer. Why won't he pick up?

"Easy, pet." A big hand settles over my palm and squeezes. Anders's forest-green eyes catch me in their spell. "The lad is fine. Just try and enjoy yourself."

I return his soft smile. "I am. Tonight's been so amazing."

Anders squeezes my hand. "I'm glad." His gaze drifting away, Anders blows out a breath, as if he's trying to calm himself down, then meets my gaze with determination. "Jamie... I never thought anywhere would feel like home. Not until I found you."

I can't wipe the smile from my face. I feel the same. Ever since Anders came along, he's brightened my world and made my broken family feel so complete.

Taking in a shaky breath, Anders says, "I may have fought him, but my wolf knew at a glance that you were the one I was destined for. I wish to spend the rest of my life proving how I was made for you as you are for me. So..." His voice wavers, but Anders pushes on, and I know whatever he asks, my answer will be yes. "Jamie, will you—"

My phone rings, making us both jump. When Janet's name flashes across my screen, my heart sinks. She's the mother of Jace's friend. Why would she be calling me unless something's happened? "Just one moment, Anders. I'm sorry." I snatch up my phone and swipe. "Janet. Hi, is everything okay?"

"Jamie, I'm so sorry, but it's Jace. He's hurt."

And just like that, my entire world shatters to pieces.

The world blurs around me as I drive, foot glued to the gas pedal. Janet's words keep running through my head.

...pushed him down the stairs.

Bile rises in my throat.

His arm, I—I think it's broken.

My baby brother is hurt. Anguish thickens my throat, and I want to break down right then and there. Ever since we were kids, I've been looking out for him. I swore to myself I would protect my little brother.

But while I was off with my boyfriend, Jace got hurt. This should never have happened. I shouldn't have let him out of my sight.

"Jamie."

Anders's soft voice makes me jump, my fingers squeezing the wheel.

I can't look at him. The guilt feels like it'll eat me alive. I shouldn't have let Jace go. I should have—

"The lad will be fine," Anders says. His fingers curl around my arm.

I pull away, rejecting his touch. "Please don't." Guilt flares, making me feel even sicker. "Just... not now."

Anders says nothing. He doesn't have to. I know I've hurt him, but all I can think about is my brother.

I promised myself I would put my brother first, and I've failed.

My stomach writhes as I jump from the car and rush inside the hospital. The receptionist sends us to the fifth floor. I run to the waiting room, breathless with fear by the time I get to the front desk. I rush through an introduction, and she gives me papers to sign, consenting to my brother's surgery.

Fuck. He has to have surgery. This is a first for Jace, one I hoped he'd never experience. If my parents were here, this wouldn't have happened. My eyes burn as I sign the papers, and I have to pause to wipe my eyes so I don't get tears on the papers. Anders sits silently beside me. More than anything, I want to turn to him for comfort, but this isn't about me. I don't deserve comfort, not when Jace needs it the most.

Once the papers are signed, a nurse motions for me to follow her to Jace's room so I can be there for him when they put him under. Jace's face is wet with tears, which breaks my heart, but it's the sight of him lying in a hospital bed that nearly brings me to my knees. Running to him, I pull him close, mindful of the arm he's cradling to his chest. "Hey, kiddo. Are you okay? Are you in pain?" I frame his damp face in my hands.

"N-no. The doctors gave me medicine," Jace says, sniffling. "I want to go home."

I press my lips to his hair. "We'll go home soon, okay? I promise."

"Am I going to die? Like Mom and Dad?" Sobs rack his shoulders.

Being in a hospital must be bringing back terrible memories for him. "No, bud. It's just a broken arm. The doctors are going to help you get some sleep, and by the time you wake up, you'll feel much better."

"Will you be here when I wake up?"

I wipe away his tears with my thumbs. "Of course. I'll be right here."

The doctor comes in. She's a lovely woman and explains everything to Jace in a way that's reassuring and easy to understand, answering all of his questions. She encourages him to lie down and places a mask over his face. A tear spills down Jace's cheek, and I squeeze his hand tight. In only seconds, my little brother is asleep, and I'm asked to leave the room so they can wheel him off into surgery.

Outside the room, Anders paces, wringing his hands. "Jamie—"

I turn away, unable to even look at him without guilt consuming my insides. "I need to be alone right now, Anders." Before he can answer, I escape into the nearest bathroom and lock myself in a stall.

Finally alone, I let my tears cascade down my face as I fold in on myself and gasp for air.

Because I was selfish and focusing on myself, my little brother got hurt. I promised I would put him first, always. It's time to keep that promise.

No matter how much it hurts.

Chapter 22
Anders

Dread racks my insides.

Jamie will barely look at me, and he hasn't said a word since Jace went into surgery. Children and their parents come and go, the little ones crying and distressed by their injuries. Their wails, the metallic tang of blood, all the people coming and going—it's too much for me to bear.

"Be right back." I rise, resisting the urge to give Jamie a comforting touch. It's clear he needs space. He's only rejected comfort when he's hurting deeply, and it terrifies me and my wolf that our mate won't let us give him what he needs.

Since neither of us had supper, I stop by a vending machine and feed it a few dollars in exchange for whatever snack catches my interest, making sure to get more for Jamie than for myself. My mate needs to be nourished right now, and he never thinks of himself.

When I return, Jace's healer is speaking to Jamie. He grips the arms of his chair tight, shoulders stiff. I run to his side, almost dropping the snacks. "Is he well?"

The doctor smiles. "The surgery went great. Jace is in recovery now. I'll let you know as soon as he starts to wake up, but he's going to be fine."

All the tension bleeds from Jamie's body, and he slumps back into his chair. "Thank you so much."

She squeezes his shoulder. "I know how you feel. I was devastated when my son broke his arm."

My fingers curl. Jamie will accept a stranger's touch before he accepts mine?

He hides his face in his hands, sniffling. "I feel so awful."

"These things happen, Mr. Sullivan."

Hopelessness claws at me. Jamie's blaming himself for Jace's injury, but it wasn't his fault. How can I make him see that?

Once we're alone, I sit down beside him and hand him a package of snacks. "Eat, pet."

"Thanks..." Jamie tears open the package and scoops up a handful of nuts and raisins. His eyes fall shut as he chews, his head tilting like he's on the cusp of sleep.

"Get some rest." I squeeze his leg. "I will wake you when Jace is up."

Forcing his eyes open, Jamie shakes his head. "I need to be there. I promised I would."

I want to argue, but the tone of his voice implies he won't take no for an answer. "The healer was right. This wasn't your fault."

Jamie swallows with effort, then crams the snacks in his pocket after only eating a handful. "I'm responsible for him, and because I wasn't there, he got hurt." His voice wobbles.

"You can't always be there, Jamie." I pull him to me. He's stiff in my arms, and he doesn't return my touch. Fear makes my insides tremble. Why is he pulling away from me?

"I should have..." Jamie's throat clicks when he swallows. "I should have made him stay home."

"No. You can't restrict his freedom because something bad might happen." My poor mate isn't thinking rationally right now. Gods, I wish I knew what to say to ease his guilt. If Wulfric were here—

Jamie leaps up when another healer rushes up to us. "He's waking up," he tells us.

We arrive in Jace's room and sit by his bed. Several layers of bandages cover his arm, but he sleeps peacefully, so he can't be in much pain. I brush some dark hair away from his forehead. "Brave lad."

Jace's long lashes flutter, and he opens his eyes.

"Hey, bud." Jamie leans over the other side of the bed. "Feeling okay?"

"My throat hurts," Jace rasps.

The healer brings him a paper cup of water and tells us that Jace can go home. He gives Jamie and me a list of instructions and a bottle of medicine, but everything he says goes over my head. Jamie listens raptly, nodding or asking questions. I wish I could give the boy some wolf furs. That would heal his arm in no time at all.

Once Jace is up and dressed, Jamie escorts the sleepy boy back to the car. As we drive home, Jace falls asleep in the back seat. Jamie puts the car in park and slumps against the wheel. "Home. Finally."

It feels like an age since we've been home. "I'll get the boy." Stepping out, I walk around to the rear passenger door. Movement across the street catches my attention. There's a figure reclining against the window of a store. The burn of magic hits my nose, making my spine stiffen as my wolf growls low in my chest.

What is a witch doing here? They must be part of the coven that gave me trouble.

"Anders?" Jamie's waiting by the door.

Tearing my gaze away reluctantly, I carefully maneuver Jace from the back seat. The figure hasn't moved when I look up. Giving them a final glare over my shoulder, I follow Jamie inside. I help carry the lad upstairs, and Jamie unlocks the front door for me. "Wait," I growl and hold Jace out to him. Frowning, Jamie takes him from me. I ease open the door just enough to poke my head inside and draw in a deep breath. The apartment is dark and quiet, devoid of the stink of magic. That doesn't mean a witch hasn't cast a compulsion spell to mask their presence and ambush us. "Stay," I command Jamie, not giving him time to answer as I proceed deeper into the apartment.

Only once I've checked every room do I decide it's safe enough. "Come in," I say and take Jace from him and carry him to his room. Slowly, I lay Jace in bed. He grimaces, eyes fluttering. The poor boy must be exhausted.

"Are we home?" His voice still sounds scratchy.

"Aye. Safe and sound." Hopefully, that witch across the street is just observing me. "Are you in any pain?"

Jace shakes his head. "Tired."

"I'm sure you are. You were very brave." Pride warms me.

A sweet smile lights up his face. "Really?"

Kneeling, I run my fingers over his soft hair. "Braver than most warriors I know."

Jace yawns big and wide, making me chuckle. "Can I see Jamie before I sleep?"

"Of course." Leaning down, I plant a kiss to his cheek. I don't want to leave his side. All I want is to stay and watch over him in case he needs anything. "Sleep well, pup."

Gods above, but I adore this little boy as if he were my own son. This cold heart of mine has only grown twice its size to fit how much I love Jamie and his little brother. They are my family, my pack.

"He okay?" Jamie is right outside the door, worrying his bottom lip.

"Tired but all right. He wants to see you."

Jamie sweeps past me without another word, and all the warmth of seeing Jace turns cold in my chest. Why is he being so distant? To distract myself, I wash my face and brush my teeth, then head into our bedroom to change. By the time I'm dressed, the bedroom door opens behind me.

"Is the lad asleep?" I ask as I turn, only to freeze. Jamie's looking at me in a way he never has before, eyes narrowed and lips in a tight line. The scent of anger pours off him. By the nine realms, what's happened now?

"You taught my little brother how to throw a punch."

It's not a question. No blade is as sharp as Jamie's words.

Oh Hel. What have I done? The ground feels unsteady beneath me as I fold my arms across my chest. "To protect himself, aye."

Jamie rolls his eyes skyward. "You had no right."

Shit. Damn it!

"I only wanted the lad to be able to stand up for himself!"

"And guess who he decided to hit at the party?" Jamie snaps. "Guess!"

"I don't know! A frost giant? Maybe Odin himself?" My jests bounce right off him.

"Kevin. The brat who bullied him. He's the reason Jace broke his arm, because Kevin shoved him down the stairs after Jace hit him."

My heart drops into my stomach. Oh gods. "I... I'm sure Jace had his reasons."

Jamie barks a harsh laugh. "Oh, I'm sure he did, but that's not the point. I've always told Jace to get an adult if he needs help so shit like this doesn't happen!"

"He's ten! He's not a toddler. Any child of mine will know how to fight back!"

"He's not *your* child!" Jamie's shout makes me flinch, but it's his words that hurt the most, cutting me to the very core. I must look as devastated as I feel. Tears suddenly flood Jamie's eyes. "He's mine, and he got hurt because I wasn't there to protect him." The tears spill over despite Jamie's best attempts to dash them away.

I'm moving before I can stop myself, my hands on his shoulders. "You can't always be there, pet."

"No." Jamie untangles himself from my arms and backs away from me. "After our parents died, I promised Jace I'd protect him. I swore to myself he would always come first. I told my—my grandmother the l-last time I saw her alive that I'd take care of him." Jamie heaves in a shuddery gasp as tears drip down his chin. "I let myself get distracted. I've been selfish."

"Jamie..." I don't know what to say, speechless as he falls apart right in front of me. "Jace didn't get hurt because you put yourself first for once."

But Jamie shakes his head, furiously wiping his face. "I can't do this, Anders."

Dread rises within me. "We can find ways to include Jace in our outings. We—"

"No. I can't—I can't be with you."

I try to speak, but all that escapes is a pitiful little gasp.

Jamie's rejecting me. My mate is rejecting our bond.

"You don't mean this." My voice is barely louder than a whisper.

Sniffling, Jamie pulls the necklace over his head.

What can I say? How can I convince him to give us a chance, that it's all right to put himself first? A lump aches in my throat.

Jamie takes my hand, fingers trembling. "Take it. Go home and be with your family. I won't force you to stay here anymore." He presses the necklace into my palm.

"You *are* my home." I grip his hand tight, desperate to keep him here with me. "You are my family. Do not send me away. Please."

Jamie's mouth shakes, and he wipes away tears as he tugs his hand free.

My heart cracks to pieces in my chest. I'd fall to my knees and beg if I thought it would change his mind, but the devastation in those watery blue eyes tells me all I need to know. He's made his choice, and it wasn't me.

A broken sound I didn't know I was capable of falls from my lips. The pain has me folding in on myself as my very heart itself feels as if it will shatter.

Our mate doesn't want us, my wolf howls, and the pain brings me to my knees.

My gasps turn to snorts and pants as the pain morphs to a fury that burns me from the inside out. Claws burst from my fingertips, carving into the floorboards. No. No, no, no! My berserker is coming out, and I can't control him.

"A-Anders?" Jamie's heart races fast in my ears. He's scared.

"Get back," I snarl, voice deep and distorted. My body grows, clothes straining before they tear to threads. A red haze falls over my eyes. Thick fur sprouts all over my body. I've got to get out of here before I hurt him.

"Anders, wait! I'm sorry. I'm so sorry!" He reaches for me, and my eyes latch onto the veins in his wrist. I imagine them bursting beneath my fangs, how sweet his blood would taste as it fills my mouth, the crunch of his delicate bones.

"Get back!" I roar through my fangs, and Jamie scrambles across the room, face pale and eyes wide and damp. He smells so sweet. I want to tear him apart and devour him piece by piece...

I charge, rushing past him toward the window. Glass shatters, cutting into my flesh as I hurl myself from the bedroom. The wind roars in my ears, whipping my fur back. I land on my clawed paws, shaking the earth. Drawing in a lungful of air, my mouth salivates as I catch the scent of prey nearby. Human prey. I push myself onto my back legs, claws scraping the ground as I prowl from the alley, shoulders brushing along the walls.

There they are, across the road. A man and woman argue, their shrill voices hurting my ears. They haven't seen me yet. Licking my lips, I drop to all fours and lope toward them. The woman's perfume makes my mouth water. She will taste so sweet.

Something moves behind me. My nose burns, making me growl. Suddenly, an immense weight bears down upon me, forcing me to the ground.

"Easy there, Anders. I've got you." A witch I vaguely recognize stands over me. I snarl, hungry for his blood. If I kill him, the stink of magic will go away.

The witch's face pinches in pity. "Shit. There's not much time left. I must get you to your brothers."

With a snap of his fingers, the portal bursts open, the light blinding me. My paws are ripped out from beneath me as the portal pulls me toward it. I drive my claws into the concrete, but I'm not strong enough to fight the portal's magic as it draws me in.

White light obscures everything I know.

Chapter 23

Jamie

When I wake up, there's an Anders-shaped hole in my chest.

Tears dampen the pillowcase as images torment me of Anders being hunted down by the police and shot dead, hurting himself or others, running off into the wilderness never to be found.

He dropped my gran's necklace when he went berserk. It's all I have to remind me he was here at all. I touch the necklace against my chest, eyes stinging.

There's a howling in my soul. My wolf is mourning the other half of his heart. I want to howl out all my anguish until Anders hears me and comes home.

Chest aching, I force myself from the bed. I can't focus on myself. Jace needs me. Falling apart isn't an option. I dry my eyes as I leave the bedroom, trying to look like I haven't been crying all night. In the kitchen, I crack some eggs in a bowl. Yesterday, Anders and I cooked breakfast together. I'd laughed when he cracked the egg too hard and got yolk all over his hand.

Shaking the memory from my head, I scramble the eggs in a pan. Jace comes out of his room, yawning. I force a smile. "Hey. Sleep well?"

Jace shakes his head. "My arm hurts."

"Sorry about that. I'll get you your meds. Have a seat. Food's almost done."

Frowning, Jace looks around the room. "Where's Anders?"

My breath hitches. How do I even answer that? Unwilling to speak, I plate the eggs, butter the toast, and bring our plates to the table. Next, I fill a glass with water, grab Jace's meds, and bring them to him. He gulps down the water and meds but doesn't eat right away, looking in confusion at Anders's empty seat. The table looks too big without him here, slurping down bacon and shoveling down his eggs, making us laugh with his enthusiasm for the food. A lump rises in my throat. What have I done?

"Isn't Anders eating?" Jace asks.

"Jace... Anders and I had a big fight. I don't think he's coming back." My voice shakes, and I cram eggs in my mouth to avoid saying anything else.

Jace stares at me with such a look of betrayal I have to tear my gaze away. "Because I got into a fight with Kevin? But he's the one who attacked me. I didn't start anything. I swear! It wasn't Anders's fault!"

"Hey, no, that's not what happened." Crossing the table, I put my hand on his shaking shoulder. "We didn't break up because of you, kiddo."

Jace bucks my hand off. "But if I hadn't gotten hurt, you wouldn't have fought!" He lurches from the seat and makes for his room.

"Jace!" I stop him by the door, turning him around to face me. Tears streak his face, and he hangs his head with a miserable sob. "Things wouldn't have worked out anyway. Anders was always going to return to his home." My voice breaks from how hard I'm trying to convince myself.

"So he just left us?" Jace asks, the pain in his voice making me flinch.

"Yeah, he, um... he probably got on a boat and went back to his time."

"And you didn't even try and stop him!" Jace says accusingly. "You just let him go! Every time you're finally happy, you always ruin it!"

Is that really what he thinks?

"That's not true—"

"It is! You were really happy with Anders, but you made him leave! All because I broke my stupid arm?" He's yelling now, catching me completely by surprise. "That's so dumb!"

"How is putting my family first dumb?" I snap.

Jace shouts over me. "You're not putting me first! You're just scared!"

I'm struck speechless by how perceptive my brother is. Is that what this is? Have I been using Jace as a shield to protect myself from committing to the guys I've dated?

"That's not... Jace—"

"We were finally a family again, and you ruined it." Jace sniffles. "Leave me alone."

His bedroom door slams in my face.

I thought I was doing the right thing. Now, I just feel like an even bigger asshole.

I call out from work to stay home with Jace, but even though we're in close proximity, we barely speak a word to each other. I hurt Anders. Not only that, but I also hurt Jace. I feel like a colossal failure. Beside me, Jace watches *Avatar: The Last Airbender*, a show he loves, but his face is blank as an anticipated battle unfolds on the screen.

Reaching out, I squeeze his knee. He barely reacts to my touch, but at least he didn't push me away. "Need anything, bud?"

"Can I have a sandwich?"

I jump up, thrilled to be of use. "Sure. What kind?"

He shrugs. "Ham and cheese."

"Coming right up."

In the kitchen, I prepare the sandwiches, one for myself, one for Jace, and one for—

A lump thickens my throat. Anders isn't here. He's not coming back. Tears sting my eyes as I wrap up the third sandwich and put it in the refrigerator. I take a few deep breaths to get my emotions under control. I made my choice. I've got to bear the consequences.

I set the plate of sandwiches on the coffee table and try and focus on the show. Anders's reaction to seeing a movie for the first time had been so cute and funny. I wish I'd been able to show him the other two *Lord of the Rings* movies. He would have loved them.

Eventually, Jace falls asleep beside me, the lights from the screen highlighting the tear tracks on his cheeks. My heart breaks open, unleashing a dam of anguish. Leaning down, I kiss his cheek, wiping away a tear that falls from my cheek to his.

"I'm so sorry, kiddo."

For so long, I'd wanted a partner who would love and support Jace as much as I did. I'd found all that and more in Anders, so why did I fuck things up? Why did I push him away?

My phone rings, and I answer without checking who it is so the noise doesn't wake Jace.

"Hello?"

"Hey, Jamie!" Jess grins at me from the screen, surprising me. She doesn't usually FaceTime.

"Shh! Jace is sleeping."

"Oops, sorry," she says, lowering her voice.

"Slacking off?" I tease, managing a small smile.

"Yup. The shop's burning down, and Bailey's dancing in the ashes." She takes a bite of a sandwich. She must be at the cute little sandwich place around the corner from the café. "Just checking in. How's Jace?"

I glance at my brother, heart aching at the sadness that pinches his face even in sleep. "He's, uh... Fine. Just needs to rest and take his meds—"

"Were you crying?" Jess leans closer to the screen, a frown puckering her brows.

Shit. I attempt a laugh. "What? No."

She fixes me with a hard stare. "You had better not be blaming yourself for Jace's injury," she says.

My throat thickens, and I blink away the burn of tears. "I... Of course I am, but it's not just that. It's Anders. I think I messed up, Jess."

"Talk to me," she urges, voice soft and comforting.

The smile falls off my face. I confess everything that happened last night: Jace's injury and surgery, my argument with Anders, then my conversation with Jace this morning.

Jess says, "I guess Jace is doing okay if he can give you shit."

I give a defeated nod. "Yup. No broken arm is going to stop him from wrecking me emotionally, apparently."

"He's right, though. What's going on? I thought you wanted a boyfriend."

I wince. "I did, but—"

Blowing out a sigh, Jess sets her coffee down out of sight. "You felt guilty about Jace getting hurt, so you pushed him away to punish yourself. Jamie, being alone for the rest of your life won't bring your parents back."

A lump rises in my throat. "That's not—"

"They wouldn't want you to keep beating yourself up over their deaths."

Blinking fast, I say, "I promised them I'd look after my brother." From the moment I held him, all I'd wanted was to keep him safe. Sometimes I'd noticed the strain that raising two kids had put on my parents. How tired they were, the frustration they'd let slip. I'd felt bad and wanted to lighten their burden, so I'd taken it on myself to care for Jace: bottle-feeding him, being the first to comfort him when he cried at night, constantly keeping him in my sight so my parents could shop or do other chores. Even when they'd assured me Jace was their responsibility, I'd still been determined to help them.

"You're allowed to be happy." Jess's soft, empathetic gaze makes it hard to hold in my tears. She sees through me to my very core, always has. "It's fine to accept help, to trust another person to look after both of you. But denying yourself happiness? Is that really what they'd want?"

No. Of course not. My parents would want me to be happy, but that doesn't make forgiving myself any easier. "If it weren't for me, they'd still be here." I wipe away the tear that spills free. "Ugh. This sucks. I hate being wrong."

Jess smiles. "You must really love the guy if you're this torn up about him."

"I do." My heart clenches. I love Anders more than anything or anyone. But do I love him more than my guilt? Do I love him more than my own self-loathing?

Of course I do.

Even if I never forgive myself, I want to be better. For Anders. For Jace. And maybe a little bit for me too.

Jess gives me a knowing smile. "You've got that I'm-gonna-make-things-right look."

How *do* I make things right? I have no idea where Anders is. He couldn't have gone back to his time without my necklace. He could be anywhere, and if he went berserk, can he even come back? Oh god. Have I lost him forever?

I won't know unless I try.

We say goodbye, and I end the call. Jace continues to sleep beside me. Exhaustion wears at me, so I snuggle in close and put my arm around him. "I'll fix this, bud. I promise."

When I open my eyes, the sky outside is stained with red and orange as the sun sets. Shit. I must have been really tired if I slept the day away. I sit up and realize I fell onto my side while I was sleeping because my Jace-sized prop left at some point.

I stretch out an ache in my neck as I cross the room and knock on his bedroom door. "Jace? You want dinner?"

No answer.

The door squeaks when I open it, light spilling in through the gap and pooling on an empty bed. Something doesn't feel right. He's probably in the bathroom. With a heavy feeling in my stomach, I knock on the bathroom door and try the handle when nobody responds. The door opens, revealing an empty bathroom.

My chest tightens.

"Jace?" My voice echoes through the apartment as I jog to my bedroom and throw open the door. He isn't here. "Jace, come out, now!" I check under the bed. Look in all the closets. Behind the shower curtain.

An iron band wraps around my lungs. I can't find him. He's not in the apartment. With shaking hands, I dial the police, stammering and panting my way through the conversation. Jace is gone. I don't know where he is or when he left. Where would he go? Was he really so angry that he'd storm out without telling me?

The operator assures me that the police will be there soon, but the ringing in my ears drowns her out as my knees buckle.

Where is he?

Where's my baby brother?

Is he hurt? Is he safe?

I grip at my chest, pulling at my shirt to try and ease the pressure on my chest.

And then, I notice it.

My necklace is gone, and I understand.

Jace took it.

My little brother has gone to bring Anders back himself.

Chapter 24

Anders

Waves roar and gulls cry out as I come to, lying on hard stones. Cold seawater sloshes over my boots, making me jolt up onto my elbows.

I'd recognize these shores anywhere. I'm on Ulfheim, and I'm not alone. I direct a glare at Arlo. He sighs with relief. "Perfect, you're back to your regular snarly self."

The rage has indeed lost its grip on me, but my berserker still lurks close to the surface, making my fangs and claws sharp. Filling the void of my heart, however, is a bone-deep ache. Jamie rejected me. Remembering makes me want to roar my rage and heartache to the skies, as cold and gray as steel.

"Sorry to whisk you away like that. Couldn't have you taking bites out of the locals."

I sit up, tugging off my boot and emptying it of water. "Why did you bring me here?"

Arlo tugs at my arm. "You haven't got much time left. Staying among humans isn't an option, not if we want to keep people safe *and* protect our secrets. Being around your pack will help. Now, come on, up-up!"

I snort. "My pack exiled me, remember?"

Arlo rolls his eyes. "I do, but regardless of how you feel, your wolf will know his pack and should settle down long enough for a decision to be made. Isn't that how those bonds of yours work?"

I rise, stumbling. "The only decision that will be made is whether I will be put down like a dog or you will rip my wolf from me with your magic."

I'd rather die than lose Fenrir's great gift or live without Jamie.

Arlo grimaces as if he dislikes the idea as much as I do. "Wolves from an Alpha bloodline can't be soothed by pack alone? It has to be a mate to tame your berserker?"

"Aye. Pack bonds can help slow the process, but the stronger the wolf, the harder he or she is to control." And considering my bonds with my pack are in tatters, there may truly be no hope for me to recover. But if today will be the last day I have with my mind intact, then I won't waste it.

I've got too much to make up for. Walking upright is difficult, the beast within yearning to prowl on all fours, but I push myself to move. I've got to see my brothers. There is too much I have to say to them. "Coming, witch?" I snap.

With Arlo behind me, I walk the familiar path toward the village. Smoke rises from chimney stacks, and the wind carries the distant sounds of life as usual. As the huts come into view, I hold up an arm. "Wait here. They won't take kindly to you just waltzing in. Let me announce your presence first."

Arlo folds his arms, sparing the village a wary look. "I appreciate it."

"Not doing it for your benefit," I grumble, forcing myself to move faster toward the village. Gods, what if they refuse to speak to me? I've earned their ire, I know that without a doubt, but I want so badly for a chance to apologize.

Heart racing fast, I force my trembling legs to march toward the village. Wolves lope through the streets, and children run and play while their parents haggle at stalls. Wulfric's longhouse is the easiest to spot as it is the biggest building in the village. My knees knock together as I take one step and then another toward my family home. Heads turn, and a lull falls over the streets until whispers fill the air around me. Eyes narrow as the peasants glare at me. Wolves growl. Parents tug their children close. I want to disappear into the ground but make myself hold my head high and continue onward.

I'm only ten paces from the longhouse when the door is thrown open. As Wulfric's eyes lock with mine, they blaze with shock and then fury.

"Wulf?" Kieran appears in the doorway, but Wulfric shoves him back.

"Stay behind me," Wulfric snarls, voice deep and throaty.

My heart sinks, and I try to get my tongue to move, but the damn thing feels fat and heavy.

Wulfric puts one hand on his axe. "Why have you returned? *How*? I banished you. You were never to come back!"

"Aye, that's what banishment usually entails, isn't it?" As Wulfric snarls at my sarcasm, I internally hit myself. Now is not the time to mouth off.

Footsteps come crashing toward us. "Anders!" Lyall bursts through the door, shoving past Wulfric. A smile lights up his face, but it quickly falls as Wulfric muscles past him.

"Stay away from him, Lyall," Wulfric commands.

In the doorway behind them, Gunnar grips onto my aunt Helga's shoulders.

The whole pack is here. This will make things simple, as I don't have to seek them out individually, but also so much more complicated.

"What trickery have you brought upon my shores, Anders?" Wulfric asks. "Or should I just call you Loki?"

I snort. "You flatter me, but I am not here to trick you. I mean it." My heart races until I fear it will burst from my chest. Where do I even begin? I owe them all an apology, but none more than Wulfric. I look my little brother in the eyes. "I was here a few days ago but kept my presence a secret." At their startled looks, I quickly add, "I only wished to make sure all was well."

Wulfric's hand falls away from his axe. "You were here. Why didn't you make yourself known then?"

Gunnar scowls. "You've fallen lower than we thought if you're sneaking around like a craven, Anders."

Lyall snaps, "Would you lot just hear him out?"

Painful memories of that day claw at me, reminding me of how alone I'd felt when I'd realized they'd forgotten all about me. "I wished to survey the village, not to fight. I thought for certain that things would have changed, and not for the better."

"Because of me," Kieran states, gripping onto Wulfric's arm.

I nod. "Aye. But the village prospers more than I have ever thought possible. I deeply believed that the presence of a human would bring about our downfall, like before."

The breath leaves me in a shudder that makes my chest rattle. "I was wrong. So very wrong. About everything. I believed the worst about Kieran and refused to see how happy he has made you, brother. How much he has helped you heal the damage done to you by our father's killers and by me. I saw how happy you were, Aunt Helga, to sit down to a meal with our family without any fear of fighting. How relaxed you were, Gunnar, and how relieved you were, Lyall, not to have to choose between me and Wulfric. And I realized it was because I wasn't there. I wasn't there to divide us, to pit brother against brother and tear open old wounds or to mock and insult you, Wulfric."

In my shame, I get on my knees and bow my head. "I'm so sorry. For everything. All of it. To all of you. But most of all, I'm sorry to you, Kieran, for hurting you."

Kieran's mouth slips open. "O-oh," he says softly.

Swallowing hard, I add, "And I'm sorry to you, Wulfric." My throat tries to close as remorse thickens it, but I keep on going. I look my brother in his wide, shining gray eyes and say, "An Alpha is more than a status symbol. More than some lofty title that gives a person unfair advantage over others. An Alpha is someone who puts the needs of others before themselves. Someone who teaches, guides, and nurtures. It's who you *are*. Who you've always been. And I hated you for that for so long. Unfairly. Because even as a lad, I knew the goodness of your heart, how deserving you were of the title, and despised you for it."

My eyes sting, clouding over as I look my brother in the face and see him, finally see him. This strong, incredible man who had such responsibility thrust upon him so young, who led us out of the darkest time in our pack's history and built something beautiful out of all that darkness.

"You are my brother, Wulfric." I smile even as my voice breaks. "And I'm sorry I was never the brother you deserved. I... I know this fixes nothing between us. I don't expect it to, nor do I deserve forgiveness. I needed you all to know how I felt. Nothing more."

Wulfric blinks fast, eyes glistening. He breaks my stare and clears his throat, thumbing the corner of his eye. Kieran leans his chin on his shoulder and whispers something to him. Lyall's expression is somber, and Gunnar rubs Helga's trembling shoulders, his own head bowed.

"Get up," Wulfric says gruffly, so sharply I jump.

I scramble to my feet. My heart cracks in my chest. I tried, I did. I meant every word. Even though I told myself not to expect their forgiveness because I didn't deserve it, I wasn't prepared for the pain of my pack's rejection.

Jaw tightly clenched, Wulfric comes toward me, boots crunching over the snow. I don't know when it started snowing. Thick clumps fall from the sky in flurries, and the bitter wind blows between us as he comes to a halt only inches from me.

I can't read his expression or get a sense of what he's feeling. The bond between us has been dormant for so long. So when he reaches out, I brace myself for the impact of a punch or a shove. I'd deserve it.

Wulfric grips the back of my neck, squeezing tight. His hand trembles. "I think," he says, voice low and rough with emotion, "we've hurt each other enough, brother."

The breath escapes me in a shaky gasp, and try as I might, I can't help the tear that falls down my cheek.

Brother. *Brother.* With a single word, I am reborn. Not Anders the exile or Anders the villain. I am Anders, brother of Wulfric.

"Now," Gunnar says.

Now what?

Next thing I know, Lyall has thrown himself at me and enveloped me in a backbreaking hug. Wulfric and I end up mashed together. Laughing, my aunt joins the embrace, crushing us even tighter together. Then Gunnar's got his big arms around as many of us as he can fit in. Wulfric's body shakes as he laughs, and I join in.

The bonds burst open in my chest, and I drown in tender feelings of *pack*, *family*, and *love*. I can feel them. All of them, for the first time in so long. Lyall's mirth. Helga's relief. Gunnar's amusement. Wulfric's cautious hope in this new beginning we're embarking on together.

They've let me in, I am pack again, and I will never let them regret giving me their love and their trust.

Then Gunnar bends over, scoops up snow, and mashes it into my face. The hug dissolves into a wrestling match as I untangle myself and grab as much snow as I can hold. "Take this!" I throw the snow at Wulfric, then another clump at Lyall.

"Not the face, Anders, you ass!" Lyall exclaims, sputtering and wiping snow out of his eyes.

"Boys, that's enough!" Helga squawks, laughing as she rubs snow out of her silver hair.

"Aww, you guys," Kieran says, wiping his eyes. "I knew Jamie wouldn't settle for a jerkhole like Anders without a good reason!"

The bonds in my chest burn as if I've been stabbed with a hot branding iron, and I grip my chest. The berserker within roars. The bonds between my brothers and me are not enough. The berserker's fury consumes them, further severing my connection to my humanity.

"Anders, what is it?" Lyall's voice is high and panicked as he kneels beside me, touching my back.

"My m-mate rejected me. I hadn't had time to claim him." Harsh pants and snarls punctuate my words until I sound more wolf than man. "No time. Lock me up. Quickly! Before I hurt anyone!"

Lyall whimpers, clutching my arm. "We've only just got you back! Wulfric, do something!"

"There's nothing to be done." Pain floods Wulfric's voice. "He is too far gone."

"The witch," I snarl, clawing at the ground. "Get the witch! Left him at the western road. Hurry!"

There's confused murmuring, but Wulfric snaps, "Do as he says! Gunnar, go!"

"Got it!" Gunnar takes off past me, and I snap at his ankles, longing to chase him and rip into his flesh.

Gods, it is happening fast.

I'm not ready.

Where is my mate?

I want to see him.

To say goodbye.

One last time...

CHAPTER 25

JAMIE

I SLAM ON THE brakes and lurch from the car. Gulls cry, and the frigid river breeze numbs my throat as I run. *Please let me be in time. Please!* My lungs ache by the time I'm at the marina. He has to be here. There's no way anyone would let a little boy just get a boat and sail away.

"But I have money!" a familiar voice protests.

My heart skips as I whirl around. Jace stands in front of a ticket booth, holding up a handful of cash.

"Sorry. No unaccompanied children are allowed on board any of our tours," the ticket-taker says kindly but firmly.

"Jace!" I snap, both angry and relieved as I rush up to him.

At the crack of my voice, Jace winces, his shoulders hunching up to his ears. "Uh-oh..."

"Yeah. 'Uh-oh.'" Grabbing his wrist on his uninjured side, I tug him away from the booth and toward the car. "What were you thinking?" I snap once we're out of earshot of the lady in the booth.

Jace's cheeks flush. "I was trying to find Anders." His bottom lip wobbles. "You guys need to make up. You have to."

My heart clenches. "I will."

"Why did you two fight? Was it because of me?"

I can't tear my gaze away from his cast, can't let go of my guilt because if I'd just been there, Jace might not have gotten hurt. I was so focused on myself, lost in the love I'd found with Anders, that I'd forgotten about the promise I'd made to my parents. "No. I was the one at fault." I swallow hard and kneel, gripping his shoulders. "I promised Mom and Dad I'd look after you, and I failed. I felt like if I'd been there instead of out with Anders, I could have helped you. I used my guilt as an excuse to push Anders away. I'm sorry if you felt like you were responsible."

"We were finally a family again. You, me, and Anders. Do you... do you think Mom and Dad would be mad about that? Or sad? Like they think we've forgotten about them?"

I shake my head frantically. "No. No, of course not."

Jace nods his agreement, making a determined fist at his side. "They always said they wanted us to be happy. Remember?"

That's true. When I'd come out as gay to them, they'd both embraced me and told me that all that mattered was that I found someone who made me happy. And Anders didn't just make me happy. Anders *was* my happiness.

"I do, but..." When my throat closes, speaking becomes difficult. "I was driving when they were killed. It's m-my fault they're gone." Tears spill down my cheeks, and I hang my head so he can't see. "I don't deserve to be happy. Not when I took them from us."

Jace puts his arm around my shoulders "It wasn't your fault," Jace says, voice shaking but full of sincerity that only makes me cry harder. "It was an accident. The doctors said so. Grandma said so. Mom and Dad would too, right?"

Hiccupping, I nod into his shoulder.

"Mom and Dad wouldn't blame you. I know they wouldn't."

"Do you?" I choke out the words, suddenly feeling sick with fear. "Do you hate me, Jace? Do you blame me?"

Jace's hesitation makes more tears fall. Of course he does. How could he not? I'd feel the same if I were in his shoes.

"Why would you think that?" Jace sounds just as upset as I feel.

"I... I took our parents away from you. I got to spend more time with them than you did. How could you not hate me?"

Sniffling, Jace hugs me tighter. "I don't!" His little body shakes, and I hold him to me. "I never could. I'm—I'm so, so happy you survived. That we h-have each other."

Jace doesn't blame me. He doesn't hate me. My little brother's happy I survived, and I am too, because that means I can be there for him. For the first time in so long, I feel like I can breathe. I hold my little brother tighter as we both cry like the lost, broken boys we are. "We do have each other. Always will. I promise."

"So let's be happy. With Anders. Please?"

Chuckling, I ruffle his hair. "When did you get smarter than your big bro, huh?"

"I've always been smarter, duh!" He laughs and shoves me away. "Oh, wait! Here." He hands me Gran's necklace. "Sorry I took it. I thought maybe he went back to the past, so I wanted to go and see if I could find him."

I give him a look. "You shouldn't have taken it, and you definitely shouldn't have run off without telling me. You scared me."

"I know. Sorry." He huffs and hangs his head.

"But that's a great idea you had, Jace. I'll search there." Hopefully, I won't get eaten by territorial ulfhednar...

"Take some pictures of all the Vikings, okay?"

Grinning, I take the necklace. "You got it." Gripping his shoulders, I turn him toward the car. I've got to get him home, but as soon as I can, I'm getting Anders back and reminding him of where he belongs.

With me for the rest of our lives.

I don't know why I expected going through a portal to be, like... I don't know, as simple as walking through a doorway. It's not. My stomach lurches like I fell down a staircase as the boat soars through the portal and lands with a splash in a vast ocean. It's way colder than in the present, and frigid waterdrops spatter my clothes.

The boat rocks violently as the waves swell beneath me. Gulls cry overhead, and a light snow is falling from the gray clouds. Ahead of me, a vast island awaits. I sure hope it's Anders's home and not an island full of cannibals or something. Not sure an island full of werewolves is much better, though.

Clutching the oars, I paddle until my shoulders begin to burn. Finally, rocks scrape the bottom of the boat. I jump out and drag it the rest of the way up the rocky shore. A pine forest unfurls around me. For a moment, I'm unsure where to go until I notice multiple sets of footprints leading away from the shore in the light snow on the ground.

I take in a fortifying breath and lift my head high. Here goes. Time to win back my mate.

Gathering my courage, I set off into the woods. The double set of footprints twists and turns for a bit before a road marred by wagon wheels, hoofprints, and boot prints materializes. It isn't long before the trees thin and the ground slopes, revealing a village below the hill. Wow. If I hadn't already known I'd gone back in time, I would have believed it now. The houses are so rudimentary they couldn't have come from anywhere but the past.

My eyes snag on two figures standing outside the village. One has got to be ulfhednar; he's enormous, tall as hell with bulging muscles and black hair shaved at the sides with a long, braided beard. There are gray furs slung over his wide shoulders. He looks so similar to Anders that my heart skips, but there's something off about him. Maybe it's the curl of his fangs or the tapping of his claws at his sides. He seems more wolf than man.

And the guy beside him can only be Arlo, that guy who approached me in the bookshop and asked about Anders. Although his outfit is totally weird. He's wearing a black cloak adorned with raven feathers. It's pretty striking.

When I'm close enough, both men turn their heads. "Arlo!" My voice echoes for what seems like miles.

Arlo's eyes widen in recognition. "Goodness! Looks like Ulfheim is open for tourists, huh?"

The man I assume is Anders's brother glares at me. "You're ulfhednar. I can smell it. But I don't recognize you."

Raising both hands placatingly, I say, "I'm Anders's mate. Is he here? I need to speak with him."

Arlo goes to speak, but Anders's brother snaps, "You do not bear his mark! You will not have entry."

"Hold on, Guthark."

"Gunnar," the bear of a man says.

Arlo gives him a pinched smile. "Sorry. I'm a bit distracted by your rugged good looks. This *is* Anders's mate."

Gunnar shoots him a narrowed look. "I don't like this, but my brother needs help *now*. Otherwise, you'd both be thrown out on your asses for daring to trespass."

Fear leaves a sour taste in my throat. "Is he okay?"

Gunnar shakes his head. "Follow me." He jerks a shoulder, motioning for us to follow, then breaks into a jog.

"I'll be right behind you, enjoying the view!" Arlo singsongs, and a growl rumbles from Gunnar. A roar echoes over the trees, and my wolf howls within my soul. I need to hurry, now! Anders is in trouble. I've got to get to him.

The cold has numbed my throat by the time we arrive outside a big longhouse. Gunnar motions us onward, leading us past the house and into the woodlands beyond. Another roar shakes the forest down to the roots. It's the most furious sound, and a whimper crawls up my throat. Something is wrong with Anders. Voices get louder and louder, and through the trees, three figures come into view. Two are men, both huge and blond and clad in wolf furs. The other is an older woman, also wearing furs.

They're restraining a beast so hideous, so terrifying, it freezes me in my tracks. My heart sinks like a cold stone into my stomach as primal fear paralyzes me. The beast is a hideous conjoining of man and wolf as it towers on two muscular back legs, tail lashing at the air. With a swipe of an enormous, clawed hand, it bowls the older woman off her feet.

"Helga!" one of the men shouts, fear in his voice.

"Lyall, focus!" booms the other one. "Keep him restrained!"

Gunnar. Lyall. Then the big blond man must be...

Wulfric goes flying, back smashing against a tree. I'm not sure what cracks, the trunk or his spine.

"Anders, please, stop!" Lyall screams, clutching at Anders's huge black-furred arm.

That thing is... Anders? Oh god. What's happened to him? As the beast throws back its head and roars, making my ears ring, blazing green eyes set their sights on me. Eyes so familiar, I can't deny the truth.

I'm too late.

Anders has become a monster, and I don't know how I can get him back.

Chapter 26
Anders

A red haze of fury falls over my eyes. It feels like I am a passenger in Jamie's car, watching through a window in horror at my own actions. Against my will, I lash out. First at Helga, then at Wulfric. Wulfric's bones crack. His blood hits the air and makes my mouth salivate.

Why am I doing this? Stop! Please, stop!

Lyall screams, "Anders, don't!" His hand looks so tiny as he clutches at my arm. Oh, how his fingers tremble. How sweetly they'd crunch beneath my fangs. How his blood would water my tongue, quenching this thirst that's burning in my throat.

Another scent washes over me, tugs at my mind. Mate. My roar sends birds fleeing from the treetops as I whirl toward Jamie. As our eyes meet, my stomach lurches. Jamie's sweet face is bone white, eyes impossibly wide, and the scent of fear rolls off him in waves.

My mate is terrified... because of me.

"A-Anders," Jamie says, voice breaking. "Please, stop. Just listen to me."

Jamie is here. He came for me. Joy tempers my rage. A whimper of sweet relief rises from my chest. Gods above, how I missed him. I thought I'd never see him again after he...

After he broke my heart. Rejected me.

Fury burns anew in my veins. A growl rumbles up my throat.

"Jamie, get out of here!" Lyall shouts, tugging my arm. Trying to pull me away. To separate me from *mine*.

My twin screams again, this time in anguish. His bones crunch just like I knew they would, the sound musical. Blood gushes onto my tongue, and I slurp it down like a starving beast. It's not enough. Why aren't I sated?

"Anders, no!" Wulfric bellows.

My twin's howls of anguish pierce my ears.

Oh gods. Lyall. I am so sorry. I can't stop. I can't!

Snarling, I throw Lyall away from me. Gunnar shoves Jamie behind him. How dare they come between me and mine? No one is taking Jamie from me!

Jamie gasps. "Wait, everyone get away from me! Quickly!" Panic spikes his scent. They've scared him. Unacceptable!

I charge, spraying snow. The edges of my vision darken as my sights narrow to anyone who dares to stand between my mate and me. I slam into what feels like an invisible wall. The force of the collision sends me flying backward, spots bursting before my eyes. Whining, I cradle my head in my claws as my skull aches. Blinking until my blurry vision adjusts, I glare at a shimmering wall veined with red. The stench of blood magic makes my lip curl.

The witch holds out his palm, blood dripping from a slit in the center of his hand. A grimace of pain flickers over his face. "I can hold him for a time. We need to figure out what to do, fast, before the spell takes its toll on me."

I'm surprised when Gunnar's eyes widen. "Are you in pain?"

The witch offers a cocky smile. "Don't you worry, stud. It doesn't hurt too much."

I swear to the gods, my brother blushes like a maiden.

A growl rumbles from me as I rise, claws sweeping through the snow as I approach the barrier. Slowly, I lift my hand and touch it. It doesn't hurt, but nor does it give when I smash my hand into the shimmering wall. A flinch creases the witch's face.

They think they can contain me? Laughable. I will break free and become the villain they always knew I was. Whatever it takes, I will get what's mine.

"Speak to him!" the witch says suddenly, turning toward Jamie. "If you really are his mate, you could calm him down enough. He isn't so far gone yet. My magic could still help him."

Jamie's throat bobs. "What do I say?"

"At this point? Anything. But it needs to happen quickly, before he falls even deeper into his wolf."

Twisting his shaking fingers together, Jamie comes closer to the barrier. The growl in my throat cuts out as traces of his scent waft through the barrier keeping us apart. Lifting my clawed hand, I press it to the shimmering wall. Eyes glistening, Jamie reaches out and presses his palm to the barrier. The space where our hands should meet makes me whimper. All I long for is to touch him. Would he let me? Or would he reject me again? I couldn't endure such agony, not again. A whimper tears from my throat, pitiful and raw. I tug my hand away and clutch it to my chest.

Jamie makes a soft, devastated sound. "Anders..." A tear spills down his cheek. "Come here. Please. I won't push you away, puppy dog. Why do you think I came all this way?"

Hope tries to lift my broken heart, but I hold fast.

Leaning forward, Jamie touches his forehead to the barrier, damp eyes caught in mine. "I'm here to bring you back home where you belong. With Jace. With Jess and Bailey. With me."

"We're not..." The words crawl as a guttural growl from my throat. "F-family. Said so yourself."

"I was wrong!" Jamie cries, shaking his head. "I was scared and guilty and... and I let my own guilt and grief come between us." He tries to touch me and scowls when the barrier keeps us apart. "I'm sorry, Anders. So sorry. I've already lost most of the people in my family, and I won't lose another one. I let the pain of my past dictate my future with you, and I'm here to tell you that I choose you. I choose us and our family over everything else."

I try and fight it, but hope takes root within my broken heart. My mate is here, saying everything I wished he'd told me that horrible night.

"I'm ready to fight for us," Jamie vows. "I want to be yours." He tugs down his collar, baring the spot between his neck and shoulder. "Now and forever."

Joy casts away the darkness. My mate has chosen me. Chosen our family. I tip my head so my forehead touches the space where his would be if we were not divided. I place my hand to the barrier over his splayed palm.

"Let me in," Jamie says, already scratching at the barrier. The wall shimmers, dispersing like mist, and my mate falls into my waiting arms where he belongs. As sobs shake Jamie's body, I wrap him in my arms, mindful of my claws. His scent, like sunshine, washes over me, like rays of light bursting through the darkest of storms. My body trembles as it fights the shift. A whine escapes me. Something is wrong. I can't change back. I can't!

"Anders?" Fear makes Jamie's voice hitch.

"C-can't," I snarl, panting as panic takes hold.

What if I'm stuck this way? If I can't shift back, then I'll never be able to return to his world. I'll be exiled, not only from my pack in this time but from Jamie's world. I can't. Not again. I can't be alone again. Closing my eyes tight, pitiful whimpers escape me.

"Hey. It's okay." Warm hands frame my face. Jamie gazes at me with such tenderness, seeing through my beastliness to my very core, like he has from the beginning. "If you can't shift back, I'll stay as a wolf the rest of my life for you. I'll bring Jace, and we can just stay here. Or if you're exiled again, then we will come with you. You will never be alone, Anders. Not again. You're stuck with me, remember? I love you, Anders." He leans in and presses a kiss to the tip of my nose.

His words, his kiss, they transform me. Fur falls from me like ash. My body ripples, becoming smaller, softer. Fangs become blunt, claws retract. Lifting my bare arms, I throw them around Jamie and pull him close. His lips find mine, and I weave my fingers through his soft tresses and breathe him into my lungs, drowning in his taste.

"I love you too," I whisper against his mouth, unable to stop my smile as I wipe tears from his face. "My family. My pack. My mate."

The sky shimmers with green and blue light, bathing Jamie in breathtaking color as he leans in and captures my mouth with his.

CHAPTER 27

JAMIE

Someone coughs. Anders growls, and I chuckle, looking over my shoulder at our spectators. Lyall's cheeks are pink, but he's smiling, and Wulfric doesn't look half as grumpy when he's hiding a grin behind his fist. Gunnar averts his gaze and scuffs the snow with his weathered boot.

Arlo exhales, smiling. "Thank Freya. I really didn't want to have to do anything drastic like we usually do with berserkers. Welcome back, Anders!" Suddenly, he staggers. "Whoa. Feeling a bit dizzy... all of a sudden..." His eyes roll back.

My cry of warning has barely escaped when Gunnar swoops in and catches Arlo in his arms.

"I can take him," Wulfric says as he approaches Gunnar. "He should lie down inside."

A rumble like thunder fills the air, and I realize it's coming from Gunnar as the man huddles over Arlo's vulnerable body. Like a wolf protecting its prey.

"Gunnar," Lyall says sharply. "What's gotten into you?"

"Stay away from my mate," Gunnar snarls.

Anders tenses beside me. "*Mate*? The witch is his—"

There's a low laugh. "My, my. What big, strong arms you have, stud." Arlo blinks groggily up at Gunnar. "I'm all right."

All the tension drains from Gunnar's body, his eyes widening as he seems to come to his senses. "I... what happened?"

No one speaks. I don't blame them. I don't know what to say either.

Arlo wets his lips. The two of them are so close together, a hair's breadth away from kissing. It's such an intimate moment I feel like I should look away, but I can't. Anders's family has more drama than a soap opera, and I'm addicted.

"You said that I was your mate," Arlo says, eyes wide as he searches Gunnar's face. "Did you mean that?"

The blood drains from his face, and he lets Arlo fall into the snow. Gunnar stumbles back, his chest rising and falling quickly. He says, "No. I have no mate. Not anymore."

I can almost feel the devastation on Arlo's face. It's the look of a man whose heart has been broken.

Gunnar turns and takes off into the woods, leaving a heavy silence in his wake.

"Here you are, dear!" Helga rushes over with a change of clothes. She frowns at all our shocked faces. "What did I miss?"

"Thank you," Anders says with a gruff clearing of his throat, accepting the clothes. "I'm going to dress, pet, but wait here for me. I have an evening planned."

"Really?" I ask distractedly, watching Arlo as he stumbles up with Kieran's help and quickly shoos him away.

"Aye. Wait for me, pet." With a kiss to my cheek, Anders walks buck-ass naked to the longhouse. I shamelessly ogle him until he's out of sight.

Lyall offers a smile. "Thank you for your help. We were worried about him."

I shrug. "I didn't do much…"

Wulfric snorts. "You saved him from his berserker rage and looked after him in your time." My wolf instincts rush to the surface, and I bare my throat to the pack Alpha. He's not *my* Alpha, but he's pack. I can feel it. Squeezing my shoulder, Wulfric says, "You are welcome among us, always."

"Thank you."

Wulfric's mustache tips when he offers a small but respectful smile. "Now, I've got to go find Gunnar and make sure he's all right."

"Are you hungry?" Helga asks Arlo. She's eyeing him with interest behind her friendly smile, like he's a species of bird she wants to observe.

"Huh?" Arlo looks away from the woods where Gunnar had run off. "Oh. Yes. Thank you."

"Come in, come in. Have some mead and a meal. You need food to recover your magic, do you not?"

Arlo chuckles. "Well, food can help a little, but it's the act of lovemaking that replenishes our magic quickly. A shame the man I'd love to have it with just rejected me in front of his whole family," he adds in a mutter, then goes inside after Helga.

For a few minutes, I linger, watching the northern lights swirl.

An arm encircles me, and Anders rumbles, "Come. We can watch the lights anytime you wish, but I can hear your stomach growling from here. You must eat."

I notice a basket hooked over his other arm. "What's in there?" It smells good, like cheese, bread, and a bunch of other things.

Anders's smile is mischievous when he replies. "You'll see. Now, follow me."

We leave the village behind and walk among towering pines. After some time, Anders stops in a clearing beneath the stars. A hot spring awaits us, the aurora staining the water shades of blue and green. Anders approaches with a playful smile and covers my eyes. "Close your eyes."

Smiling, I obey even after Anders's calloused palms slide from my face. There's rustling and thoughtful mumbling.

Curiosity makes it hard to keep my eyes closed, but I squeeze them tighter.

"All right! Open them!"

A blanket has been spread out on the forest floor, where a small banquet of food awaits us. Bowls of stew, hunks of meat and cheese, a loaf of bread, and two mugs of mead make my stomach roar in anticipation. The clouds part, revealing the full moon above. It's so damn romantic, tears sting my eyes.

"Anders," I say but can't find the words.

"Come, sit." Anders takes my hand and guides me to the picnic. We kneel on the blanket, and I try again to find the right words. Nobody has done something like this for me before. Anders squeezes my hands. "Happy birthday, Jamie."

I blink fast. I can't crumble. "I don't—" I bite off the words, knowing I probably should save my future therapist some time by stopping with the negative self-talk.

But Anders growls, "You don't what?"

"Deserve this."

A muscle ticks in Anders's jaw. "Listen to me." He takes my hands and holds on tight. "I understand why you feel that way. But it's time to stop blaming yourself for something that was never your fault. I wished every day for years that I had been the one to die instead of my father. I know now that is the last thing my father would have wanted. It's time to start living, Jamie, and there's no one else in all the world I want by my side but you."

I want to believe him, I do. Just as he wants to overcome his past and be better for me, I too want to be a man deserving of his love.

No.

I *am* worthy of his love.

I *am* worthy of life.

I deserve happiness.

I deserve *him*.

And I'm going to fight for him, for us.

No matter what.

Reaching out, he wipes away a tear that's escaped down my cheek. "I want to live with you. Every day, for the rest of my days, until we both leave this world and Odin welcomes us into Valhalla." Anders frames my face in his hands. "You are not undeserving of love, Jamie. I am living proof of that because I have never loved another like I love you."

"I love you too." Anders is it for me. This man is my ride or die, now and forever. "Claim me," I whisper.

Anders's eyes darken, arousal spicing his scent. "Are you sure?"

"Why wouldn't I be?"

"There's no going back." His hands slide down my chest and settle on my waist. My jeans tighten as my cock thickens. "Once we've claimed each other, you're mine in body and soul. No one else can have you. I will kill them if they try."

My wolf growls low in my chest. He feels the same way about Anders. He'll be mine and mine alone, forever. I angle my neck, exposing my throat to the only man I'll ever submit to. "Please, Alpha. Make me yours."

When Anders snarls, eyes blazing, I know we've passed the point of no return. Good. Black fur covers Anders's hands, which are suddenly fitted with claws. With a swipe, he cuts open my shirt without leaving a scratch on me. It falls open to expose my chest, and when Anders's mouth attacks my skin, my eyes close in bliss. His fangs dimple my neck, and I groan, needing him to bite down and temper the fire burning beneath my skin.

"Please," I whimper, but he leaves me hanging and mouths his way up my neck. His fangs nip my skin, leaving behind little love bites. Clawed fingers curl in my hair and tug, and our lips mash together. His tongue teases my lips, and I open to him, moaning as our tongues tangle.

With a shove, Anders pushes me down onto the blanket. He grips my waist and tugs, and I lift my hips. My pants and underwear slide down past my thighs. I wriggle out of them, and Anders's dark eyes comb over every inch of me. Reaching down, I tug on my cock, biting my lip as pleasure arcs through me.

Anders's low growl raises the hairs on my arms. "Gods, but you are eager, pet, aren't you?"

I grin. "Only for my Alpha."

"Do not touch yourself," he growls and grabs my wrist, stilling my hand. "The only one to make you come tonight will be your Alpha. Am I clear?"

I squirm, trying to free myself. "Then less talking and more doing."

Anders brings his lips to my sternum, then licks and kisses a trail down my body, inch by inch. He sucks on one nipple, encasing it in his hot, attentive mouth, then pinches the other so hard I gasp like I've been electrified. He goes lower, nipping my hip bone. My cock twitches and throbs with anticipation. When Anders's hot breath hits the sensitive head of my cock, my hips jerk. He grabs a vial off the blanket and coats his fingers with the oil inside.

"Open for me," he commands, and I obey, spreading my legs wide for him. "Good." A shiver runs through me as those dark eyes take in every exposed inch of my skin. Just knowing he's seeing me, every piece and part, makes me pant and tremble.

"Fuck, I need you," I whimper.

He leans down and claims my lips, long and sweet, until we're both breathless. "You have me," he whispers, "all of me."

His finger presses in. Just the tip, but I moan as my body opens to him like he never left. He swirls his finger, crooking it, and I writhe beneath him. I roll my hips, and he slides deeper into my body, up to the third knuckle, as deep as he can go.

Anders breaks the kiss, panting. "Gods, you are so perfect."

Another of his fingers presses in, and I can't hold back my cry. More. I need more. I need *him*. Need him to fuck me, fill me, come inside me.

Slowly, Anders pumps his fingers in and out of me. His breaths come short and fast, and I realize it's because he's as turned on as I am just from pleasuring me. I pull him down, and our lips meet, stifling our gasps and groans as he massages my prostate and strokes my inner walls. My toes curl, my balls tightening.

"Anders," I snarl. "Now. Hurry."

Anders pulls his fingers out and douses them with oil. He gives his cock a few quick strokes, his knot already quite swollen. This won't last long, but that doesn't matter. All that matters is that I'm his and he's mine.

Suddenly, Anders hauls me into his lap. I straddle him and wrap my arms around his shoulders, curling my fingers in his hair. Our breaths mingle, foreheads touching. When our eyes meet, my heart nearly bursts in two. I crush my lips to his, pouring as much tenderness and love into the kiss as I can. Then I lower my hips and he's there, right where I need him, filling me just the way I crave.

Growling, Anders seizes my hips and grips hard enough to bruise as he bucks into me, setting a desperate rhythm that unhinges me. I drop my hips, taking him deep, hard, fast, and the sounds we make fill the forest around us. "Close," Anders says breathlessly, snapping his hips up into me. His knot fills me so intensely I almost come then and there before it pops back out. "You want it, don't you, pet? Want my knot? Want to be tied to me as I fill your tight hole with my seed? Want my fangs in your skin as I claim you?"

"Yes," I cry. "Yes, Anders! All of it. Please. Make me yours."

"Then hold on. Now." I wrap my arms around his shoulders, and Anders seizes my hips and holds me in place. With a hoarse snarl, he pounds into me so hard and fast my eyes roll back and I lose the ability to speak. It's perfect. Everything I needed. He always knows how to give me what I crave.

Anders lets out a guttural animal noise as his knot locks inside me at last. Then his fangs are in my skin, biting down as he climaxes. I howl my pleasure and pain as my fangs elongate and my hands sprout claws. Panting, Anders looks up at me, eyes wide, mouth tinged with red. He's gorgeous in all his wildness, and he's *mine.* So close to the edge of my own release, I bounce up and down on him, making us both moan when his knot tugs at my rim.

"Claim me, love," Anders pants against my lips. "Possess me, body and soul."

His words detonate me, and I come messily between our bodies. I lunge, piercing his neck with my fangs. His blood fills my mouth, the taste surprisingly sweet, and something locks into place deep within my chest. If I had any doubts, they're nothing but dust now.

I've claimed the man I love. He's mine, and nothing but death can separate us.

Gasping, we lie together beneath the stars. Anders gazes at me like he's truly seeing me for the first time. "My berserker, he's finally at peace," Anders whispers as he thumbs away my tears. His eyes are bright and wet. "Gods. Why did I ever hold back?"

Sensing his regret starting to build, I take his hand and kiss his knuckles. "It doesn't matter anymore. I forgive you, Anders."

"I'm not perfect. I'll probably make more mistakes. There's still so much to learn about your world."

"That's okay. Neither am I. I'll forgive those too. Here, now. I don't need perfect. Just you."

Anders exhales softly, lacing our fingers together. "I'll try, Jamie. I want a place in your world, with you."

"So will I. I'll talk to someone about all the guilt and grief I'm still carrying around. We'll work on ourselves. Work in the shop together. It will be great."

A smile bursts across Anders's face like the sun through dark storm clouds. "There's nothing I would love more, pet."

Anders yanks me into a kiss, right where I want to be.

Neither of us is perfect. We've got our scars. That's okay. With Anders by my side, I'm confident we can face anything that comes our way.

Once we return the boat, we seek out the nearest subway and ride to Kate's apartment. I'm so tired I almost fall asleep on Anders's shoulder. Hand in hand, we leave the train and hurry through the streets until we're at her building. Anders rushes up the stairs, following Jace's faint scent, shuffling restlessly as I climb the final steps. He wants to see Jace.

I ring the doorbell, and Anders fidgets beside me.

Kate smiles when she answers the door. "Come in, come in. He's brushing his teeth now."

The apartment is dark except for the glow of lamplight in the living room.

"Thank you so much for taking him at such last minute." I give her a quick hug she returns.

A door creaks open. "Anders?" Jace's hopeful voice flips a switch in Anders. He whirls around to face Jace, who is frozen in the middle of the doorway.

"Lad," Anders says, voice so soft and gentle it's almost a whisper.

"You came back!" Jace charges across the room, and Anders drops to his knees and wraps my brother in his arms, carefully avoiding his injury. He nuzzles into Jace's shoulder, but not before I notice the tear that falls down his cheek.

"Aye. Of course I did, pup."

Jace's narrow shoulders heave with overjoyed sobs. "You can't ever leave again, Anders. You're our family, okay? Family sticks together, no matter what."

Anders makes a sound between a laugh and a sob. "And you're mine too, Jace."

I wipe my eyes, smiling so wide it hurts.

As I pull them both into a hug, my heart has never felt so full.

For so long, it was just Jace and me against the world. I never could have imagined a Viking werewolf was the missing piece my little family was missing.

I wouldn't have it any other way.

Epilogue
Anders

"This is a bad idea."

Jamie waves a hand. "Oh, hush, puppy dog. It's a great idea."

Sometimes I question my mate's sanity. "They'll never approve."

Jamie just folds his arms defiantly. "Give them a chance."

My stomach won't stop churning as I count down the minutes until Jess and Bailey arrive. Somehow, I let Jamie convince me to show Jess and Bailey my true self. Jamie assured me he'd "come out" to them as a wolf as well. I don't know what I was thinking.

So far, I've been wrong in many of my assumptions about the human world, but if there's anything I've learned, it's that humans are unpredictable in the best and worst ways.

"Hey. Look at me." Jamie tilts my chin and offers a smile. "Hiding who you are from those you love is no way to live."

"Sometimes it is the only way to stay safe."

"I know." He kisses my cheek. I lean into the touch of his lips, seeking sanctuary from my worries. "But you are safe. I promise."

"What will I say?"

Jamie takes my hand and squeezes. "Let's save the time travel stuff for another time. I think learning about time travel and werewolves in the same day would be a lot."

I huff. "I would imagine so. What if they panic?"

Jamie points to the window. Outside, Arlo gives a cheery wave. "Then Arlo will wipe their memories of the event, and it'll be like it never happened."

Outside, Jess's and Bailey's familiar voices get closer and closer. My heart sinks. They sound happy, and I'd hate to be the one to turn their happiness to fear.

Jamie gives my shoulders a squeeze. "I love you, Anders. You're so brave, and I'm proud of you."

I cough around the suspicious lump in my throat, then lean in to kiss his forehead. "Love you too."

When the key turns in the lock, I'm so nervous I'm worried I'll vomit. Jess and Bailey enter the café, smiling and laughing. Bailey waves. "Hello, lovelies!"

"Morning, guys," Jess says, locking the door behind her.

I try and smile.

Bailey gives me an odd look. "Why do you look constipated, Andy?"

"*Anders.*" I really don't hate the nickname as much as I should.

Jamie clears his throat. "Hey, can we talk to you real quick?"

Bailey and Jess exchange looks before Jess asks, "Is everything okay?"

"Oh, let me guess. You're engaged!" Bailey squeals.

"Sort of," I say, and Jamie elbows me.

"Let's sit down," Jamie suggests, leading the way to a booth by the window. He and I remain standing while Jess and Bailey sit.

Jamie clears his throat. "So. Uh. There's really no easy way to say this... Werewolves are real."

Jess and Bailey exchange amused looks, and then Bailey laughs. "This is cute. I have no clue what you're doing, but I'm here for it. Go on."

They think we're joking, and it's disheartening. "It's the truth, though where I'm from, we call them ulfhednar."

"Like those Vikings who'd wear the skins of wolves and go berserk?" Jess says, eyes lighting up with interest.

"Aye!" I say, feeling more optimistic. "That's it! That's me."

Bailey coos. "Aww, bless. I love how committed you are to this bit, Andy."

"I think," Jamie says, cutting in, "it would be easier to show you." He motions to me.

Heart racing, I pull up my fur hood. Jess and Bailey shout in shock as the fur comes alive, consuming me. I drop to all fours, and when I look up, they're both gaping at me.

"You saw that, right?" Jess whispers.

Bailey gawks at me. "Think I put too many shrooms in my cereal..."

"Bailey! You do drugs?" Jamie asks.

Bailey looks around nervously. "No! Okay, just a little. I'm not high or anything. It just... opens my mind more."

"Shut up about drugs. There's a big fucking wolf in here!" Jess shrieks, standing on top of the table in her panic.

"He's not going to hurt you!" Jamie holds up both hands placatingly.

"He's a freaking wolf!"

"I know that!"

I frightened her. That's not what I wanted at all. Ducking my head, I lie down on my belly to make myself smaller and unimposing. Did I scare my friends away for good? They hate me. They must. I'm a monster to them. A whimper escapes me. This was a terrible idea.

"Babe, you made him sad," Bailey says, pity in their voice. "Jamie. Is he... like, safe?"

"Of course he is. He can still understand you. Right, Anders?"

Lifting my head, I look only at Jamie and woof softly. I'm too nervous to look at anyone else.

"Holy shit..." The floorboards creak, making me whip around to look at Bailey. They freeze, eyes wide. "H-hey, Anders. Remember me?"

My tail wags. Of course. How could I forget them?

Bailey laughs softly, shaking their head. "Un-fuck-ing-real..." Slowly, they offer their hand.

"Bailey," Jess whimpers, looking petrified.

"It's okay, babe. He won't hurt me." Despite their confidence, Bailey's scent is heavy with fear. They're scared, but they aren't attacking. They're giving me a chance. Accepting me.

Hope brings me to my paws, and I approach until I'm just close enough to bump my nose into the pink palm of Bailey's hand. Bailey gasps, and then a smile spreads over their face, bright and joyful. "This is so freaking cool!" They laugh when I lick their fingers. My tail can't stop wagging, happy whines escaping me.

Bailey accepted me. They accepted me! I've never been happier to be wrong.

"You are so fluffy!" Bailey throws their arms around my neck and hugs me tight. I lick their ear, making them laugh. Jamie laughs too. The only one seemingly not amused is Jess, watching from the top of the table with suspicion.

"Bailey, that's enough. Get away from him."

My tail droops. I suppose it was too much to hope that they'd both accept me.

"But—" Bailey says.

Jess carefully gets down from the table. "Move over, Bailey." A smile lights up her face. "I want a turn."

Next thing I know, Jess's warm arms are around me, then Bailey's. My heart aches as they hold me tight, their touches gentle, their voices soothing. They tell me how beautiful I am. How soft. How amazing it is to meet a real werewolf. I never knew humans could be so fearless, so kind. I'm grateful to be in my shifted form. If I were in my human form, I'd have cried tears of joy.

"Uh, guys. I can shift too." Jamie sounds like he's pouting.

Jess gives him a challenging look. "Prove it."

Jamie grabs his fur hood. "Okay, but just a heads-up, I'm way more adorable than Anders."

I growl. As if.

Jess ruffles my fur. "Let Bailey and me be the judge of that."

As Jamie shifts to his beautiful wolf and they fuss over him, I can't even be sore that he is, in fact, cuter than me.

I've never been so happy. It's like I can finally breathe after years of suffocating. Even if every other human in the world fears me, it doesn't matter. As long as I have my pack, I can take on the world.

Snow falls around us in gentle flurries as Jace, Jamie, and I approach my village. It's been a long time since I was able to have a proper dinner with my pack, and this time, I'm not coming alone. Jamie will get to know my brothers and my aunt. I have no doubt they'll adore him almost as much as I do.

Jamie exhales beside me and squeezes my hand.

"Nervous, pet?"

"A little bit. I've never had dinner with a guy's family before."

I pull him close and kiss his hair. "They already like you. There is nothing to fear." I wrap my arm around his waist. "I take it your first session went well?"

Jamie has started seeing someone called a therapist. They're supposed to help people like Jamie cope with intense feelings of trauma. I picked him up from his session, and we came straight to Ulfheim. He'd been quiet on the walk to the piers, but he hadn't seemed troubled, more... reflective.

"It was pretty good. She's nice, and I feel comfortable talking to her."

I wish I knew the perfect thing to say that would free him of his guilt and pain.

As if sensing my thoughts, Jamie bumps his shoulder into mine. "It's not your job to fix me, Anders. Besides, you help me a lot, in your own way."

"I do?"

Sighing exasperatedly, Jamie turns me toward him and stands on his toes. Looping his arms around my neck, he pulls me down for a sweet, brief kiss in the middle of the village square. The crowds disappear as I melt into his affection, and I sweep my arms around his back and slender waist, holding him close to me.

"Yeah, puppy dog, you do. You remind me I deserve love." Patting my chest, Jamie steps back. I take his hand in mine and we walk the final stretch to Wulfric's longhouse. "Maybe I'll always feel guilty, but as long as I have you and the tools to help me deal with it, then that's good enough for me."

"Come on, guys! Hurry!" Jace waves at us. He's already run ahead.

"Jace, I told you not to run!" Jamie calls. "If you fall, you'll have to stay in that cast even longer."

I knock on Wulfric's door.

Helga calls, "Come on in! We've got warm food and drink to chase the cold out of you."

Jamie sniffs the air as we enter. "Smells great in here. What's cooking?"

Kieran laughs. "What *isn't*? We've got stew, bread, cheese, and meat, vegetables from the garden."

"So, enough food for a whole pack of wolves," Jamie says.

A roar of greetings comes at us from the dining table. Wulfric and Gunnar are there, and so is Helga, of course. They all greet Jace as if he's a pup of their own while he bombards them with questions of all sorts.

Gunnar looks over at me, then leans to the side, trying to get a glimpse of the door.

"Arlo isn't here," I say.

Gunnar tenses, color rushing to his cheeks. "I wasn't looking for him," he insists, but the disappointment is written all over his face as he slumps in his chair.

Oddly, Lyall is absent. I feel a pang of disappointment. I'd hoped to see him.

Kieran asks, "How's the café?"

"Great." Jamie takes a seat at the table. "I'm training Anders to become a barista."

Kieran looks at me with interest. "Wow. I can't say I ever expected to hear Anders and barista in the same sentence."

I pull up a seat beside Jamie. "Neither did I," I admit honestly. Emotion swells in my throat. "Thank you for giving me a seat at your table. All of you." My gaze holds Wulfric's. When I look upon my little brother, I no longer feel envy or contempt.

Kieran elbows Wulfric, and my brother coughs to clear his throat. "It is... it's good to have you back, brother." His smile is warm and sincere. "And it is wonderful to see Jamie again. Thank you for putting up with my brother."

Jamie grins. "My pleasure."

"I am sitting right here," I grumble, but when Jamie squeezes my hand, I smile with more ease than ever before.

I can't believe I'm at this table, surrounded by the family I thought I had lost in one world and a family I've found in another.

The gods themselves have blessed me with a second chance at happiness, and this time, I will be the father Jace needs, the most supportive brother in the world, and the lifelong companion my mate deserves.

It's late by the time we're ready to go. Jace fell asleep, so I carry him as Jamie and I walk back to our boat. "To think, one day he'll be too big to carry," I say, chest aching at the thought.

Jamie laughs softly. "Don't remind me."

The ocean roars, and gulls cry as we walk over gravel and sand toward our boat.

"I'll take him if you get the boat in the water," Jamie offers.

I snort as I carefully pass Jace over to him. The lad will be grumpier than a draugr if we wake him. "You just don't want to get wet."

"Of course not. These shoes are brand-new!" Jamie gives me a playful wink as he hoists Jace into his arms.

As I carefully lower the lad into the boat, a bright flash out in the water makes us wince. A portal shimmers not far from shore.

Jamie arches a brow. "Did you do that?"

"No." I hadn't even touched his necklace.

"Who is that?" Jamie asks, eyes wide.

I turn toward the ocean as someone rows a boat from the portal and out into the sea. Even at this distance, I'd recognize Lyall's golden hair anywhere. "It's Lyall. What was he doing in that portal?" I'd wondered why he wasn't at supper tonight. What was so important that he'd miss out on dinner? I wave at my brother, and either he sees it and ignores me or doesn't notice. I make for him, calling out to him as he moors his boat.

Lyall steps onto dry land and looks up at me. I freeze. His eyes are red-rimmed, as if he's been crying. Despite his obvious distress, he still tries to smile, but it's a mockery of his usual jovial grin. "Evening, brother. Sorry, it looks like I missed you."

What in Hel's name is he doing? Does he think I'm stupid?

"What happened?" I ask. "Did someone hurt you?" My gaze darts all over his body, looking for a wound, though I can't smell any blood.

"It's nothing." Lyall tries to brush past me, but I grab his arm.

"Are we in danger? Did something happen?"

Lyall's face twists in dismay. "Gods no! Would you just leave it?"

He tries to dart around me, but I block his path. "How am I supposed to believe you when you're obviously hiding something?"

With a sigh, Lyall's shoulders slump. "If I tell you, you must keep this between us."

My suspicion deepens, but so does my concern. "Aye. You have my word. Now, tell me what ails you."

"I found my mate."

My heart leaps with joy for him, but as his words sink in, they make less sense to me. "But you claimed Soren, did you not? So how could you have found a new mate?" Understanding makes my breath catch, and when Lyall hangs his head, anger rises within me. "You went to find *him*? The traitor who destroyed our family?"

Lyall's head snaps up, his hands in fists. "Don't you dare call him that! Soren never betrayed us!"

Jamie grips my arm when I try to close the distance between us. "He admitted as much! He'd used us all those years, then led his father and those hunters right to us!"

"No!" Lyall snarls, and I step back, alarmed by the sight of his fangs and claws. "He lied. All those years, he thought his father had died with his mother. He was as shocked as I was when his father raided our village."

"Nonsense, all of it! Why would he have lied about such a thing?"

"To protect me!" Lyall's voice echoes along the beach.

I don't understand. Everything I'd believed so fiercely about the most tragic day in our lives has been thrown into question.

Lyall inhales, forcing his claws and fangs to become blunt on his exhale. "After the attack, we were lost, grieving, and desperate for someone to blame. Many suspected Soren once we realized it was his father who'd led the attack, but they also suspected that I'd been in on it."

"I remember that." A rush of anger makes me grind my teeth. "I punched a farmer in his face when I overheard him accusing you of having something to do with the attack."

"Soren didn't want me to take the blame for his father's actions. So he lied and made all of you believe he alone was in on it." I open my mouth to deny it, but Lyall snaps, "Think, Anders. Really think now that your mind isn't besieged by grief and shock. Soren grew up among us, became ulfhednar, let me claim him as mine. Why do all of that for a lie?"

My hands ball into fists. Damn it. Lyall has a good point. If Soren was planning on betraying us all that time, why go so far as to mate with Lyall?

"Please, Anders." My twin takes my hands. "Put aside your anger. I would never lie to you about this. If Soren had always intended to hurt us so deeply, the Norns would not have chosen him as my mate. I could never believe that."

No. No, this isn't true.

If Soren was truly innocent, then I let my brother be separated from his mate. My actions have hurt him all these years. Gods. Can I do nothing but hurt the ones I love?

"Anders." Jamie takes my hand. "It's okay. It's not your fault."

I take in a breath as I hold Lyall's pleading gaze. I don't know what to believe anymore, but I trust my brother. Mayhap before I met Jamie, I would have clung to my anger and rejected Lyall's version of the story. For years, I've blamed others so I wouldn't have to face the parts of myself I hated most. That isn't who I am anymore.

There's an ache in my throat as I tug Lyall close and hold him tight. "I'm so sorry." The ocean beyond Lyall's shoulder becomes a blur through tears of shame. "I failed you."

Lyall shudders against me and croaks, "I finally found him, and he doesn't... he doesn't remember me."

Alarmed, I hold Lyall at arm's length. "What?"

Tears leave a wet sheen in Lyall's eyes. "I don't know why or how, but he didn't know who I was. He looked at me like I was a stranger, even when I told him my name."

Jamie shakes his head. "I'm sorry, Lyall."

"All these years, I've searched for him!" Lyall dashes his tears away and paces, kicking gravel out of his path. "Only to lose him once I'd found him."

I huff, making Lyall scowl at me. "You're just going to give up? After all that? I had no idea you were so weak-willed."

Lyall's nostrils flare. "What in Hel's name would you have me do?"

I arch a brow at him. "Isn't it obvious? Make him remember you, of course!"

"Is that even possible?" Lyall asks.

"You're mates. Of course it is. This is merely an obstacle on the path you must walk to be together again."

"Anders is right." A grin springs across Jamie's face. "And we'll help you!"

"Truly?" My twin looks from Jamie to me, eyes lighting up with hope.

"Aye." I clap him on the shoulder. "You won't be alone in this."

Laughter tumbles from Lyall's lips. "Thank you. Both of you." He squeezes my shoulder, then Jamie's. "Until we meet again. I hope it will be under better circumstances." Lyall walks off toward the village, and I watch him go with an ache in my chest.

"I hate that I didn't have his back when he needed me. I was so blind."

"Hey." Jamie turns me toward him, one hand cupping my cheek. "You were grieving. Besides, you know now."

I touch my forehead to his, drinking in his scent until the guilt ceases to ache. "Aye. I do. I'll help my brother find happiness, no matter what."

Jamie grins, giving me an excited shake. "There we go! Operation Loren has just begun!"

His enthusiasm makes me chuckle. "What is Loren?"

"It's their ship name. You know. Lyall. Soren."

I'm at a loss. "Jamie, how will buying them a ship solve any of their problems?" Besides, I barely have enough coin to pay for it.

I don't know what I said, but Jamie doubles over into me, laughing. His smiling mouth takes mine in a kiss that leaves me dizzy and warm all over.

"I love you so much." Jamie's smile is blinding, and the warmth in his words fills me with love. This beautiful man has filled my once dark heart with light.

"And I you." I envelop him in my arms, sighing in contentment when he wraps his arms around me too. My life has taken such a drastic turn since I landed at Jamie's feet in the ruins of my rowboat.

"Guys, hurry up!" A very cranky-looking Jace glares at us from the boat. "I wanna go home and sleep."

I take Jamie's hand. "Of course, lad."

We join Jace in the boat, and I hoist the oars. "Let's go home."

"Right there with you, puppy dog." Jamie squeezes my hand. "Always."

"You guys, stop!" Jace groans, and Jamie and I burst into laughter.

With my family in the past a part of me again and the family I've found in the future at my side, I set sail for the horizon.

Thank you for reading! I hope you enjoyed Anders and Jamie.

What happens when Jamie asks Anders to roleplay a scene from his favorite Omegaverse book? Scan the code to sign up for my newsletter, and get access to a whole library of spicy, bonus epilogues for all of my books.

About CJ

CJ Ravenna loves to tell stories where the ordinary meets the extraordinary. Her books often feature an explosion or two, possessive and protective werewolves who adore their mates, steamy and swoony romance, and of course a happy ending.

Scan the code to connect with me on my socials, read my books, and more!

The Lycanthrope Protection Agency Series

To Hunt A Moonborn Beast (Gabe & Max)

Child Of The Moon (Gabe & Max)

The Moon Aways Rises (Gabe & Max)

The Moon Over The Oak (Zach & Ryan)

Redemption Under The Moon (Ben & Isaac)

Fire and Moonlight (Eddie & Vico)
A Paranormal Yakuza Duet

Secrets & Sake (A Paranormal Yakuza Duet Book 1)

Curses & Kitsune (A Paranormal Yakuza Duet Book 2)
Viking Wolves